JOSH BILLINGS (Henry Wheeler Shaw)
in a don't-give-a-damn pose

America's Phunniest Phellow
Josh Billings

The Delightful, Funny
Stories & Sayings
Of Our Wisest
American Humorist

Edited and Introduction by
JAMES E. MYERS

Illustrated

Lincoln-Herndon Press, Inc.
 # 1 West Old State Capitol Plaza
Springfield, Illinois 62701

First Edition
Manufactured in the United States of America.

For information write to:

LINCOLN-HERNDON PRESS, INC.
1 West Old State Captitol Plaza
Springfield, Illinois 62701

Library of Congress Cataloguing in Publication Data.

Library of Congress Catalog Card Number:
85-081677

ISBN 0-942936-07-8 (Softcover)
ISBN 0-942936-05-1 (Hardcover)

Acknowledgments

To Edith Sarah Myers, without whose counsel, editing—and laughter—this tribute to Josh Billings could not have been completed.

The editor is grateful to the following individuals and institutions for their cooperation in providing needed information and photographs—with permission to publish them—for the completion of this book.

The Rare Books Room of the University of Illinois library, Champaign, Illinois, holds the largest collection of materials published by Henry Wheeler Shaw (Josh Billings) available to the editor. These materials were generously made available by the most excellent staff, especially its director, Mr. Frederick Nash.

Mr. Frank Lorenz, Special Collection Librarian of HAMILTON COLLEGE, Clinton, N.Y., where Josh Billings spent nearly a year, his only year in higher education. Mr. Lorenz provided counsel and photographs from the College holdings, and gave us permission to publish them.

We are grateful to the excellent staff of both the Reference Department and the Interlibrary Loan department of the Lincoln Library, Springfield, Illinois, for their tireless efforts to locate and procure materials needed from other libraries for the completion of this book.

Contents

Introduction*

Thrice armed is he who hath his
quarrel just (Christopher Marlowe)
and four times he who gits hiz
fist in fust. (Josh Billings)

Josh Billings/Henry Wheeler Shaw was born 12 April 1818 in Lanesboro, Massachusetts, of an illustrious father and grandfather both of whom served several terms in the United States Congress. And Josh's father, Henry Shaw, was a member of his State Senate for twenty-five years.

Josh's schooling in Lanesboro was typical of its day, some three months in winter at a district school, and a few weeks more in Spring and Fall. Then came a finishing touch at some academy where enough Greek and Latin were taught the properly motivated youth to enable him to enter college.

Josh wasn't much of a scholar. He loved pranks, practical jokes, and to fish and hunt—lifelong hobbies—so that neither Sunday religious school nor weekday public school presented him, as he put it, with his "best holt". Or, as he described it: "I alwus went to school bi the way of somebodys orchard, and green apples and me waz the best ov friends. . . stealing watermelons on dark and rainy nights was a pius duty in thoze days."

Despite his fondness for practical jokes, hunting and fishing and the exploration of just about all the land out of doors, Josh's father sent him on to a finishing school at the academy at Lenox, just north of Lanesboro. There Josh got a working knowledge of those two languages that every boy from a cultured family was expected to know—Latin and Greek—and he learned as well, from the taciturn and crusty schoolmaster, that pithy, punchy, brief Yankee aphorism: "Whatever you git. . . git it got!"

---

* A major source of information for the introduction was JOSH BILLINGS, YANKEE HUMORIST, Clemens, Cyril. 1932. International Mark Twain Society, MO.

When he was fifteen, and without much enthusiasm for it, Josh entered Hamilton College in Clinton, New York. Here, too, Josh was far readier for a joke or prank than for the banality of study. Still, he did get through his freshman year. But then his mischievous and independent spirit—always mixed with the bizarre—intervened to compete with scholarship. It seems that attending morning chapel at college was a daily duty required of all students. The campus chapel had a devastatingly clangorous and arousing bell that worked like a cold shower to drive students out of bed and to church. The bell was a daily morning peremptory summons to rise and shine and pray. Finally, Josh had had enough of it. He climbed up the lightning rod cable attached to the bell tower, removed the bell's clapper, climbed down with the offensive iron tool and went back to bed.

Somehow, the news of that peccadillo leaked. The President of the college peremptorily expelled Josh who returned to Lanesboro to resume the more important skills of hunting and fishing. But, as with many youngsters of his time and status, Josh hankered to see the wild American frontier to the west, to join with the broad movement of Americans looking for land, for adventure, for something better—or at least different—than had been theirs back home.

Resigned to his going, Josh's father said: "Henry, I guess you had better go. You're not doing any good around here." He gave Josh ten dollars, a bundle of clothes, letters of commendation from Ex-President John Quincy Adams; also Senator Henry Clay and Martin Van Buren, Vice-President and soon to be President. Then Josh was on his way, not to return for ten years.

Slowly he worked his way west, landing in St. Louis where he joined some congenial young fellows who were organizing a group to explore the South Pass of the Rocky Mountains. By the time the group hit Topeka, Kansas, bad luck had swamped them, bringing fever and various other illness, one death, Indian depredations, short rations, all contributing to the end of the matter. They turned back because the going was unbelieveably tough. It was so tough that a successful similar expedition was not to be completed for seven years and then it took General George Fremont and his well-planned, trained and equipped expedition to do it.

Josh headed for Toledo, Ohio where he made two new friends. They pooled their money, bought a boat and supplies, then proceeded to explore the Maumee River. They were broke when they hit Napoleon, Indiana where, to feed themselves, they devised a lecture on a popular form of hypnotism called Mesmerism. Josh delivered what was apparently a hilarious performance, his friend sang songs and the show proved an enormous success earning them $13.40, a good sum of money in those days. Their advertisement for the show was as follows:

MORDECAI DAVID,
the last surviving relative of David, the original author of
the David Psalter, will read a

LECTURE ON MESMERISM

to the citizens of Napoleon on

FRIDAY NIGHT

and the lecture will be prefaced by some characteristic songs by

OTTO HAYWOOD,

the sweet singer from the East

The three young men performed throughout the Midwest and their success was a revelation to Josh, and a beginning. These early performances qualified Josh as one of our earliest stand-up comedians, a style of art and entertainment popular to this day.

Those wandering years, from 1835 to 1845, were semenal to Josh's life. He learned to turn a kindly if skeptical—and at times satirical—eye on the ways and means—both the noble and the less-than-noble aspects of American life then evolving on our western frontier and our eastern seaboard. He learned much about the vagaries of human nature.

Once again in Lanesboro, in 1845, Josh wooed and won his childhood sweetheart, Zilpha Bradford. Doubtless his later essay on "Courting" and "How To Pick Out A Wife" were based on that courtship. Soon there came the first of two baby daughters to be born to the couple and this, doubtless, created the inspiration for his essay, "The First Baby".

In 1854 the family moved to Poughkeepsie, New York, where Josh continued his career as a successful auctioneer and real estate agent. Writing and lecturing as a vocation had not yet offered itself to him as a promising way to support his family!

But those ten years on the frontier had brought to Josh a certain restlessness; a kind of dissatisfaction with his status quo, as well as a penchant for chance-taking that was now a fixed part of his character. He went to Pittsburgh, bought a paddle-wheel steamer, and began to work his way back home in mid-winter. The Ohio River was not hospitable and offered Josh and his crew daily jousts with disaster. First came a cold wave while they were en route up the river. Then ice. Then snow. Then the boat became firmly stuck on a sandbar. Matters looked gloomy as ice piled up all around him. An entry in his diary reveals the state of things: "The ice broke our wheel badly." Then came more ice. And more heavy snow. And illness among the crew. Then another entry in his diary: "This is the seventeenth day on the bar. . . Ice piled up three feet high." On and on went the anguished daily entries until finally, on 27 July, we read: "By cash received from steamer. . . $1450.00. As with the Rocky Mountain episode so with the effort at steam-boating. . . failure. But Josh was learning, gaining experience, looking at the world through both amused and dour glasses that began to develop in him a satirical streak that was later to be a major factor in his successful career as a humorist.

Back in Poughkeepsie, Josh began to do very well as an auctioneer and real estate dealer. Everybody like him. His neighbor for thirty years said of him: "Every man, woman, child, dog and billy-goat in Poughkeepsie knew and loved that great and good man."

And now Josh had begun to write in his "phunny" way with busted grammar and odd, phonetic spelling. But before he began to use the odd spelling, he wrote only in the accepted, correct way, and that, he figured, had been the cause of his failure at the comedy game. An example of this was his Essay on the Mule, a piece that bombed! Taking a cue from the phonetic spelling of enormously successful Artemis Ward, he rewrote the piece using the popular odd spelling and grammar. Now, wonder of wonders, the piece was successful, was picked up and reprinted across the nation and suddenly Josh was not only famous, he was enormously encouraged. A few successful local lectures brought him an agent who offered to represent him nation-wide. They commenced a tour that was not very successful but it once again gave Josh that chance to satisfy his wanderlust while trying to make money. He continued this national lecture tour annually for the rest of his life.

Curiously, in our generation, stand-up comedians are once again popular. They perform today in night spots with odd names like: Laffs, Mr. Gags, The Comedy Connection, Yocks, The Punch Line, Ha-Ha-A-Go-Go. However, most of these latter day comedians are put-down artists or smut jokesters, full of pessimism and disdain for their fellow man. They lack the optimistic humor, the horse sense humor that marked comics like Josh Billings whose satirical but kind and helpful style reflected his own satirical yet optimistic, and hopeful assessment of mankind. We see this in his adaptation of Psalm 8: "Man was created only a leetle lower than the angels. But one day he fell out ov hiz kradle and aint hit bottom yit."

Josh was not an immediate success as a comic lecturer. He had to build a following. Early, at one lecture hall with nearly 500 seats, all vacant except for one customer, Josh graciously addressed that single, paying auditor: "Will the audience please move a little closer and occupy front seats?" The "audience" complied. Then Josh asked: "Would the audience like to go around the corner with the lecturer and have some fried oysters with catsup?" The entire audience smiled, arose and departed with Josh for a delightful evening.

The above incident with poor audiences was by no means unusual so that theatrical critics, in their usual waspish way began to demean, to belittle Josh and his performances in their reviews of his show. Fortunately, Josh was an instant and permanent success in France and England. They loved his written material and their reviews of his work were glowing. Josh bundled these reviews into several packets and mailed them to the snide reviewers, and to the theatre owners who had rejected him. Here is his accompanying letter.

"My dear Sir;"

"I have sent you by today's mail a copy of the London Spectator, containing an extended criticism on 'Josh Billings', and as you will observe, of a most flattering character. I have done this, not expecting that you would alter your opinion in reference to him, but to show you what consummate asses those English papers are making of themselves."

But he soon became famous and a beloved comedian who commanded capacity audiences wherever he went. And he went just about everywhere his agent could find a town with a population of 20,000 or more. And sometimes Josh would insist on going to towns much smaller than that. Even the President of the United States was taken with his wit: Abraham Lincoln read his *Essa on the Muel* to his entire cabinet (to the impatient chagrin of the more literal-minded among them), and Mr. Lincoln invited Josh to visit him at the White House. President Lincoln is said to have remarked: "Next to William Shakespeare, Josh Billings is the greatest judge of human nature the world has ever seen."

Josh had begun to make considerable money from the ten books he had published. His "Allminax" sold more copies than any other book up to that time—over a million. There were 44,000,000 Americans between 1860-1870. Today there are more than five times as many as then. Thus, on today's market, with one out of forty-four Americans buying copies of his books, Josh would sell over 5,000,000 books in the same ten year period, a tremendous sale for any writer and a good indication of the popularity of his humor and of the great affection the American people had for Josh.

After achieving wealth and fame, Josh abandoned his auctioneering and real estate business and moved with his family to New York, the center of publishing, of theatre and theatrical agents. Too, the greatest newspapers in the nation were there and Josh still published in them. He loved New York, found pleasure and humorous material there through his observation of the heterogeneous population and its cosmopolitan ambience.

In the Fall of 1885, Josh was exhausted. His physicain recommended an extended vacation. Josh took his advice and, with Zilpha traveled west to Monterey, California where he settled down to an easy, carefree time of rest, conversation, but no work. There, on October 14, 1885, he suffered a massive heart attack and died within the hour. He was sixty-seven years old.

Thus ended the useful and fascinating career of America's then most famous and most American humorist. In terms of

American literature, Josh Billings is second only to Mark Twain and there are some who place this "Yankee Solomon" on a level with the younger Twain. Actually the two were friendly and corresponded regularly.

Josh is our pre-eminent Yankee humorist/moralist and was described by his biographer, Cyril Clemens, in 1932, as follows: "Josh Billings is as American as apple pie or the corncob pipe. . . Yankee of the Yankees, he smacks of his region just as much as did the old clippers that put out from Nantucket and Gloucester for all parts of the world."

Poet-anthologist Max Eastman called Josh "A poetic humorist of genius," and wrote: "He possessed these two gifts, the comic vision and the liberated taste for foolishness, in a degree that enabled him to create a new artistic form. . . he was the father of imagism, the first man in English literature to set down on his page, quite like a French painter reared in the tradition of art for art's sake, a series of tiny, highly polished verbal pictures, and leave them there for what they might be worth." Eastman considered some of Josh's metaphors "Homeric".

As his hometown newspaper declared in its funeral eulogy for Josh: "In his quaint way he preached the Ten Commandments; held up the follies of life that men might abandon them and live wisdom; gave advice marvelously sugar-coated with refined humor; scattered all over the world profound truths in two-line pearly paragraphs. He has done his day and generation good." And today, after knowing this wonderful man's writing and humor, we can say "amen" to that. For our dour, pessimistic and disillusioned generation needs the upbeat, wise and grinable humor of Josh Billings to lift us from the doldrums, out of the slough of despair at what confronts man today, in the here and now of our common danger, our common humanity.

"A Solomon in cap and bells," Josh Billings is one of our most neglected literary artists and he is here offered to Americans and to the world for the wise, witty, absolutely and incomparably funny man he was. . . and is. He will do future generations good, as well as our own.

A brief word about the odd spelling and grammar that Josh Billings affected. The editors have eased the spelling a bit, made it less extreme for ease of reading by our hurried, impatient generation. But in the main, Josh's spelling remains intact. It was funny

then and it is still funny, adding much to the humor and, as Josh said, h
had as much right to spell words the way they sounded as the dictionar
had to spell them the way they didn't!

But not everyone agreed. His good friend, Mark Twain, loathed th
most popular form of written humor that involved misspelled words. Jo
knew that and, to tickle his friend, Josh addressed a letter to him, writin
it as if Mark Twain had written to Josh. The letter follows:

> "Dear Josh:—I think a very great deal of you, as a per-
> sonal friend of long standing; I admire you as a
> philosopher; I actually revere you as almost the only
> specimen remaining with us, of a species that used to be
> common enough—I mean an honest man.
>
> "Therefore you can easily believe that if I don't write
> the paragraphs you desire for your department of the
> paper, it is not because there is any lack in me of either
> the will or the willingness to do it.
>
> "No, it is only because my present literary contracts,
> and understandings debar me.
>
> "I am thus debarred for three years to come. But after
> that—however, you wouldn't want to wait, perhaps.
>
> "I wish we could compromise; I wish it would an-
> swer for you to write one of these books, for me, while
> I write an almanac for you.
>
> "But this will not do, because I cannot abide your
> spelling.
>
> "It does seem to me that you spell worse every day.
>
> "Sometimes your orthography makes me frantic.
>
> "It is out of all reason that a man, seventy-five years of
> age, should spell as you do.
>
> "Why do you not attend a night school? You might at
> least get the hang of the easy words.
>
> "I am sending you a primer by this mail which I know
> will help you, if you will study it hard.
>
> "Now is the most favorable time that you have had
> for seventy years, now that you are just entering your

second childhood.

"It ought to come really easy to you.

"Many believe that in the dominion of natural history you stand without a peer.

"It is acknowledged on all sides that you have thrown new light on the mule, and also on other birds of the same family; you have notably augmented the world's admiration of the splendid plumage of the kangaroo— or possibly it might have been the cockatoo—but I knew it was one of those bivalves or the other; that you have uplifted the hornet, and given him his just place among the flora of our country; and that you have aroused an interest never felt before, in every fur bearing animal, from the occult rhinoceros clear down to the domestic cow of the present geologic period.

"These researches ought not to die; but what can you expect?

"Yale University desires to use them as text books in the natural history department of that institution, but they cannot stand the spelling.

"You will take kindly what I am saying; I only wish to make you understand that even the profoundest science must perish and be lost to the world, when it is couched in such inhuman orthography as yours.

"Even the very first word of your annual is an atrocity: "Allminax" is no way to build that word.

"I can spell better than that with my left hand.

"In answer to your other inquiry, I say 'No' decidedly.

"You can't lecture on 'Light' with any success.

Tyndall has used up that subject.

"And I think you ought not to lecture on 'Nitro-Glycerine, with Experiments.' The cost of keeping a coroner under salary would eat up all the profits.

"Try 'Readings.' They are all the rage now. Yet how can you read acceptably when you cannot even spell correctly.

"An ignorance so shining and conspicuous as yours.—Now I have it —go on a jury.

"That is your place.

Your friend,
Mark Twain."

With the bad reputation today's graduates have, perhaps it is time once again to joke about, and to use in humor, the technique of bad spelling. After all it IS funny and it mirrors today's condition.

So here he is, that great soul and superbly wise and phunny phellow: JOSH BILLINGS.

■   ■   ■

Thare iz no medicine like a good joke; it iz a silver-coated pill that frolicks and physics on the run.

CHAPTER I

THE REALITIES OF LIFE

A good dokter iz a gentleman to whom we pay three dollars a visit, for advising us to eat less, and exercise more.

■   ■   ■

BILLING'S LEXICON

Blush—The cream ov modesty.
Man—Live dirt.
Friends—Books, paintings, and stuffed birds.
Bashfulnes—Ignorance afraid.
Conservatism—A bag with a hole to it.
Radicalism—A hole with a bag to it.
Aristocrat—A democrat with hiz pockets filled.
Politics—The apology ov plunder.
Tin watch—Faith without works.
Mule—A bad pun on a horse.
Patience—Faith waiting for a nibble.
Sparking—Picking buds off from the bush.

Malice—A blind mule kicking by guess.
Eternal—God's epitaff.
Faith—The soul riding anchor.
Bliss—Happiness boiling over and running down both
    sides ov the pot.
Quack—A doctor whose science lays in hiz bill.
Hash—A boarding-house confidence game.
Twins—2 much.

■   ■   ■

Love iz like the meazles, we can't have it bad but once, and the
later in life we have it the tougher it goes with us.

■   ■   ■

The miser who heaps up gains tew gloat over, iz like a hog in a
pen, fatted for a show.

■   ■   ■

Most every one seems tew be willing to be a fool himself, but he
cant bear to have any body else one.

■   ■   ■

The man who haint got an enemy, iz really poor.

■   ■   ■

Advice iz like castor oil, easy enough to give but dredful uneasy
tew take.

■   ■   ■

WHISSLING

I have spent a great deal ov searching, and some money, tew find
out who waz the first whissler, but up tew now i am just az much
uncivilized on the subject az I waz.

I can tell who played on the first Jews harp, and who beat the fust
tin pan, and i kno the year the harp ov a thousand strings waz discovered in, but when whissling waz an infant, iz az hard for me
tew say, az my prayers in low Dutch. Whissling iz a wind instrument, and iz did by puckering up the mouth, and blowing
through the hole.

There aint no tune on the whole earth but what can be played on
this instrument, and that celebrated old tune, Yankeedoodle haz
bin almost whissled tew death.

Great thinkers are not apt tew be good whisslers, in fact, when a man cant think ov nothing, then he begins tew whissell. We seldom see a rascal who iz a good whissler, there iz a great deal ov honor bright, in a sharp, well puckered whissell.

Good whisslers are gitting scarce, 75 years ago they waz plenty, but the desire tew git rich, or tew hold office, haz took the pucker out ov this honest, and cheerful amusement.

If i had a boy, who couldn't whissell, i don't want tew be understood, that i should feel at liberty, tew giv the boy up for lost, but i would mutch rather he would know how tew whissell fust rate, than to know how tew play a second rate game ov cards.

I wouldn't force a boy ov mine tew whissell against his natural inclinashun.

Wimmin az a kind, or in the lump, are poor whisslers, i don't know how i found this out, but i am glad ov it, it iz a good deal like crowing in a hen.

Crowing iz an unladylike thing in a hen tew do.

I hav often heard hens try tew crow, but i never knew one tew do herself justice.

A rooster can crow well, and a hen can kluk well, and i say let each one ov them stick tew their trade.

Klucking iz just az necessary in this world az crowing especially if it iz well did.

But i want it well understood that i am the last man on record who would refuse a woman a chance tew whissell if she waz certain she had the right pucker for it.

I never knew a good whissler but what had a good constitution. Whissling iz composed ov pucker and wind, and these two accomplishments denote vigor.

Sum people always whissell where thare iz danger—this they do to keep the afraid out ov them. When i waz a boy i always considered whissling the next best thing to a candle to go down cellar with in the nite time.

The best whisslers i have ever heard have bin among the negroes (i make this remark with the highest respect to the accomplishments ov the whites), i have heard a South Caroliny darkey whissell so natural that a mocking-bird would drop a worm out ov hiz bill and talk back to him.

I dont want any better evidence ov the general honesty there iz in a whissell than the fact that there aint nothing which a dog will answer quicker than the whissell ov hiz master, and dogs are az good judges ov honesty az any critters that live.

It iz hard work to fool a dog once, and it iz next to impossible to fool him the second time.

I aint afraid to trust any man for a small amount who iz a good whissler.

I wouldn't want to sell him a farm on credit, for i should expect to have to take the farm back after awhile and remove the mortgage myself.

You cant whissell a mortgage off from a farm.

A fust rate whissler iz like a middling sized fiddler, good for nothing else, and tho whissling may keep a man from gitting lonesome, it wont keep him from gitting ragged.

■   ■   ■

I thank God most fervently for one thing, and that iz, when everbody else iz happy, i am sure to be.

■   ■   ■

Love iz sed tew be blind, but i know lots ov fellows in love, who can see twice az much in their sweethearts as i can.

■   ■   ■

If yu want tew git a sure crop, and a big yield, sow wild oats.

■   ■   ■

The chains ov slavery are none the lighter for being made ov gold.

■   ■   ■

In youth we run into difficulties, in old age, difficulties run into us.

■   ■   ■

DISPATCH

DISPATCH iz the gift, or art ov doing a thing right quick. To do a thing right, and to do it quick iz an attribute ov genius.

Hurry iz often mistaken for dispatch; but there iz just az much difference az there iz between a hornet and a pissmire when they are both ov them on duty.

A hornet never takes any steps backwards, but a pissmire always travels just as tho he had forgot sumthing.

Hurry works from morning until night, but works on a treadwheel.

Dispatch never undertakes a job without first marking out the course tew take. and then follows it, right or wrong, while hurry travels like a blind hoss, stepping hi and often, and spends most ov her time in running into things, and the balance in backing out again.

Dispatch iz always the mark ov great ability, while hurry iz the evidence ov a few brains, and they, flying around so fast in the head, they keep their owner always dizzy.

Hurry iz a good fellow tew fight bumble bees, where, if yu have ever so good a plan, you cant make it work well.

Dispatch has dun all the great things that have been did in this world, while hurry has been at work at the small ones, and haint got thru yet.

■ ■ ■

To make boarding-house hash, take a little ov everything, a good deal ov nothing, and throw in a chunk ov sumthing; jam to a mush, cook over a cold fire, season with hair pins, and serve it up on the jump.

■ ■ ■

To bring up a child in the way he should go, travel that way yourself once in a while.

■ ■ ■

To find the solid contents ov a mule's hind legg, feel of it closely.

■ ■ ■

I have finally cum to the conclusion that the best obituary notiss, for all practikal purposes, is a good bank ackount.

■ ■ ■

OUR OLDEST INHABITANTS—TWO OF THEM.

JOHN BASCOMB

JOHN Bascomb iz now living in Coon Hollow, Raccoon county, State ov Iowa.

He iz 196 years old, and can read fine print by moonlite 33 feet off.

He remembers Gen. Washington fust rate, and once lent him 10 dollars to buy a pair ov calf skin boots with.

He fit in the revolushun, also in the war ov 1812, likewize in the late melee, and sez he won't take sass now from any man living.

He iz a hard shell Baptiss by religion, and sez he will die for his religion.

He waz converted 150 years ago, and thinks the hard-shell iz the toughest religion thare iz for every day wear. He sez that one hard shell baptiss can do more hard work on the same vittles during a hot day than 15 Episcopalites.

He haz always used plug tobbaco from a child, and sez he learnt how teu chew by watching a cow chew her cud.

He has never drunk any intoxicating licker but whiskey, and sez that no other licker is healthy. He thinks 3 horns a day iz enough for health.

He has always voted the dimocratik ticket for the last 170 years, and walked, last fall, in sloppy weather, 18 miles to vote for Jim Buchanan.

He haint never seen a rail-road yet, nor a wimmin's rite convention.

His greatest desire, he tells me, iz to see Gen. Jackson, and sez that he shall go next year down to Tennesee to see him.

He fatted a hog last year, with hiz own hands, that weighed 636 pounds after it waz drest and well dried out. He iz very cheerful, and sez he won 7 dollars on the weight ov this hog, out ov one ov the deacons ov the hard-shell church. He declares this to be one ov the proudest accidents ov hiz life, for the deacon waz known far and near az a tite cuss.

He tells me that for 90 years he haz went to bed at just 17 minnits after 9, and has arisen at precisely 5 o'clock the next day.

The fust thing he duz in the morning iz to take a short drink, about 2 inches, and then for an hour before breakfast he reads the allmanax. (*I will here state that it iz "Josh Billings' Farmers' Almanax" that he reads.*)

I asked him hiz opinion ov gin and milk az a fertilizer. He pronounced it bogus, and sed that the good old hard-shell drink, *whiskey unadorned*; was the only spirits that never went back on a man.

Hiz habits are simple. For breakfast he generally et fat slices ov psalt pork, 3 biled pertatoes, a couple ov sausages, 5 hot biscuits, a dozen ov hard biled out eggs, 2 cups ov rhye coffee, a small plate ov slapjax, sum few pickles, and cold cabbage and vinegar, if there was any left from yesterday's dinner.

Hiz dinner waz always a lite one, and he seldom et anything but sum boiled mutton, sum corned beef, sum cold ham, and sum injun pudding tew top off with.

Hiz suppers were mere nothing, and consisted simply ov cold psalt pork, cold corned beef, cold boiled mutton, and, once in a grate while, a phew slices ov cold ham, with mustard and hoss reddish.

I examined hiz head and found that he had all the usual bumps in a remarkable state ov preservation.

He haz a good ear for musik, and whisselled me Yankee Doo-dle, with variations.

He waz born a shumaker, but hasn't done anything at the trade for the last 125 years. He enjoys the best ov health, but just now he iz teething, which he tells me iz his 7th set.

He iz a firm beleaver in the Darwin theory, and sez he used tew hear his great-grandfather tell ov a race ov men somewhere down on the coast ov Florida, who had sum little ov the caudle appendix still remaining.

On the subject ov marriage his head seems tew be dead level. He sed "that he had been married 15 times, and proposed again tew Hannah Campbell, a lady in the naberhood, who was 28 years old."

I asked him what he thought his chances were for obtaining the lady's hand, and he sed "it lay between him and one Theodorus Whitney, a travelling corn doctor," and added "if Whitney didn't look out he would enlarge his head for him."

Upon my asking him what he attributed his immense life and vigor to, he sed, in a clear and distinct voice:

"To 3 small horns ov whiskey a day, beleaving in the hard-shell doctrine, and voting unanimously the dimocratik ticket."

I thanked him very much for the information he had given me ov himself, and asked him if he had any objection to my putting it into print, and he manifested a great desire that i should do so, not forgetting teu make special mention ov what he had sed about en-larging Whitney's hed for him, for he thought that would clear him out ov the neighborhood.

I left John Bascomb after a deliteful visit ov four hours, and thought over teu myself, if there waz any two rules for long life that had been thus far discovered that waz alike.

The more i thought ov this, the more i wished i could come accrost Methuseler for a few minutes, and hear him tell how he managed.

■   ■   ■

ELIZABETH MEACHEM.

Lib Meachem (az she iz familiarly called in the township where she resides) iz one ov the rarest gems ov extenuated mortality that has ever been my blessed luck tew encounter.

She iz not so old az Bascomb by about two years, being only about 194 years old. Next to Lot's wife she iz the best preserved woman the world contains.

I reached her place ov residence early in the morning, and in one minute after i told her my bizzness her tongue had a full head of steam on, and for 3 hours it run like a stream of quicksilver down an inclined plain.

I asked her a thousand questions at least, but not one ov them did she answer, but kept talking all the time.

Az near az i could find out she had lived 194 years simply because she couldn't die without cutting short one ov her storys.

I asked her tew show me her tongue—I wanted to see if that member waz badly worn; but she couldn't stop it long enough tew show it.

This woman haz reached her enormous age without any particular habit.

She haz outlived every body she haz cum acrost, so far, by out-talking them.

The only subject that I could for a moment arrest the flood ov her language with, was the fashions; but this was a subject upon which i unfortunately wasn't mutch.

As a last hope ov drawing her out upon sum facts az tew her mode ov life, i touched upon that all-absorbing topic teu both old and young—i refer now tew matrimony.

Her fust husband it seemed, was a carpenter, and, tew use her own words, "was too lazy tew talk, or tew listen while she talked, and so he died."

Her second husband was a pretty good talker but a poor listener, and, therefore, he died.

Her third husband waz a deaf and dumb man, and, az she remarked, "either he or she had got tew die, and the man died."

Her fourth husband undertook tew out-talk her, and died early.

In this way she went on describing her husbands, 12 in all.

As i rose tew depart i sed tew her solemnly:

"ELIZABETH MEACHEM, yu hav been much married, and

much an inconsolate widder—at what time ov life do yu think the married state ceases tew be preferable?''

She replied:

"You must ask sumboddy older than i am.''

■　　　■　　　■

MORE OF BILLING'S LEXICON

Experiment—Energy out ov a job.

Perfection—God in man.

Virtue—That ingredient which needs no foil, and without which nothing else is valuabel.

Solitude—A good place tew visit, but a poor place tew stay.

Sloth—Life in a tomb.

Health—A call loan.

Memory—The shadow that the soul casts.

Politeness—Sixty day paper.

Poverty—The only birthright that a man cant lose.

Accidents—The dismay ov fools, the wize man's barometer.

Ease—Discounted time.

Wealth—Baggage at the risk ov the owner.

Fortune—The aggregate ov possibilitys; a goddess whom cowards court by stealth, but whom brave men take by storm.

Economy—A fust mortgage on wealth.

Enough—Jist a leetle more.

Dignity—Wisdom in tights.

Mischief—The malice ov fun.

Cook—One who manufactures appetites.

Diseases—The whipping posts and branding irons ov luxury.

Drunkenness—Shame lost and shame found.

Cowardice—Pluck on ice.

Glutton—A man with a drunken appetight.

Examples—Foot prints in the wilderness.

Ignorance—Raw happiness.

Sin—A natural distemper, for which virtew has been discovered to be an antidote.

Friendship—One ov love's pimps.

■　　　■　　　■

MY FUST GONG.

I never can eradicate wholy from mi memory the sound ov the first gong I ever heard—i was setting on the front stupe ov a tavern in the city ov Bufferlo, pensively asmoking.

The sun was a going tu bed, and the heavens far and near was blushing at the purformance.

The Erie Canal with its golden waters was on its winding way tu albany, and i was perusing the line boats afloatin by, and thinkin ov Italy, (where i used tu live,) and her gondoliers, and showy wimmin.

Mi entire sole was, as it were in a sweat, i wanted tu climb, i felt great, i actually grew.

There are things in this life too big tu be trifled with, there are times when a man breaks loose from hisself, when he sees spirits, when he can almost touch the moon, and feels as tho he could fill both hands with the stars ov heavin and almost swear he was a bank president.

Thats what ailed me.

But the course ov true love never did run smooth, (this iz Shakesperes opinion too, i and he often think thru one quill) just az i was doing my best, dummer, dummer, spat, bang, beller, crash, roar, ram, dummer, dummer, whang, rip, rare, rally, dummer dummer, dummer dum, with one tremendous jump, i struck the center ov the side walk, with another i cleared the gutter and with another, i stood in the middle ov the streets snorting like a injin pony, at a band ov music; i gazed in wild dispair at the tavern stand, mi heart swelled up as big as an out door oven, mi teeth were as loose as a string ov prairie beads.

I thought all the crockery in the tavern stand had fell down, i thought ov phenomenans, i thought ov gabriel and his horn.

. I was just on the point ov thinking ov sumthing else when the landlord come out to the front stupe ov the tavern stand holding by a string the bottom ov an old brass kettle.

He called me gently with his hand i went slowly and sadly tu him, he calmed my fears, he said it was a gong; i saw the cussed thing, he said supper was ready, he asked me if i would have black or green tea and i said i would.

■   ■   ■

ADVERTIZEMENT

I can sell for eighteen hundred and thirty-nine dollars, a palace, a sweet and pensive retirement, located on the virgin banks ov the Hudson, containing 85 acres. The land is luxuriously divided by the hand of nature, and art, into pasture and tillage, into plain and declivity, into stern abruptness and the dalliance ov moss-tufted meadow; streams ov sparkling gladness, (thick with trout,) dance through this wilderness ov beauty, tew the low music ov the cricket and grasshopper. The evergreen sighs az the evening zepher flits through its shadowy buzzum, and the aspen trembles like the love-smitten heart ov a damsell. Fruits ov the tropics, in golden beauty, melt on the bows, and the bees go heavy and sweet from the fields to their garnering hives. The mansion iz ov Parian marble, the porch iz a single diamond, set with rubies and the mother-ov-pearl; the floors are ov rosewood, and the ceilings are more beautiful than the starry vault of heavin. Hot and cold water bubbles and squirts in every apartment, and nothing is wanting that a poet could pray for, or art could portray. The stables are worthy of the steeds ov Nimrod or the studs ov Achilles, and its henery waz built expressly for the birds of paradise; while somber in the distance, like the cave ov a hermit, glimpses are caught ov the dorg-house. Here poets have cum and warbled their lays—here sculptors have cut, here painters have robbed the scene ov dreamy landscapes, and here the philosopher discovered the stone, which made him the alchemist ov nature. Next northward ov this thing ov beauty, sleeps the residence and domain ov the Duke John Smith; while southward, and nearer the spice-breathing tropics, may be seen the baronial villa ov Earl Brown, and the Duchess, Widder Betsy Stevens. Walls ov primitive rock, laid in Roman cement, bound the estate, while upward and downward, the eye catches far away, the magesty and slow grandeur ov the Hudson. As the young morn hangs like a cutting ov silver from the blue breast ov the sky, an angel may be seen each night dancing with golden tiptoes on the green. (N.B. This angel goes with the place.)

■　　■　　■

JOSH BILLINGS INSURES HIS LIFE.

I come to the conclusion, lately, that life waz so unsartin, that the only way for me tu stand a fair chance with other folks, was to git my life insured, and so i called on the Agent of the "Garden Angel life insurance Co.," and answered the following questions, which was put tu me over the top ov a pair of gold specks, by a slick little fat old feller, with a little round gray head, az pretty az any man ever owned:—

QUESTIONS.

1st— Are yu male or female? if so, Pleaze state how long you have been so.

2d—Are you subject tu fits, and if so, do yu have more than one at a time?

3d—What is your precise fighting weight?

4th—Did yu ever have any ancestors, and if so, how much?

5th—What iz your legal opinion ov the constitutionality ov the 10 commandments?

6th—Do yu ever have any nite mares?

7th—Are you married and single, or are yu a Bachelor?

8th—Do yu believe in a future state? if yu do, state it.

9th—What are your private sentiments about a rush ov rats tu the head; can it be did successfully?

10th—Hav yu ever committed suicide, and if so, how did it seem to affect yu?

After answering the above questions, like a man in the confirmative, the slick little fat old fellow with gold specks on, said i was insured for life, and probably would remain so for a term ov years. I thanked him, and smiled one ov my most pensive smiles.

■   ■   ■

KOLD KUTS.

The more humble a man iz before God, the more humble he will be exalted,—the more humble he iz before men, the more he will git rode rough shod.

■   ■   ■

The only really natural thing there iz about any man, iz hiz conscience.

■   ■   ■

Enough good luck will ruin any man.

■   ■   ■

Where there iz one man obstinate becauze he iz wise, there iz 4,695,853 obstinate becauze they are ignorant.

■   ■   ■

Trust in God first, your nabor next, and yourself last.—AMEN

■   ■   ■

LONG BRANCH IN SLICES.

L ONG Branch iz the eastern terminus ov sum real estate on the
west side ov the Atlantic Ocean, and iz located close down to
the edge ov the water.

The population iz homo genus, woman genus, girl and boy
genus, young one genus, and divers other kind ov genus.

The divers genus are sum plenty. They go into the Atlantic
Ocean, hand in hand, man and wife, fellow and gal, stranger and
strangeresses, dressed in flowing robes, and cum out by-and-by
like statuary in a tite fit.

The Atlantic Ocean iz a great success. The author and proprietor
ov it never makes any blunders.

There iz a great deal ov morality here at Long Branch. There
iz some isolated cases ov iniquity, and a clever sprinkling of innocent deviltry.

I am pleased to state that the *iniquity* iz principally in first hands,
and finds but few takers.

The fluid ov the Atlantic Ocean iz psalt, and haz bin so for more
than three hundred years to my knowledge. I state this as a stubborn fact, and the "*oldest inhabitant*" may help himself if he can.

The occasion ov this psaltness has bothered the clergy for years.
Sum ov them say that large lumps ov psalt waz deposited in the
ocean, at an early day, bi the injuns, for safe keeping, and sum say
that the great number ov codfish and number 2 mackrel that travel
in its waters haz flavoured the ocean.

I endorse the codfish and mackrel job, not becauze i think it iz
true, but becauze i think it iz the weakest, and i hav always been in
the habit ov standing up for the weak and oppressed.

Flirtations are thick here, but principally occur amung those
who have wore the conjugal yoke until their necks hav begun to
get galled.

Theze flirtations are looked upon az entirely innocent, and are
called "*recruiting.*"

They are considered by some (who call themselves good judges)
more *braceing* than the sea-airing.

Millionaires are numerous, besides others who put on a million ov airs more or less.

Now and then yu will see a foreign snob just over from the other side ov the Atlantic Ocean. They wear long shirt-collars, turned down, and short noses turned up.

The landlord tells me, they have all paid their bills thus far, and he sez, the last thing he does at nite, before he goes tew sleep, iz tew pray—they will continue on to do so.

The prayers ov the righteous are said tew be heavy, and weigh well, and the landlord being ov a righteous turn ov mind, i think he will win.

The Continental Hotel iz the principal one here, and iz infested, just now, by eight hundred and fifty innocent creatures, who eat 3 meals per day.

The female portion ov these dear innocent creatures, roll up their sleeves, and go down once a day, to the keel ov their trunk, and drag out by the nap ov the neck some clothes, that would make the Queen ov Sheba sorry that she hadn't postponed living until Long Branch had been invented, so that she could have got the style.

I advise all of my friends to come to the Continental Hotel, and bring their best clothes with them.

Long Branch haz many things to interest the scholar, and the philanthropist, among which iz the race course, just built.

I attended this race-course lately, and saw some very good rotary movements on it.

I didn't bet, because i have always been principled aginst loseing any money.

I think i could win any quantity ov money, and not spoil my morality, but the loss ov a few dollars, would git mi virteu out ov repair for ages.

Long Branch iz also the home ov the miscellaneous crab, and the world-renowned mosquito.

The crab iz caught in endless confusion at *Plezzure Bay,* close by Long Branch.

He iz caught by tying a hard knot on the other end ov a string, and then dropping the string down in the water, and tickling the bottom ov hiz feet with the knot, in this way, sometimes he iz caught, and sometimes he iz knot.

The mosquito iz az natral to New Jersey az Jersey litening iz.

The mosquito iz a marvelous cuss, but why he ever waz allowed tew take out hiz papers, and travel, iz unknown to me, or any ov my near relashuns.

If he haz any destiny tew fill, it must be his stomach, for he iz the biggest bore, according tew the size ov hiz gimblet, i hav ever met seldom. It dont look well for a philosopher tew be fractious at any thing, not even a bug, but if any body ever hears me swear (out loud) he may know there haz bin a cussed musketeer on mi premises.

I come tew Long Branch (in company with mi wife) at the opening ov the season, and put up at the Continental Hotel, and intend now to keep putttin up there, untill the house shuts up, if i hav tew climb the flag-staff to do it.

Every body who puts up at this hotel, iz allowed tew put up regular, once a week, for hiz board, and promiscuous things.

There iz a blessed privilege, which sum folks can't never enjoy, until they are deprived ov it.

It will then be forever too late.

I am one ov them cunning critters, who, when they find a good hotel, a 225 pound landlord, and polite officials, dwell with them heavily.

I have said before (in writing about hotels) that almost any body thinks they know how tew keep a hotel (*and they do know how*) but this accounts for the great number of cussed poor hotels, all over the country.

■   ■   ■

JOSH SETTLES UP WITH HIS CORRESPONDENTS SUMMARILY.

"Philander."—If you borrow ov the Devil, you must keep your eye peeled wide open, for the Devil always takes a mortgage, and seldom takes one, that he fails tew foreclose.

"Plato."—My experience, az far az i have got, iz this, that i can most always find out the style ov milk in any man's moral coconut by hearing his opinion ov his nearest neighbors, for men are quite apt tew dam in others, what they have got the most ov themselfs, and praise what they have got the least ov.

"Pan."—Fame iz very much like good health, them men who hunt for it the most find it the least.

"Pilot."—A man may hav a great deal ov education and

not be very wise, after all; jist az he may have a heap ov strength, and not know the best holts.

"*Pilgarlick.*—You ask me the best way tew make balony sausage. Here iz the best, and only way:

Take an eel, about six feet in length, and about one feet in wideness, (git a lively eel if possible); skin the eel lengthways from head to foot, and stuff the skin with pulvarized gutta percha and equal parts ov merino wool; seazon with Scotch snuff and assafidity, hang it up by the tail in a Dutch grocery for 4 months, for the flies tew give it the trade marks; it iz then awl ready for use, and can be cut up into right lengths, and sold for police clubs.

This kind ov sausage iz the only one who took a gold medal at the Paris imposition.

"*Pharaoh.*"—It iz an actual fact that most ov us work harder, tew seem happy, than we should have to, to be happy.

"*Pedro.*"—Before you buy the hoss you speak ov, look him over close, but don't examine him much afterward, for fear you may come across sumthing that you are looking after. This iz a good rule tew follow when you take a wife.

"*Palmer.*"—In reply to your kind and numerous letter, i am happy tew state that mi age iz a profound secret, but i waz born in the old-fashioned way in the old ov the moon, am long, but crooked, don't believe in spirits (not even Jamaica spirits;) am married, or waz twenty years ago, and have every reason to beleave that I am now; have never raised any boys to my knowledge, on account ov their liability tew git out ov repair; have turned my attenshion tew girl children; have two ov that specie, one ov whom iz now boarding with a young feller; mi hair iz black, and quite tall behind; i wear a moustache, and number 10 pegged boots; have a sanguinary temperament, and a bilious nose; eat az other folks do, except roasted goose; roasted goose iz not one ov mi weaknesses, I can eat two ov them, and then take a little more ov that there goose; I work for my bread and roast goose; have a grey eye, and am always az ready tew wag az the next dog—this iz me. I forgot to state that I waz brought up by a Presbeterian Church in Massachusetts, and am a good job.

■   ■   ■

AND MORE OF BILLING'S LEXICON

Envy—A disease original with Cain, but which hiz brother Abel afterward caught, and died suddenly ov.

Belle—A female boss ov the situation.

Fancy—The flirtashun ov truth.

Sarcasm—An undertaker in tears.

Sulks—Deaf and dumb madness.

Fiction—A lie with holiday clothes on.

Hen—A lay member.

Law—The shackels ov liberty.

Science—The literature ov truth.

Deceit—A dead wasp with a live tail.

Babys—Dividend.

Miser—A wretch who haz dug out his heart tew stow away his money in.

Misfortunes—A band ov vagrants, who live on what they can steal.

Inheritance—Second-hand goods, other people's leavings.

Grave Yard—A small patch ov land, cultivated by the dead, lieing between time and eternity.

Lap Dogs—A nucleus for affection out ov a job.

Society—Burning on an alter natural rights, and then sacredly watching over the ashes.

Jealousy—Selflove.

Stingyness—The bran ov economy.

Buck Saw—An instrument ov torture.

Bragadocio—One who pulls hiz own courage by the nose.

Anxiety—Milking a kicking heifer with one hand, and holding her by the tail with the other.

Swearing—The metalic currency ov loafers.

Judicious Benevolence—The brains ov the heart.

Blue Jay—The fop ov the forest.

Policy—"Honesty iz the best policy," but policy iz not always the best honesty.

Bachelor—The hero ov a cot bedstead.

Club Houses—Where the hen-pecked go tew swear and smooth out their feathers.

Lie—The cowardice ov truth.

Skunk—An athletic animal, stronger than an elephant.

■   ■   ■

HABITS OF GREAT MEN.

Habits are like corns on the little toes; the result ov tite boots.

Habits are likewise the crooks in an ordinary dorg's tale, natural az life, but seldom useful, or ornamental.

George Washington Crab, Esq., the wonderful astronomer ov the 4th century, always took his observashuns ov the suns perigammut on one bended knee, with his eye tooth buried to the core in a sour apple, and hiz left shin-bone bandaged, with a solution ov sheet iron.

In this way he discovered cancer, one ov the signs of the zodiac, and it haz ever since bore his name in English.

George also wore an uprite collar, about one foot in upriteness and always used cats intestines, for shoe strings.

He waz a great man, and had some habits.

He died in due time.

And haint bin seen since.

His widow waz inconsolable for a large amount. Hiz widow iz also no more now, she coiled off this mortal shuffle in good shape, at the reasonable age of 86.

If her actual ashes are still extant, i say boldly, "peace tew her ashes."

If her ashes cant be found, i am willing to be one ov ten to make any other arrangements that will pay.

Rev. Moses Bickerstaff wrote those famous sermons ov hiz that shook the moral firmament from dan to beersheeba upon the head ov a flower barrel, with a bony pen made from the dorsal feather finish ov an untamed ostrich.

He used ink made from an extract ov mid-nite, combined with the perspiration ov a confirmed Ethiopian.

He also cultivated the ambition ov his little finger nail which grew to be about 8 feet in longevity.

He had a way ov leering with hiz left eye, when he preached, which history sez was cussed good.

Bickerstaff haz had a host ov immitators, but they are like the millers who fly at a candle, he cooks them all.

Bickerstaff wore hiz hat without any brim to it, nor any crown, and always put on hiz left boot last. He,like all those who lived before the flood, iz now departed to death, but hiz way ov doing things (on the head ov a flower barrell), tho often tried on, haz never bin badly beat yet.

Doctor Henry Magnum, M.D., waz a doctor.

He waz rather a weak sister, and always rode sideways on a side-saddle.

He had one strong point, he never give up a patient until he waz plumb dead.

His eccentricitys waz there.

He always used a wooden spoon, made out ov wood.

When he eat, hiz mouth always flew open, to the crook ov hiz elbow.

He never et any mollassis during his sweet life.

He made all ov his pills down cellar.

He iz sed to hav had, during his life, a thousand students ov medicine, but history sez, they didn't any ov them equal Magnum, only in his odditys.

Doctor Magnum worked in physick about 46 years after the landing ov the pilgrims, on Mount Ararat, and i presume iz now fully dead, and gone, or too old for a full days work.

He wrote a book on rats (as a dire necessity) which waz a standard work for many generations ov rats.

This book waz translated into Hindoo, and thus waz lost, by being burnt with a widder, in a funeral scrape.

Ebenezer Smile waz probably one ov the most talented eccentrics that ever smiled.

He waz a landlord on the Himmalaya mountains, and waz the author ov *Gin*.

Ten thousand funny things ov his hav bin handed down, and all lost.

The most truly wonderful odd awkwardness ov all hiz peculiarness waz hiz way ov smiling.

He could smile and drink a gin cocktail at one and the same time.

This natrality ov his has bin imitated so much since, that the original idea iz all wore out.

He haz had several imitators who have outsmiled their daddy.

History sez, he could smile a pint ov gin a day, without any water in it.

But a pint ov gin, now days, would hardly raise a smile ov contempt.

Ebenezer Smile was a bachelor, and history sez, his father waz also one before him.

This oddness haz also its immitators.

Ebenezer died with a smile on his countenance, or just after one.

I hav cum tew the conclusion that the excentricities ov great men iz the work ov art, and is mistaken by the owners ov it for nature, and has made more phools, (bi thoze who hav imitated them,) than the Lord ever haz.

Ebenezer Smile was a cussed poor original any how.

Ebenezer haz vacated life, but he haz left a bitter smile behind him.

Oh! the sarcasm, in the smile ov a gin cocktail.

■   ■   ■

TIGHT BOOTS.

I WOULD jist like to know who the man waz who first invented *tite boots*.

He must have been a narrow and contracted cuss.

If he still lives, i hope he haz repented ov hiz sin, or iz enjoying great agony ov sum kind.

I have bin in a great many tite spots in mi life, but generally could manage to make them average; but there iz no such thing az making a pair of tite boots average.

Any man who can wear a pair ov tite boots, and be humble, and penitent, and not indulge profane literature, will make a good husband.

Oh! for the pen ov departed Wm. Shakespear, to write an anathema aginst tite boots, that would make ancient Rome wake up, and howl again az she did once before on a previous occasion

Oh! for the strength ov Hercules, to tear into shoe strings all the tite boots ov creation, and scatter them tew the 8 winds ov heaven.

Oh! for the beauty ov Venus, tew make a big foot look handsome without a tite boot on it.

Oh! for the patience ov Job, the Apostle, to nurse a tite boot and bless it, and even pray for one a size smaller and more pinchfull.

Oh! for a pair of boots big enough for the foot ov a mountain.

I have been led into the above assortment ov *Oh's!* from having in my possession, at this moment, a pair ov number nine boots, with a pair ov number eleven feet in them.

My feet are az uneasy az a dog's nose the fust time he wears a muzzle.

I think mi feet will eventually choke the boots to death.

I live in hopes they will.

I supposed i had lived long enough not to be fooled agin in this way, but i hav found out that an ounce ov vanity weighs more than a pound ov reazon, especially when a man mistakes a big foot for a small one.

Avoid tight boots, my friend, as you would the grip of the devil; for many a man has caught for life a first rate habit for swearing by encouraging his feet to hurt his boots.

I have promised my two feet, at least a dozen ov times during mi checkered life, that they never should be strangled again, but i find them to-day az full ov pain az the stomach ache from a sudden attack ov tite boots.

But this iz solemly the last pair ov tite boots i will ever wear; i will hereafter wear boots az big az mi feet, if i have to go barefoot to do it.

I am too old and too respectable to be a fool any more.

Easy boots iz *one* of the luxurys ov life, but i forgit what the other luxury iz, but i don't know az i care, provided i can git rid ov this pair ov tite boots.

Any man can have them for seven dollars, just half what they cost, and if they don't make his feet ache worse than an angle worm in hot ashes, he needn't pay for them.

Methuselah iz the only man, that i can call to mind now, who could have afforded to have wore tite boots, and enjoyed them, he had a great deal ov waste time tew be miserable in, but life now days, iz too short, and too full ov actual bizzness to fool away any ov it on tite boots.

Tite boots are an insult to any man's understanding.

He who wears tite boots will have to acknowledge the corn.

Tite boots hav no bowels or mercy, their insides are wrath, and promiscious cussing.

Beware ov tite boots.

■　　　　■　　　　■

BRISTOW'S SOWING MASHEEN.

Buy Bristow's double-thread, cross-stitch, rivet-seam, dove-tail-hammer, lighting-movement, crank–motion sowing machine. These machines took all the premiums at the late lamented Paris imposition, and one ov them, which waz sent tew a farmer in

Tiogy county last fall, on trial, sowed up the whole family in a hard knot in less than three days, besides sowing fourteen acres of winter rye.

■   ■   ■

BRAVERY.

TRUE bravery iz very eazy tew detect, for it iz az much a part and parcel of a man's every day life az hiz clothes iz.

Everything that a truly brave man duz iz did from principle not impulse, and when no one sees him he iz just az heroic az he would be if he waz in the eyes of the multitude.

There iz a great deal ov bravery that iz simply ornamental, and if it wasn't for its spurs and cockade wouldn't amount tew much.

It iz not bravery to face what we can't dodge, but it iz true courage tew face all things that are honest and dodge nothing.

True bravery exists among the lowly just az much az among the great, and a man really haz no more right tew expect praise for his courage than he haz for hiz virtue.

It often requires more bravery tew tell the simple truth than it does tew win a battle.

He who fills to the brim the station in life, which nature or fortune haz given him, iz a hero; i don't care whether he iz a peasant on the hillside, or a chief in the tented field.

The most sublime courage I have ever witnessed, have been among that class who waz too poor to know that they possessed it, and too humble for the world ever to discover it.

When I want to see a hero, or commune with one, i don't go tew the pages ov history; i can find them in among the bi-paths ov every day life. i have known them tew live out their lives and die without any record here; but hereafter, when the great sorting takes place, they will be found among the jewels.

■   ■   ■

Nature never makes any blunders; when she makes a fool, she means it.

■   ■   ■

Thare iz sum folks in this world who spend their whole lives a hunting after righteousness, and can't find any time tew practice.

■   ■   ■

Human happiness iz like the Hottentot language, anybody can

talk it well enough, but there aint but few can understand it.

◼ ◼ ◼

Great transgretions seem tew baptize themselfs,—if the Devil had only bin guilty ov petit larceny, he never would have bin heard ov agin.

◼ ◼ ◼

I dont know ov any thing more remorseless, on the face ov the earth, than 7 per cent interest.

◼ ◼ ◼

The only way tew truly enjoy anything iz tew be willing tew quit it when the bell rings.

◼ ◼ ◼

Time iz like a fair wind—if we don't set our sails, we lose that breeze forever.

◼ ◼ ◼

HOSS SENSE

There is nothing that haz been discovered yet, that iz so scarce as good hoss sense, about 28 hoss power.

I don't mean race hoss, nor trotting hoss sense, that can run a mile in 1:28 and then break down; nor trot in 2:13, and good for nothing afterwards, only to brag on; but I mean the all-day hoss sense, that iz good for 8 miles an hour, from rooster crowing in the morning, until the cows come home at night, clean tew the end ov the road.

I have seen fast sense, that was like some hosses, who could git so far in one day that it would take them two days tew git back, on a litter. I don't mean this kind neither.

Good hard-pan sense iz the thing that will wash well, wear well, iron out without wrinkling, and take starch without cracking.

Many people are hunting after uncommon sense, but they never find it a good deal; uncommon sense iz ov the nature of genius, and all genius iz the gift of God, but cant be had, like hens eggs, for the hunting.

Good, old-fashioned common sense iz one ov the hardest things in the world to out-wit, out-argue, or beat in any way, it iz az honest az a loaf ov good domestic bread, always in tune, either hot from the oven or 8 days old.

Common sense can be improved upon by education—genius

can be too, sum, but not much.

Education gauls genius like a bad setting harness.

Common sense iz like boiled vittles, it is good right from the pot, and it is good next day warmed up.

If every man waz a genius, mankind would be az bad off az the heavens would be, with every star a comet, things would git hurt badly, and nobody tew blame.

Common sense iz instinct, and instinct don't make any blunders much, no more than a rat duz, in coming out, or going into a hole, he hits the hole the first time, and just fills it.

Genius iz always in advance ov the times, and makes some magnificent hits, but the world owes most ov its tributes to good hoss sense.

■   ■   ■

Mankind loves mysteries—a hole in the ground excites more wonder than a star up in heaven.

■   ■   ■

Just about az ceremonys creep into one end ov a church, piety backs out at the other.

■   ■   ■

Blessed are they who have no eye for a key hole.

■   ■   ■

Don't mistake vivacity for wit, there iz about az much difference as there iz between lightning and a lightning bug.

■   ■   ■

Watching one's health all the time iz like watching the weather—a great deal of time iz lost, and there iz just az many showers after all.

■   ■   ■

If a man haz got a good reputation, he better git it insured, for they are dreadful risky.

■   ■   ■

When a man proves a literary failure, he generally sets up for a critic, and like the fox in the fable, who had lost hiz brush in a trap, cant see a nice long tail without hankering tew bob it.

■   ■   ■

CONTENTMENT

CONTENTMENT is the gift ov God, as it can be cultivated a little, but it is hard tew acquire. Contentment is sed to be the same az happiness, this accounts for the small amount ov happiness laying around loose, without any owner. I don't beleave that man was made tew be contented, nor happy in this world, for if he had bin, he wouldn't have hankered enough for the other world.

When a man gits perfectly contented, he and a clam are first couzins.

Contentment iz a kind ov moral laziness; if there wasn't anything but contentment in this world, man wouldn't be any more of a success than an angleworm iz.

When a man gits so he don't want anything more, he iz like a raccoon with his intestines full ov green corn.

Contentment iz one ov the instincts, i admit it tew be happiness, but it iz kind ov spruce-gum-chawing happiness.

We all find fault with Adam and Eve, for not being contented, but if they had bin satisfied with the garden ov Eden, and themselfs, they would have been living there now, the only two human beings on the face ov the earth, az innocent as a couple of vegetable oysters.

They would have bin two splendid specimens ov the handy work ov God, elegant portraits in the vestibule ov heaven, but they would not have developed reazon, the only God-like attribute in man.

When a man is thoroly contented, he iz either too lazy to want anything, or too big a fool tew enjoy it.

I have lived in neighborhoods where everybody seemed to be contented, but if the itch had ever broke out in them neighborhoods, the people would have scratched to this day.

I am in favor of all the vanitys, and petty ambitions, all the jealousys and backbitings in the world, not because i think they am hansome but becauze I think they stir up men, and wimmin, git them onto their muscle, cultivating their venom and reason at the same time, and proving what a brilliant cuss man may be, at the same time that it proves what a miserable cuss he iz.

I had rather see two wimmin pull hair, than tew see them set down, thoroughly satisfied with an aimless life, and never suffer any excitement, greater than bleeding tears together, through their nose, for a parcel of shirtless heathen on the coast ov Madagaskar, or, once in a while, open their eyes, from a dream ov young hyson contentment tea, tew search the allminac, for the next change in the moon. Contentment, in this age of the world, either means death, or decay, in the days ov Abraham, contentment was simply ignorance.

The world iz now full ov learning, the arts, and sciences, and all the thousand appliances ov reason, these things make ignorance the exception, and no man has a right tew cultivate contentment, any more than he has tew cut off his thumb and set quietly down, and nurse the stub.

Show me a thoroughly contented person, and i will show you a useless one.

What we want iz folks who won't be contented, who cant be contented, who git up in the morning, not simply to have their bed made, but for the sake ov gitting tired; not for the sake ov nourishing contentment, but for the sake ov putting turpentine in some dead place, and stiring up the animals. Contentment was born with Adam, and died when Adam ceased tew be an angel, and became a man.

I don't say that a man couldn't be hatched out, and, like a young owl, set on a dry limb, all hiz days, with his brains az fast asleep az a mudturtles, but i do say, that 10 generashuns ov such guise of contentment, but i do say, that 10 generashuns ov such men would run most of the human race into the ground, and leave the balance as lifeless, and as base, as a currency made out ov pewter ten cent pieces.

I would like just az well as the next man, tew crawl into a hole, that just fitted me, head first, and thus shutting out all the light, be contented, for i know how awfully unsoothening the aims, and ambitions ov life are, but this would only be burying mi few talents, and sacrificing on the dead alter ov contentment, what was given me, to make a fire or a smudge with.

There aint no sich thing as contentment and reason existing together; those who slip out ov the crowd, into some alley, and pretend they are chawing the cud of sweet contentment, the very best specimens ov them, are no better than pin cushions, stuck full.

They have just as many longings as anybody, they have just as many vices, their virtews are too often simply a mixture ov jealousy and cowardice.

Contentment is not designed, as a steady bizziness, for the sons ov man, while on this earth.

A yeller dog, with a tin kettle tew his tail, climbing a hill, at a three minute gait iz a more reasonable spectacle for me, than a slimy snail, contented and happy.

■ ■ ■

Pedantry iz ignorant knowledge.

■ ■ ■

Thare iz this difference between modesty and bashfulness, one iz paint under the skin, and the other iz paint on the outside ov it, liable tew wash off.

■ ■ ■

Fortune iz no holyday goddess she don't simper among arcadian scenes, she dwells in rugged places, and you can't wear her favors without winning them.

■ ■ ■

Confess your sorrows, your fears, your hopes, your love, and even your deviltrys tew men, but don't let them git a smell ov your poverty—poverty has no friends, not even among paupers.

■ ■ ■

Gold seems tew be the standard of all values in this world. Even virtew in a poor man, iz quoted 75 per cent below par.

■ ■ ■

A man who cant fiddle but one tune, i don't care how well he can do it, ain't a permanent success.

■ ■ ■

Every time a man laffs he takes a kink out ov the chain ov life, and thus lengthens it.

■ ■ ■

Three score years and ten iz mans furlough, and it iz enough,— if a man cant suffer all the mizery he wants in that time he must be numb.

■ ■ ■

Man iz mi brother, and i consider that i am nearer related tew him through his vices, than i am through his virtews.

■ ■ ■

We should not forgit one thing—there is not a sure thing on this footstool,—even the best tooth in our head may fall tew aching before sunset and hav tew be jerked out.

■   ■   ■

Take the humbugg out ov this world, and you won't have much left tew do bizzness with.

■   ■   ■

LOST ARTS.

Some ov our best and most energetic quill jerkers, have written essays on the "Lost Arts," and have did comparatively well, but they have overlooked several ov the missing articles, whitch i take the liberty, (in a strikly confidential way) tew draw their attention to.

"Pumpkin Pi."—This delitesum work ov art *iz,* (or rather *was*) a triumphant conglomeration ov baked dough, and boiled pumpkin.

It waz discovered during the old ov the moon, in the year 1680, by Angelica, the notable wife ov Rhehoboam Beecher, then residing in the rural town ov New Guilford, State of Connecticut, but since departed this life, aged 84 years, 3 months, 6 days, 5 hours, and 15 minutes.

Peace tew her dust.

This pi, immediately after its discovery by Angelica, proceeded into general use, and waz the boss pi, for over a hundred years.

In the year 1833 it was totally lost.

This pi hain't bin heard from since. Large rewards have been offered for its recovery by the Governor ov Connecticut but it haz undoubtedly fled forever.

Some poor imitation ov the blessed old original pi are loafing around, but pumpkin pi az it waz, (with nutmeg in it) is no more.

"Rum and Tanzy."—Good old New England rum with tanzy bruised in it, was known to our ancients, and drank by the deacons and the elders ov our churches, a century ago.

It iz now one ov the lost arts.

A haff a pint ov this glorious old mixture upon gitting out ov bed in the morning, then a half pint jist before sitting down tew breakfast, then thru the day, at stated intervals, a haff a pint ov it, and some more ov it just before retiring at night, iz what enabled our fourfathers tew shake off the yoke of Great Britain, and gave the American eagle the majestic tread and thundering big back bone, which he used tew have. But, alas ! oh, alas ! we once had spirits ov just men made perfect, but we have now, (o alas !) spirits ov the damned!

One half-pint ov the present prevailing rum would ruin a deacon in twenty minutes.

Farewell, good old New England rum with some tansy in you, thou hast gone! yes, thou hast gone tew that bourn from which no good spirits come back.

"Rum, requiescat, et liquorissimus."

"Early to bed, and early to rize."

When our ancestors landed on Plymouth Rock out ov the May flower, and stood in front ov the great landscape spread out before them, reaching from the boisterious Atlantic to the bosom ov the plaintive Pacifick, they brought with them, among other tools, the art ov getting up in the morning, and going tew bed at nite in decent season.

This art they was az familiar to them, az codfish for breakfast.

They knew it by heart.

It waz the eleventh command in their catechism.

They taught it tew their children, their young men and maidens, and if a young one waz any ways slow about learning it he was invited out to the corn crib, and there the art was explained tew him so that he got hold ov the idea for ever and amen.

I am sorry to say that this art iz now lost, or missing.

What a loss was here, my countrymen!

I pause for a reply.

Not a word do I hear.

Silence iz its epitaph.

Perhaps some profane and unthinking cuss will exclaim— "Let her rip!"

Early tew bed and early tew rise, is either a thing of the past or a thing that ain't come—it certainly don't exist in these parts now.

It has not only gone itself, but it has took off a whole lot ov good things with it.

This art will positively never be discovered again; it waz the child ov innocence and vigor, and this breed ov children are like the babes in the wood, and deserted by their uncle.

"Honesty."—Honesty iz one ov the arts and sciences.

Learned men will tell you that the above assertion iz one ov Josh Billings infernal lies, and you have a perfect right tew believe them, but i don't.

Honesty iz jist az much an art az politeness iz, and never waz born with a man any more than the capacity to spell the word Nebuddkenozzer right the first time was.

It took me seven years to master this word, and i and Noah Webster both disagree about the right way now.

Sum men are naturally more addicted tew honesty than others, jist az some have a better ear for music, and learn how tew hoist and lower the 8 notes, more completely than the next man.

Honesty iz one ov the lost or mislaid arts—there may be exceptions tew this rule, but the learned men all agree that "exceptions prove the rule."

The only doubts i have about this matter iz tew locate the time very close, when honesty was first lost.

When Adam in the garden of Eden was asked, *"Where art thou Adam,"* and afterwards explained his abscence by saying, *"I, waz afraid,"* iz az far back az I hav been able tew trace the first indications ov weakness in this grand and noble art.

I shouldn't be surprised if this art never waz fully recovered again during my day.

I aint so anxious about it on my own account, for i can manage tew worry along somehow without it, but what iz agoing tew become ov the great mass ov suffering humanity?

This iz a question that racks my simpathetic bosom!

■   ■   ■

CALCULATIONS OV A PROGNOSTIC NATURE.

Whenever yu see a flock ov geese all standing on one leg, except the old gander, and he chawing hiz cud, look out for a south-west wind tewmorrow, or the next day, or the day after, or at some future time.

Should there be cold weather during Febuary, and should roosters refuse to crow, and the taxgatherers forget tew call on you, you will have tew trust in Providence and go it blind, for there aint no man can prognostix what will come next.

Whenever dogs are seen travelling around with nothing to do and old maids refuse their tea, and hop vines won't climb, and grind stones won't grind, then you may expect a lite crop ov oats, and beans won't pay for harvesting.

If the sun rises in the east, and sets in the west, and the bull frogs sings psalms in the marshes, and there aint no pulling hair in the family circle, things are about as near right az you can git them.

Should there be no dew on the grass, in the morning before sunrise, it iz an infallible prognostix, that there didn't any dew fall.

■　　■　　■

FEAR.

Some folks think fear iz the result ov education, but i dont.

I notice that those who are educated the most, and those who are educated the least, are troubled with fear just alike.

Fear and courage are instincts.

A man who iz a coward iz born so, and, when he iz full ov scare, his hare on his head will git up on end, and I dont care how much education you pile on top ov it.

The greatest cowards in the world are the men ov the most genius—they are the most silly cowards.

One ov these kind ov men will quake with fear when a mouse gnaws in the wainscote at night, but they will face an earthquake the next day with composure.

I dont know ov a more terrible sensation than fear; it iz death when it exhausts itself and ends in despair.

I am a great coward myself, and believe i was born so, and yet there is nothing which i despise so much as cowardice.

I would give all the other virtews i hav got (provided i have got any), and throw in a hundred dollars in money besides, for an unlimited supply ov courage.

I would like tew have courage enough tew face the devil him self, if he was the least bit sassy tew me.

I am satisfied that courage iz an instinct, for i notice all the animal creation have it well defined.

■　　■　　■

When a rooster crows, he crows all over.

■　　■　　■

A new milk Cow is stepmother tew evry man's baby.

■　　■　　■

Whenever i can find a real handsome woman engaged in the "wimmins rights" bizzness, then i am going tew take my hat under my arm and join the procession.

■　　■　　■

Debt is a trap, which a man sets, and baits himself, and then deliberately gets into—and catches a cursid fool!

■   ■   ■

QUESTIONS AND ANSWERS

Qu.—How fast will the *"come-ing man"* probably travel?

Ans.—It iz impossible tew say, but if he cant beat 2:25 he'd better stay where he is, for there is no glory left for a slow cuss, in these parts, but to run foot races with the crab family.

Qu.—What iz the most carniverous animal?

Ans.—Death.

Qu.—What iz the easiest thing tew digest?

Ans.—A good joke.

Qu.—Do yu think that females can ever practice medicine successfully?

Ans.—Why not! they can beat the world bleeding a pocket book.

Qu.—Iz there anything that iz proof against ridicule?

Ans.—Nothing that i know ov, except fashion, and mosquitos.

Qu.—Iz it proper tew speak tew a lady acquaintance in the street first, or last?

Ans.—I should think first, for they tell me that wimmin will hav the last word.

Qu.—Who are the only real temperance folks in the world?

Ans.—The Greenlanders, whiskey never thaws out there.

Qu.—Iz it proper under any circumstances tew use the word *Damn* as a tonic?

Ans.—It might possibly be proper, in speaking ov a river that was dry eleven months in the year, to state carefully that it wasn't worth a dam.

Qu.—What iz one ov the principal dutys we owe to our country?

Ans.—The customs.

Qu.—Which do yu consider the most general passion ov the human heart?

Ans.—The love ov applause; it sticks tew evrybody during life, and repeats itself on the tombstone.

Qu.—If you was *blest*! with a boy, which ov the lernt professions would yu dedicate him to?

Anw.—The shoemakers.

Qu.—Iz there any rule to obtain long life?

Ans.—Only one; live virtuously; a good life, if ever so short casts a lengthning shadow back upon time, and forward into eternity.

Qu.—Which do yu count the happyest time in a man's life?

Ans.—Immediately after he has did a square thing.

Qu.—Is whiskey a tonic?

Ans.—No, it iz an alterative; it alters dollars into pence, and men into brutes.

Qu.—Iz revenge a victory?

Ans.—Kill a hornet after he has stung yu, and see if the wound heals any quicker.

Qu.—Don't you think that nearly all the shrewd sayings and snug fitting maxims, in support ov morality, and for the scourgeing ov vice and folly are simply a rehash ov what haz been written long ago bi the ancients?

Ans.—I do, but that iz no argument against their reputation; there iz just az much use for phisick now az there was when castor oil was fust invented.

Qu.—What is the difference between a mistake and a blunder?

Ans.—When a man sets down a poor umbrella and takes up a good one he makes a mistake, but when he sets down a good umbrella and takes up a poor one he makes a blunder.

Qu.—If i couldn't have but one thing, what do you think it would be?

Ans.—Contentment, for with that i could buy all the rest.

Qu.—Which do yu think iz the best representative man, the lively or the sorry Christian?

Ans.—There aint nothing in my practice so hard tew judge ov as pious heft, but i don't think the Lord ever takes the length of a man's face for a suit of heavenly clothes; he measures the soul.

Qu.—What iz the best cure for love?

Ans.—Tew live on it.

Qu.—What iz the best cure for pride?

Ans.—A fall on the ice before folks.

Qu.—What iz a sick old bachelor like?

Ans.—A cocoon.

Qu.—What iz an excuse?

Ans.—The finesse ov reason.

■   ■   ■

PRIVATE OPINION.

Mi private opinion iz—that politeness iz about the only profession ov humans that i endorse without looking into.

Mi private opinion of *Fame* iz—that it consists in being praised wrongfully while you live, and being damned incorrectly when you are dead, and the very best it can do for any man, iz tew make him respectably forgotten.

Mi private opinion iz—that a bad joke, iz like a bad eg, all the worse for being cracked.

Mi private opinion iz—that manufacturing fun for other pholks amusement, iz like hatching out eggs a sober, steady bizzness.

Mi private opinion iz—that originality in writing was played out long ago, and the very best that any man can do, iz tew steal with good judgement, and then own it like a man.

Mi private opinion iz—that the most that learning can do for us, iz tew teach us how little we know.

Mi private opinion ov civilation iz—that it always ends in luxury, and luxury always ends in destruction. The barbarians have always outlasted the Christians, i am dreadful sorry for this, but i cant help it.

Mi private opinion iz—that a young man oftner neglects hiz genius for sawing wood than he does for writing poetry.

Mi private opinion iz—that adversity and temptation are the very best kind ov tests ov virtue.

Mi private opinion ov human happiness iz—that it iz like Jonah's gourd, it often looses in a nite all that it grew in a day.

Mi private opinion ov a braggart iz—that he iz a sheep in wolf's clothing.

Mi private opinion ov a prude iz, that their greatest anxiety iz tew have their propriety tempted.

Mi private opinion ov woman iz, that she iz a natural brick, and she iz a fool just in proportion that she don't know it.

■   ■   ■

GOOD RESOLUTIONS FOR 1872, 1873, & 1874 [or 1984, 1985, 1986]

THAT i wont smoke any more cigars, only at somebody else's expense.

That i wont borry nor lend—especially lend.

That i will be polite tew everybody, except muskeeters and bed-bugs.

That i wont advise any boddy, until i know the kind ov advice they are anxious tew follow.

That i wont eat any more chicken soup with a one-tined fork.

That i wont object tew any man on account ov hiz color, unless he happens to be blue.

That i wont swear any, unless i am put under oath.

That i wont believe in total depravity, only in gin at 4 shillings a gallon.

That poverty may be a blessing, but if it iz, it iz a blessing in dis-guise.

That i will take mi whisky hereafter straight—straight tew the gutter.

That the world owes me a living—provided i earn it.

That i wont swop any hosses with a deacon.

That no man shall beat me in politeness, not so long az polite-ness continues tew be az cheap az it iz now.

That i wont hav any religious creed miself, but will respect every body else's.

That if a lovely woman smacks me on one check, i will turn her the other also.

That if a man calls me a fool, i wont ask him to prove it.

That i will lead a moral life, even if i lose a good deal ov fun by it. That if a man tells me a mule wont kick, i will beleave what he sez without trying it.

That if i ever do git a hen that can lay 2 eggs a day, i shall insist upon her keeping one ov the eggs on hand for a sinking fund.

That it iz no disgrace tew be bit by a dog unless he duz it the sec-ond time.

That it iz just az natural tew be born rich az poor, but it iz seldom so convenient.

That one ov the riskiest things tew straddle iz the back ov a 60-day note.

That the best time tew repent ov a blunder iz just before the blun-der is made.

That i will try hard tew be honest, but it will be just my darn luck tew miss it.

That i won't grow any cats. Spontaneous cats have killed the business.

That i will love my mother-in-law if it takes all the money i can earn tew do it.

That i believe real good lies are gitting scarser and scarser everyday.

That i will respect public opinion just az long az i can respect myself in doing it.

That when i hear a man bragging on hiz ancestors i won't envy him, but i will pity the ancestors.

That i wont believe in any ghost or ghostesses unless they weigh about 140 pounds and can eat a good square meal.

That i will brag on mi wife all the time, but i will do it silently.

■　　　■　　　■

About the last thing a man duz tew correct hiz faults iz tew quit them.

■　　　■　　　■

Fool and drunken men always make this mistake, the one thinks they are sensible, and the other always thinks they are sober.

■　　　■　　　■

MISSELLANEOUS

Mi private opinion iz—that when a man haint got any thing tew say, then iz the best time not tew say it.

Mi private opinion iz—that some men did actually spring from the monkey, and didn't hav far tew spring neither.

Mi private opinion ov *Rum* iz—that the man who sells it to hiz fellow man iz worse than a hiwayman—the hiwayman demands your money or your life—the rumseller demands both.

Mi private opinion ov "*Wimmin's Rites*" iz—that nature haz fixed them jist about *rite*, and nature never underlets a contract, nor backs out ov a posishun.

Mi private opinion ov sectarian religion iz—that it iz like cider drawn from a musty cask, it always tastes ov the cask. Thoze who at last enter Heaven may find the outer walls placarded with creeds, but they wont find any on the inside.

Mi private opinion iz—that virtue iz better than gold; but i also have bin told that 10 dollars in gold will go farther towards bilding a church, or a hoss railroad, than all the piety ov Moses.

Mi private opinion ov boys iz, if i hadn't been one once myself, and a tuff one at that, i should feel like sending the whole ov them, for life, to Botany Bay.

Mi private opinion ov girls iz, the same az it was 40 years ago, when i first fell in luv with one ov them.

Mi private opinion ov the mass ov mankind iz, that they have got more brains in their hearts than they have in their heads, and i ain't sorry for it neither.

Mi private opinion iz, that politeness haz won more sudden victorys than logic haz.

Mi private opinion ov dogs iz, that their affections ought almost tew make them immortal.

Mi private opinion ov cats iz, that Judas Iskarriot ought tew hav owned the first one, and the last one too.

Mi private opinion ov myself iz that while i keep both eyes on mi neighbor I hope they wont fail tew keep one eye on me.

Mi private opinion iz that here iz a good place tew halt, and i am a big fool if i don't.

■   ■   ■

Pills will sometimes refuse to act on the liver, but sawing wood never will.

■   ■   ■

When i waz 20 i knew twice az much as i do now, and the way things are going on, if i should live to be 75, i don't expect to know nothing.

■   ■   ■

There iz no radical cure for lazyness, but starvation will cum the nearest to it.

■   ■   ■

I am satisfied that the 2 greatest bores in the world are the Hasiu tunnel and the author who iz hunting up a publisher for his first book.

■   ■   ■

Living on Hope iz like living on wind, a good way tew git full, but a poor way tew git fat.

■   ■   ■

Experience don't make a man so bold az it duz so careful.

■   ■   ■

Advice iz like kissing—it don't cost nothing, and iz a pleazant thing to do.

■   ■   ■

We laff at sheep because when one ov them leads the way all the rest follow, however ridiculous it may be, and i suppose sheep laff, when they see us doing the vary same thing.

■   ■   ■

Hiprocrasy is one ov the vices that yu cant convert, ya might az well undertake tew git the wiggle out ov a snake or the grease out ov fat pork.

■   ■   ■

Solomon remarked "that there wasn't anything new under the sun," and it duz really seem that if a man sez anything nu he haz got tew lie a leetle tew do it.

■   ■   ■

I suppose the reason why we all ov us admire the Atlantic Ocean so much iz because it don't belong tew any body in particular; for what we cant own, iz about all that we aint jealous ov.

■   ■   ■

I suppose that why advice is such a drug in the market iz because the supply alwus exceeds the demand.

■   ■   ■

A LAFF

Men who never laff, may have good hearts, but they are deep seated,—like some springs: they have their inlet and outlet from below, and show no sparkling bubble on the brim.

I don't like a giggler, this kind ov laff iz like the dandelion, a feeble yeller, and not a bit ov good smell about it.

It iz true that any kind of a laff iz better than none—but give me the laff that looks out ov a man's eyes fust, to see if the coast is clear, then steals down into the dimple ov his cheek, and rides in an eddy there awhile, then walzes a spell at the corners ov his mouth, like a thing ov life, then busts it bonds ov beauty, and fills the air for a moment with a shower ov silvery tongued sparks,—then steals back, with a smile, to its lair, in the heart, tew watch again for its prey,—this is the kind ov laff that i love, and aint afraid ov.

■　　　■　　　■

HONESTY

Honesty iz like money, a man haz got to work hard to get it, and then haz got to work harder to keep it. Honesty iz the best card in the pack; it iz always trumps, and there iz no man big fool enough but what he can play it right every time. Honesty haz been praised more, and practiced less, than any ov the virtews, but it stands in need ov no ones praise, and fears no ones rebuke. Honesty iz all the virtew that a man needs, and all that an angel has. Honest men are scarce and what i am afraid ov now iz, they are goin to be scarcer. From Adam's day to ours, and from now until the judgement time, an *Honest man* has been, and will be, *"The noblest work of God."* Pope's description ov an honest man iz the simplest, and yet the strongest language, that ever has been used.

■　　　■　　　■

FUN

Fun is the cheapist physic that has bin discovered yet and the eazyest to take. Fun pills are sugar-coated, and no change ov diet iz necessary while taking them. A little fun will sometimes go a great ways, i hav known men to live to a good old age on one joke, which they managed to tell az often az once a day, and do all the laffing themselves besides that was done. But there iz lots ov folks who cant see any fun in any thing, you couldn't fire a joke into them with a double-barrell gun, 10 paces off, they go thru life az sollum az a cow. Many people think it iz beneath their dignity to relish a joke, such people are simply fools, and dont seem to know it. The Billings family are allways on the lookout for fun, it iz sed ov Dexter Billings, one ov our pristines, that he had to be kept under 500 dollar bonds all the time, to keep him from laffing in church. Accordin to all account this Dexter Billings waz a cuss. Fun iz the pepper and salt ov every day life, and all the really wise men who have ever lived, have used it freely for seasoning.

■　　　■　　　■

LAUGHING.

I T never haz been proved, that any ov the animal creation have attempted tew laff, (we are quite certain that none have succeded;) thus this deliteful episode and pleasant power appears tew be entirely within the province ov humans.

It iz the language ov infancy—the eloquense ov childhood,—and the power tew laff is the power to be happy.

It is becoming tew all ages and conditions; and (with the very few exceptions, sacred tew sorrow) an honest, hearty laff iz always agreeable and in order.

It is an index ov character, and betrays sooner than words—Laffing keeps off sickness, and haz conquered az many diseases az ever pills have, and at much less expense.—It makes flesh, and keeps it in its place. It drives away weariness and brings a dream ov sweetmess tew the sleeper.—It never iz covetous.—It accompanies charity, and iz the handmaid ov honesty.—It disarms revenge, humbles pride, and iz the talisman ov contentment.—Some have called it a weakness—a substitute for thought, but really it strengthens wit, and adorns wisdom, invigorates the mind, gives language ease, and expression elegance.—It holds the mirror up tew beauty; it strengthens modesty, and makes virtue heavenly.

It iz the light ov life; without it we should be but animated ghosts.

It challenges fear, hides sorrow, weakens despair, and carries half ov poverty's bundles.—It costs nothing, comes at the call, and leaves a brite spot behind.—It is the only index ov gladness, and the only beauty that time cannot effase.—It never grows old; it reaches from the cradle clear tew the grave.

Without it, love would be no passion, and fruition would show no joy.—It iz the fust and the last sunshine that visits the heart; it was the warm welcom ov Eden's lovers, and was the only capital that sin left them tew begin bizzness with outside the Garden ov Paradise.

■   ■   ■

Every time a man laffs hearty, he takes a kink out ov the chain that binds him to life, and thus lengthens it.

■   ■   ■

BRAINES

BRAINES are a sort ov animal pulp, and by common consent are supposed tew be the medium ov thought.

How any body knows that the braines do the thinking, or are the interpreters ov thought, is more than i can tell; and, for what i know, this theory may be one ov those remarkable discoverys ov man which aint so.

These subjeks are tew mutch for a man ov my learning tew lift. i cant prove any ov them, and i hav too much venerashun tew guess at them.

Braines are generally suposed tew be located in the head but investigations satisfys me that they are planted all over the body.

I find that a dancing master's are situated in his heels and toes, while a fiddler's all center in his elbows.

Sum people's braines seem tew be placed in their hands and fingers, which explains their grate genius for taking things which they can reach.

I have seen cases where all the braines seemed tew congregate in the tongue; and once in a great while they inhabit the ears, and then we hav a good listener, but these are seldom cases.

Sum times the braines ain't any where in particular, but all over the body in a minnit. These fellows are like a pissmire just before a hard shower, in a big hurry, and always trieing tew go 4 different ways tew once.

There seems tew be cases where there aint any braines at all but this is a mistake. i thought i had cum across one ov these kind once, but after watching the patient for an hour, and see him drink 5 horns ov poor whiskey during the time, i had no trouble in telling where hiz braines all lay.

I hav finally cum tew the conclusion that braines, or sumthing else that iz good tew think with, are excellent tew have, but you want tew keep your eye on them, and not let them fool away their time, not yours neither.

■ ■ ■

Americans love caustic things; they would prefer turpentine tew colone-water, if they had tew drink either.

So with their relish of humor; they must hav it on the half-shell with cayenne.

An Englishman wants hiz fun smothered deep in mint sauce, and he iz willing tew wait till next day before he tastes it.

If you tickle or convince an American you have got tew do it quick.

An American loves tew laff, but he don't love tew make a bizzness ov it; he works eats, and hawhaws on a canter.

I guess the English have more wit, and the Americans more humor.

We havn't had time, yet tew boil down our humor and git the wit out ov it.

    ■   ■   ■

The time tew be carefullest iz when we hav a hand full ov trumps.

    ■   ■   ■

Imagination, tew much indulged in, soon iz tortured into reality; this iz one way that good hoss thiefs are made, a man leans over a fence all day, and imagines the hoss in the lot belongs tew him, and sure enough, the fust dark night, the hoss does.

    ■   ■   ■

There is quite a difference between a *luminous* and a *vo*luminous writer, altho many authors confound the two.

    ■   ■   ■

A man who haint got any imagination at all, iz just right for a hitching post.

    ■   ■   ■

Mankind ain't apt tew respect very much what they are familiar with, it iz what we don't know, or cant see, that we hanker for.

    ■   ■   ■

Tew enjoy a good reputasion, give publickly, and steal privately.

    ■   ■   ■

Jealousy don't pay, the best it can do, iz tew discover what we don't want tew find, nor don't expect to.

Blessed are they who hav no eye for a key hole.

There iz nothing like a sick bed for repentance, a man bekums so virtewous he will often repent ov sins he never committed.

Natur never makes enny blunders; when she makes a phool she means it.

Thare iz sum pholks in this world who spend their whole lives a lusting after righteousness, and kant find enny time tew praktiss it.

When a man gits to going
down hill, it duz seem,
az tho every thing had
been greased for the oekashun.
                    Josh Billings

CHAPTER II

MEN IN THEIR REALITIES

Falling in luv, iz like falling down stairs.— we never kan tell exackly how the thing woz did.—

In Haste, Josh Billings

■   ■   ■

I don't believe in fighting; i am solemly aginst it; but if a man gits to fighting, i am also solemly aginst hiz gitting licked. After a fight iz once opened, all the virtew there iz in it iz tew lick the other party.

■   ■   ■

I never knew anybody yet to git stung by hornets, who kept away from where they was—it iz jist so with bad-luck.

■   ■   ■

There are but few men weak enuff tew admit their jealousys-even a disgraced rooster, in a barn-yard, will git a little further off and begin to crow up a new reputashun.

■   ■   ■

THE HAPPY MAN.

The happy man iz a poor judge of hiz own bliss, for he kant set down and describe it.

Happiness iz like health—thoze who hav the most ov it seem to know it the least.

You cant go out in the spring ov the year and gather happiness along the side ov the road just the same az you would dandylions—nobody but a natural born fool can do this, they are always happy, ov course.

When i hear a man bragging how happy he iz, he dont cheat me, he only cheats himself.

■   ■   ■

THE ONE IDEA MAN

The one idea man iz like the merino ram, he shuts up both eyes and goes for things incontinently. He misses, ov course, oftener than he hits, but don't know the difference, and is always ready to argue the question. You cant convince him that he iz wrong any more than you can a hornet.

Cne idea men are their own wust enemys, and there iz but one cure for them, and that iz to agree with them. If you think just az they do, they will soon want to think sum other way, and that lets two ideas git into their head, which makes them perhaps endurable.

■   ■   ■

An enthusiast iz an individual who beleaves about four times az mutch az he can prove, and who can prove about four times az mutch az any body else believes.

■   ■   ■

Diogoneze hunted in the day time for an honest man, with a lantern; if he had lived in theze times, he would hav needed the head lite ov a locomotive.

■   ■   ■

Thare iz no cure for vanity, gitting thoroly wet cums the nearest to it, for the time being.

■   ■   ■

A *poor, but dishonest cuss* iz about az low down az any man can git, unless he drinks whiskee too.

■   ■   ■

The man who can set himself to work, at anything, on 5 minutes notiss, haz got one of the best trades i know ov.

■   ■   ■

THE OFFICIOUS MAN.

The officious man stands around rubbing his hands, anxious for a job.

He seems tew ache for something tew do, and if he gits snubbed in one place, it don't seem to discourage him, but like the fly, he lights on another.

The officious man iz az free from malice az a young pup, who, if he cant do anything else, iz ready tew lay down in front of yu and be stept on.

These kind ov men spend their whole lives trying to make friends ov all, and never suceed with any.

There iz a kind ov officious man, who iz only prompted by his vanity, hiz anxiety to be useful tew others don't arise from any goodness ov heart, but simply from a desire ov sticking hiz noze into things.

Theze kind ov individuals are supremely disgusting.

The officious man iz generally ov no use whatever to himself, and a nuisance tew everyboddy else.

I don't know ov but few more unfortunit dispositions than the officious mans, for even in its very best phase, it seldom succeeds in gitting paid for its labors with common politeness.

■   ■   ■

Man waz created a little lower than the angels, but while an infant, fell one day out ov hiz kradle, and hain't struck bottom yet.

■   ■   ■

Solomon remarked: "that thare wasn't anything nu under the sun," and it duz really seem that if a man sez anything nu he haz got to lie a leetle to do it.

■   ■   ■

When a man gits to talking about himself, he seldum fails to be eloquent, and often reaches the sublime.

■   ■   ■

When a man measures out glory for himself he alwus heaps the half-bushel.

■   ■   ■

God save the phools! and don't let them run out, for if it wasn't for them, wise men couldn't git a livin.

■   ■   ■

THE LIVE MAN.

The *Live Man* iz like the little pig; he iz weaned young, and begins to root arly.

He iz the peppersauce ov creation—the all-spice ov the world.

One *Live Man* in a village is like a case ov itch in a distrikt school—he sets everybody scratching at onst.

A man who kan draw New Orleans molasses in the month ov January, thru a half inch augur-hole, and sing "Home! sweet home!" while the molasses iz running, may be strictly honest, but he aint sudden enough for this climate.

The Live Man iz az full of business az the conducter ov a street car—he iz often like a hornet, very busy, but about what, the Lord only knows.

He lights up like a cotton factory, and haint got any more time tew spare than a school-boy has Saturday afternoons.

He is like a decoy duck, alwus above water, and lives at least 18 months each year.

He iz like a runaway hoss; he gits the whole ov the road.

He trots when he walks, and lies down at night only because everyboddy else duz.

The *Live Man* is not always a deep thinker; he jumps at conclusions, just as the frog duz, and don't always land at the spot he is looking at.

He is the Amerikan pet, a perfect mystery to foreigners; but he has done more (with charcoal) to work out the greatness of this country than any other man in it.

He is jist as necessary as the grease on an axle-tree.

He don't always die rich, but always dies busy and meets death a good deal az an oyster does, without making any fuss.

■   ■   ■

THE FAULT-FINDER.

Good Lord, deliver us from the fault-finder, one ov your cronic grunters, i mean. Theze kind ov human critters are always full ov self conceit; if they waz humble and would dam themself okasionally, i would try tew pity them. Your fault-finding old-bachelor, for instanze, orders a pair ov No. 8 boots, and then collides with his shumaker instead ov his big feet; he walks tew the depot tew save hack-hire and misses the train, and then kolides with the time-table; he courts a gal till she has tew marry somebody else tew keep from spoiling, and then he don't believe thare is a virtuous woman living. If he enjoys anything he duz it under protest, and if anybody else enjoys anything he knows they lie about it. He is like a second rate bull tarrier, alwus a fighting and alwus gitting licked. These kind ov critters never are ready tew die because thay haint never begun tew live. I never make their ackquaintanse any more than i dew somebody's small pox, bekause i am a looking after bright things and haint got any to lose. Thare aint any remedy for this dissease but hunger, and that aint parmanent unless it results in starvation. Good Lord, deliver us from the fault-finder! if yu undertake tew argue with them yu only flatter them, and if yu join in with them yu only maik them mad with themselfs.

I had rather be a target for awl the bad luck in this world than tew go thru life shooting a pizen arrow at all the good luck. The more i think ov it, the more i keep thinking that fault-finding iz verry much like bobing for eels with a raw potater; a first rate way tew git out ov conceit ov all kinds ov fishing, and a fust rate way not tew ketch any eels.

■　　　■　　　■

The reputashun that a man gits from hiz ansestors, often wants az mutch altering to fit him, az their old clothes would.=
It iz truly thus, Josh Billings.=

THE CUNNING MAN

C UNNING iz often took for wisdum, but it iz the mere scum that rizes when wisdom biles her pot, it haz not the stride ov wisdom, neither haz it the honesty ov wisdom, it iz more like instinct, than it iz like reason.

Cunning ain't good at begetting, it iz better at executing, it iz like the wisdom ov a kat, fust rate tew watch a rat hole.

The cunning man haz two virtues always prominent, patience, and energy, without these he would fall below the kat, and fail tew git his mouse.

Thare iz lots ov cunning men who are like an unskillful trapper, who knows how tew set a trap, but hain't got the wisdom tew bait it.

Cunning men alwus hav a speciality, such az it iz, i hav seen them who could ride a mule to a spot, but who set a hoss awkwardly.

Thare iz this average between a cunning man and a wise man, the cunning man's wisdom iz alwus on the outside ov hiz face, he can't hide it, it iz alwus squirting out ov the corner ov his eyes, while the wise man carrys hiz grist deep, stowed away in hiz heart, and don't use hiz wisdum tew find occasions but tew master them, when they pop up.

Cunning men have grate caution, because they suppose themselfs watched, inasmutch az they are always watching others.

They have but few brains, but what they have are petroleum, and their brains being few, and greasy, enables them to fetch them to a focus sudden.

It iz hard work to be very cunning and very honest, at the same time, i reckon this, because i don't see the two hugging and kissing each other very much.

Cunning haz a scandalous pedigree, he iz the babe ov Wisdom, and Fraud, and iz the only child they ever had, but looks and acts just like his ma.

It would take a big book to make an almanack ov a cunning man, and the changes in him, fits, starts, and doubles, and hiz windings, hiz in's and hiz outs, the parables in which he talks, and the double entenders ov hiz face, all that he duz, and awl that he thinks, are for effect.

Cunning men's advice iz hard to follow, because their wisdom iz made like a bed quilt, out ov patches, and iz also composed ov shifts, for the emergency ov an occasion, tew much for a steady diet.

If you don't understand wiggling yourself, or the rudiments ov it, you must not git your advice from the cunning man.

Cunning haz alwus passed for wisdom, and will continue on to do so, az long az phools last, and phools will last az long az anybody else does, and sustain their reputashun.

Cunning iz alwus selfish, because it iz not ov much breadth, while wisdom can afford tew be magnanimous, and hav sumthing left over.

But the ways and dodges ov cunning are past finding out, yu might az well undertake tew track a snake in the grass, when the dew iz off, or a fox, in a straight line tew hiz hole.

Cunning men are not very dangerous, they have so much vanity, and their vanity satisfied, their ambition iz. And when vanity takes the place ov ambition, we are more amused than alarmed.

Cunning men, in the hands ov wize men, are useful, more useful, quite often, than honesty, because they are more sudden and less simple.

It is safer tew entrust a secret tew a cunning man, than a clever man, the clever man is sure tew spill it, the cunning one may use it aginst yu, but he iz eazier tew watch, and control, than the good natured fellow, who, like a young pup, lays down, rolls over, and wags himself in front ov every man he meets.

Cunning men hav manny associates, but few intimates, they sometimes hunt in couples, but are apt tew fight, when they come to divide the plunder.

■　　　　■　　　　■

There iz no passion ov the human heart that promises so much and pays so little az revenge.

■　　　　■　　　　■

The man who thinks "he kant do it," iz alwuss more than haff right.

■　　　　■　　　　■

Dandys and blujays are alike, both worthless without their feathers.

■　　　　■　　　　■

THE DECEITFUL CUSS

The Deceitful Cuss—An open enemy, a hearty hater, a bold dead-beater, an imperious friend, a foolish chum, a reckless companion, anything in shape ov human, or ov brute, and even all things devlish, are mince pies with raisins in them, compared tew a slipping, sneaking *Deceit,* who, under the guise and garments ov being in love with you, chaws tobacker out ov your box, and lies tew yu every time he tells yu the truth.

These human skunks are thick in this world, their eyes are like the cats, made tew see in the dark, they have the face ov a sheep, and the heart ov a snake, they can cry at an impromptu christening, they are az full ov cunning as a she opposum, and would rather fail in an enterprise than to do it honestly.

These critters, az awkward as it may seem, are full ov vanity and ambition, and their vanity and ambition iz tew play lion under a sheep's skin.

It iz a strange ambition that a man will cultivate wisdom only for the sake ov being cunning, that he will perfect himself in the art and imagery of love and friendship for the sake ov counterfitting them, that he will study pity for gain, that he will work hard for the devil at 2 shillings a day, and finally, that he will practice the rudiments ov awl the virtews ov social life, simply for the sake ov doing with a good grace what iz shameful and wicked to do at all.

I have known men ov this brand, who where not wholly malicious, who would actually do yu a good turn to-morrow if they could cheat yu to-day, who deceive not entirely for gain, but tew keep their tools wet, who have some excellent traits, which sumtimes drop out seemingly by mistake.

But a natural crook toward deception iz like the bite ov a mad dog, it may sleep for a long time in the veins ov its victim, very well behaved poison, watching for a good time, but sooner or later, when least expected, the virus begins tew play dog by asserting its dredful prerogative.

It don't cure these vermin tew ketch them, if they was rats, which we could drown in the trap, it would be bully, but letting them go only makes them more cunning.

Deception iz one ov the sciences, it has its deacons, elders and hod carriers, the world swarms with them, all ov the pimps among them, such az the wooden nutmeg makers, and the small beer-cheats, we can punish enuff by dispising, but what reward, short ov the gibbet, or at least the whipping post, iz equal tew the villian-ous cuss who creeps on hiz body into your confidence, a subdued and shivering snake, and warms up into a viper.

Ingratitude iz one ov them diabolikal crimes that awl men hate, but leave the punishment to heaven.

■　　　■　　　■

THE GENEROUS MAN

The Generous Man.—Generosity iz an instinct—a kind ov natu-ral crook— a weird child ov the heart.

It iz different from profusion; profusion iz most always the decoy duck ov vanity.

Generosity iz diffrent from charity; charity iz the impulse ov reason.

It iz different from justice—justice iz 16 ounces tew the pound, and no more.

Generosity iz sumthing more than justice, and sumthing less than profusion; it iz the good a man does without being able to give any reazon for it.

If a man iz always genrous he will always be right, or will have a good excuse for what seems to be wrong.

Generosity iz bravery, and it iz truth; no one ever saw a generous man who was a coward or a liar.

Generosity sometimes may lack prudence, but it never lacks faith, and faith has won holier laurels than prudence ever did.

The generous man chastens his gifts with the assurance that the giver iz az happy in the gift as the receiver iz.

He takes the first swaller out ov the dipper, and smacking his lips, insists upon your drinking the balance all up.

Poverty has no power over generosity any more than it has over love.

This iz my idee ov the kind ov generosity that I am writing about.

■　　　■　　　■

Cunning men are sure tew git caught at last, and when they are kaught they are like a fox in a trap, about the silliest looking fox yu ever see.

■　　　■　　　■

To be a big man among big men, iz what proves a man's charac-ter—to be a bull frog amoung tadpoles, don't amount to much.

■   ■   ■

THE PROJECTOR

The projector iz a man with one idea and that idea iz often like a paving stone, the hardest kind ov a thing tew hatch out, and when it iz hatched out, yu can't always tell what kind ov a breed the thing iz.

He has been busy at work for the last 4 thousand years trying tew build pertetual motion, and has come within 3 quarters ov an inch ov it several times, but always slips up jist as he reaches out tew grab it.

He has done sum dreadful good things for mankind, but too often iz ov no more use in the world, than an extra pump iz.

The projector iz alway a man ov genius, but hiz genius iz frequently like the genius ov a goose, thare ain't no one can beat them at standing on one leg.

I have known these breed ov folks tew drag out a long life, richer in their own estimation than Croesus, and poorer in the opinion ov others than Lazarus.

They seldum reap any gain from their inventions, and if ever they do discover perpetual motion, they will sell the principle tew some cunning cuss, for 17 or 18 dollars, and starve tew death on the glory ov it.

I have known several ov these poor phellows in my life, and only knew them tew pity them, for they are az tender, all over, az spring lamb, and az easy tew cheat as a blind baby.

I have a friend who iz a projector. I kant tell what particular folly he iz at work at now, but there aint on the whole earth, a more busy critter than the man who iz sure that tomorrow will put the finishing touches tew his patent right plan, for threading the wrong end ov a needle, or his recipe for making soft soap out ov calfs liver.

But we can't spare the projectors, all that we can hope for iz, that too many ov them wont spend a whole life in making a jews harp that will play Yankee Doodle backwards, and finally die, and leave the tune half finished.

■   ■   ■

The biggest fool in this world haint been born yet; there iz plenty ov time yet.

■   ■   ■

Hunting after fame iz like hunting after fleas, hard tew catch, and sure tew make yu uneasy if yu do or don't catch it.

■　　　　■　　　　■

Phools, like fishes, always run in skools.

■　　　　■　　　　■

THE CHEEKY MAN

Impudence, or sumthing like it, iz the leading trait in most suck-cessful mens characters.

All the nice things that have bin said in favour ov modesty, fail tew stand the test when brought into the pull and haul of every-day life.

Bold assurance, while it may often disgust us, will win 9 times out ov 10.

We all ov us praise the modest, but our praise iz only a kind ov pity, and pity will ruin any man.

Any man will live four times az long on abuse, and git phatt, as he will on pity.

Thare iz now and then a man who iz modest, but intensely in earnest, and such men sweep everything before them.

The karakter ov the modest man iz a good thing, and a butiful thing tew frame and hang up in a private apartment, but experience teaches us that if we wait for our turn in this world *our turn* never seems tew come round.

The cheeky man never enjoys those delightful sensations which arize from having yielded tew others; hiz logick iz that the early bird gits the worm, and, regardless ov all delicacy he goes for the worm.

There seems tew be nothing now daze that will warrant success like cheek, and the more cheek the better, even if you have az mutch az a mule.

■　　　　■　　　　■

There iz many folks who are like mules, the only way tew their affections iz thru the kindness ov a club.

■　　　　■　　　　■

Suavity ov manners towards men iz like suavity ov molassis to-ward flies, it not only calls them to you, but sticks them fast after they git there.

■　　　　■　　　　■

I have larn't one thing by grate experience, and that iz, I want as much watching az my nabors do.

■   ■   ■

The most miserable people i kno ov are thoze who make pleaure a bizzness; it iz like sliding down a hill 25 miles long.

■   ■   ■

There iz just az mutch difference between precept and example, az there iz between a horn that blows a noize, and one that blows a tune.

■   ■   ■

I hav seen men so fond or argument, that they would dispute with a guide board, at the forks ov a kuntry road. about the distance to the next town. — Josh Billings
                    what fools.

■   ■   ■

THE KONDEM PHOOL.

There iz two kinds ov phools, at the date ov this article, laying around loose in the world, one iz the *natural*, and the other iz the *kondem*.

There iz sum other kind ov phools besides these, which I shall touch lightly before I git thru.

The natral phool cant help it, he iz born like the daisy, bi the side ov the road, just to nod, and to be sport for the winds.

He haz no destiny to fill, that we know ov, but hiz Heavenly

Father will care for him, for He cares for the coarse weed and the rank thistle.

The kondem phool iz a self-made man, and iz entitled tew all the credit ov the job.

Nature turns him out loose into the world, jist as she duz her other works, with all hiz facultys in good order, but like a ram in the back lot, he undertaiks tew knock down a stone fence with hiz head, and finds the stone fence too much for the occasion.

He often haz a head phull ov branes, but like a swarm ov bees, they keep up sich a buzzing they bewilder him.

The kondem phool generally lacks but one thing tew make him all the suckcess he could ask for, and that one thing iz common sense.

Common sense iz all greek tew these kind ov fellows, they kan often rite poetry that reads az smooth and sweet az oil and molassis mixt together, and kan even deliver lektures all around the country, but one dose ov common sense would take all the starch out ov them, and leave them az limpsey as the neck ov a ded goose.

The kondem phool iz the cause ov most all trouble that iz in this world, he ain't alwus malicious, but iz alwus a phool.

I divide the populashun ov the whole world into 2 heaps, and out ov respect for the parable ov the virgins in the bible, i call 5 ov them wise and 5 ov them foolish.

It is very easy tew be a kondem phool, anybody can be one, and not suspect it.

Thare iz a large invoice ov phools just now pressing upon the market, but the market for them iz steady, the demand always being full up tew the supply.

I rekolekt ov once saying, upon a memorable occasion, (i dont recollect the occasion now,) God bless the phools, and don't let them run out, for if it want for them, the rest ov the world would be bothered tew git a good living.

Among the list ov prominent phools, i take the liberty tew introduce the following:

The "Professional Phool," one who travels for a living.

The "Bizznes Phool," one who either Bulls or Bears everthing in the market.

The "Radical Phool," one who kant help it.

The "Conservative Phool," one who can help it, but wont.

The "Meek Phool," one who sez he prefers codfish balls to porterhouse stakes, or even quails on toast.

The "Hipressure Phool," one who, like the hornet, alwus keeps mad in advance, so az tew be ready for the occasion.

The "Silly Phool," one who thinks the whole civilized world iz in love with him.

The "Wise Phool," one who thinks he knows all things, and luvs everybody.

And four thousand, 3 hundred and 36 other distinct kinds ov phools, which i haint got the patience tew elucidate now.

No man iz rich who wants any more than what he haz got.

Wise men are like a watch, they have open countenances enough, but dont show their works in their face.

I hav made a close calculation on it, and i find that there aint more than 3 men, now on earth, nor never haint been, who can cultivate an excentricity with suckcess.

There are men who seem to be born on purpose to step into every thing; they kant set a common rat trap without gitting ketched in it.

When i come acrost a man who utters hiz opinions with immense deliberashun, and after they are uttered they dont amount to anything, I write him down "misterious phool."

Natur duz all her big and little jobs without making any fuss; the earth goes around the sun, the moon changes, the eclipses, and the pollywog, silently and taillessly, becomes a frog, but man cant even deliver a small-sized 4th ov July oration without knocking down a mountain or two and tareing up three or four primeval forests by bleeding roots.

A phools money iz like hiz brains, very uneazy.

THE OBTUSE MAN.

The obtuse man iz sawed off square at both ends, and iron

bound like a beetle.

He finds out the hard spot in things by running against them, and like the merino ram, shuts up both eyes when he butts.

It iz az hard tew git an idea into him az it iz tew git a wedge into a oak log.

He alwus sez "*Yes*" to what he don't understand, and iz az hard tew argue out ov a conceit az a dog iz out ov a bone.

He often sets himself up for a wise man, and sometimes a wit, but i never knew one tew think he was a bore.

He goes thru life head fust, and when he cums tew die he iz az well seasoned az a foot-ball.

If he waz a-going tew liv hiz life over again, he tells you, he wouldn't alter it, only he would eat more raw onions and be a hard-shell baptist.

Every man remembers him az a man too stubborn tew be very viscious, with a few ideas, sum ov which he inherited, but most ov which he got by sleeping with hiz mouth wide open.

■　　■　　■

THE CROSS MAN.

The cross man goes thru life like a sore-headed dog, followed by flies.

He iz az sour az a pot-bellied pickle, and like a skein of silk, iz always ready for a snarl.

He iz like an old hornet, mad all the way through, but about what, he kan't tell, tew save hiz life.

Everyboddy at home fears him, and everyboddy in the street despizes him.

He mistakes sullenness for bravery, and because he feels savage, everybody else must feel humble.

Thare iz no greater coward in the world than the cross man, nor none easier tew cure.

He iz easier tew cure than the stummuk ache, for one good knock down will do so.

■　　■　　■

THE FUNNY MAN.

The funny man can't open hiz mouth without letting a joke fly out, like ginger pop, when the cork iz pulled out.

Thare iz no genuine wit in the simply funny man, hiz only desire iz tew make yu laff, and real wit don't stoop so low.

The funny man's jokes are at best only jests, sumtimes he reaches tew the dignity ov a poor pun, and hiz vanity then absorbs all hiz humor.

It iz an awful thing tew be a funny man, it iz almost az dreadful az the counterfiting bizzness.

Thare iz no statute aginst joking, but there ought tew be, not that I think a good joke iz criminal, but they are so scarce, they are suspicious. I am the last man who wants tew see any real wit leave this world, for i think genuine wit, iz az good az religion.

■   ■   ■

> Tew swop a horse and not git beat,
>   Iz sumthing nice tew brag on,
> I tried it once, and that's the time
>   I lost a horse—and waggon.

■   ■   ■

There iz lots ov people who mistake their imaginashun for their memory.

■   ■   ■

THE POMPOUS MAN.

The pompous man iz generally a snob at home and abroad. He fills himself up with an east wind and thinks he iz grate just because he happens to feel big.

He talks loud and large, but deceives nobody who will take the trouble tew meazzure him.

He iz a man ov small *caliber*, but a good deal ov *bore*.

Hiz family looks upon him az the gratest man that the world haz had the honor to produce lately, and tho he gits snubbed often amungst folks, he recompenses himself by going home and snubbing hiz family.

■   ■   ■

One ov the hardest things to do is to be a good listener, those who are stone deaf succeed the best.

■   ■   ■

The luv ov praise never made any man worse and haz made many a man better.

■   ■   ■

How many people there iz whoze importance depends entirely upon the size ov their hotel bills.

■　　■　　■

THE HONEST MAN.

Honest men are scarse, and are a going tew be scarcer.

Thare great scarsity iz what makes them valuable.

If every body waz honest, the supply would ruin the demand.

Honesty iz like money, a man haz tew work hard tew git it, and then work harder tew keep it.

Adam waz the fust honest man we have any account ov, and hiz honesty want ov much ackount.

You couldn't put your finger on Adam, for in the garden ov Eden, when he waz wanted, he couldn't be found.

Old deacon Skinner, ov lower Pordunk village, waz an honest man, he wouldn't hunt for hen's eggs on sunday, but he waz an awful close man, he set a hen once, on three eggs, just tew save eggs.

■　　■　　■

The two richest men now living in America that i know of, iz the one who haz got the most money and the other who wants the least; and the last one iz the happiest ov the two.

■　　■　　■

Advice iz like castor-ile, easy enough to give, but dreadful uneasy tew take.

■　　■　　■

Lazy men are always the most posative. They are too lazy to inform themselfs, and too lazy to change their minds.

■　　■　　■

Married life iz too often a mere trial ov endurance.

■　　■　　■

A man who iz neither good nor bad iz like an old musket laid away, without any lock, but a heavy charge in it.

■　　■　　■

In whipping a young one, you don't never ought tew stop untill you git clean thru.

■　　■　　■

Haven't you ever seen a little child try tew pick up four apples with its little hands at once, and spill at least two ov them?

Men are constantly trying the same game, with the same kind ov success.

■   ■   ■

The man whom yu kant git to write poetry, or tell the truth, untill yu git him haff drunk aint worth the investment.— *ero siv.* Josh Billings

■   ■   ■

THE PERPENDICULAR MAN.

The perpendicular man iz half-brother tew the square man, and iz az uprite az a lamp-post.

He iz a dredful good kind ov a man tew have laying around loose, and he haint got but one fault, or rather misfortune, and that iz, he is so stiff he cant dodge good.

I don't like tew see a man dodge everything, but there are things in this world that are cheaper tew dodge than tew buck aginst.

I like the up and down, perpendicular man, you can alwus git at the solid contents ov him, by just multiplying him by himself.

■   ■   ■

THE LIMBER MAN.

The limber man iz a kind ov injun rubber specimin ov humanity, who can't tell himself how fur he can stretch without breaking.

He iz ready tew stretch, or be stretched, and tho he flies back sumtimes tew the old spot, he quite az often snaps off in such a bad place that he cant be mended agin.

Limber men aint always malishus, but they are az hard to manage az a greased pig, take a holt ov them where you will, you find them poison slippery.

Limber men are rather worse than wicked ones, for they cant even tell themselfs what they are going tew do next.

When a limber man does git tew going wrong, he iz like a blind mule, when he gits tew kicking, yu aint safe nowhere.

Limber men dont alwus lack capacity, it would perhaps be better if they did, for a still phool iz one ov the safest people we hav.

* * *

I have a grate curiosity now to know when the next flood is a going to take place, and whether thare kan be found on the face ov the earth a crew fit to man the next ark with.

* * *

I hav heard wize men prophecy, and fools guess, all mi life, but i never hav kept any count which ov them haz got it right the oftenest.

* * *

When i waz a boy i always wanted tommorow to cum, in middle life i wanted a day to last always, now that i hav got older, i look at yesterday, and to day, and compare them with tommorow, and wonder what all this fuss iz about.

* * *

There iz lots ov people in this world, who spend so much time watching their healths, that they haint got no time to enjoy it.

* * *

THE PRECISE MAN.

The precise man weighs just 16 ounces tew the pounds, and measures just 36 inches tew the yard.

He iz more particular about being *just so*, then he iz about being right.

Hiz blunders, if he ever makes any, are all chronic, and can't be cured.

He iz most alwus what we call a virtuous man at heart, but thare iz no logik kan make him alter hiz mind.

He iz az exact in hiz way az a kompass.

He knows the year, the month, the day ov the week, and sometimes the very hour that any important event took place.

He can tell yu the exact age ov every old maid in the naborhood, and can recollect distinctly ov hearing hiz great-grandfather tell what sort ov a cloud it waz that the lightning come out ov that struck the steeple ov the Presbeterian church, and knocked the weathercock on it into the shape ov a cocked hat.

The precise man iz a mere bundle ov facts, figures, and trifling incidents, which are ov the utmost importance tew him, but not ov much use tew anybody else.

He iz just about az much consequents where he lives az a last year's Farmers Allminax.

He is az set in hiz ways az an old goose trying tew hatch out a glass egg.

■   ■   ■

A boil ain't a very sore thing after all, especially when it iz on sum other fellow.

■   ■   ■

How common it iz tew see folks laff vividly without meaning anything; this i call heat lightning.

■   ■   ■

Don't borry nor lend, but if you must do one, *lend*.

■   ■   ■

Society iz made up ov the good, bad, and indifferent; and what makes so much trouble iz, the *indifferents* are in the majority.

■   ■   ■

THE LOAFER.

The loafer iz a thing who iz willing to be despised for the privilege ov abusing others. He occupys all grades in society from the judge on the bench clear down to the ragged critter who leans aginst the lamp posts, and fights flies in August. He haz no pride that iz worthy, and no delicasy that any body can hurt. During his boyhood he kills kats, and robs all the hens nests in the neighborhood. During hiz middle life he begs all the tobacco he uses, and drinks all the cheap whiskey he kan at somebody else's expense. During hiz old age he winters in the alms houses, and summers in the sugar hogsheds, and when he cums to die, he iz buried in a ditch like an omnibuss horse, with hiz old shoes on. The loafer cares nothing for publik opinyun, and this alone, will make any man a loafer. The loafer rather covets disgrace, and when a man gits az low down az this, he haz got az low down az he kan git in this world without digging. We have no reliable account ov the fust loafer, and probably shant hav ov the last one, but in mi opinyun, they hav existed just about az long az man haz. If Cain want a loafer, pray what waz he?

■　　　■　　　■

Imaginashun, tew much indulged in, soon iz tortured into reality; this iz one way that good hoss thiefs are made, a man leans over a fence all day, and imagines the hoss in the lot belongs tew him, and sure enuff, the first dark night, the hoss does.

■　　　■　　　■

The lazyest man that i kan think ov now, waz Israel Dunbar, ov Billingsville. He iz 45 years old, and hain't had the measles yet; he haz always bin too lazy tew ketch them. He had one son, who was jist like him. This boy died when he waz 18 years old, in crossing a corn-field; the punkin-vines took after him and smothered him to death.

■　　　■　　　■

THE EFFEMINATE MAN.

The effeminate man is a weak poultice.

He is a cross between root beer and ginger pop with the cork left out ov the bottle over night.

He is a fresh water mermaid lost in a cow pasture, with his hands filled with dandylions.

He is a tea-cup full of whipped sillybub—a kitten in pantylets—a sick monkey with a blonde mustache.

He is a vine without any tendrills—a fly drowned in sweet ile—a paper kite in a dead calm.

He lives as the butterflise do—nobody can tell why. He is as harmless as a cent's wuth ov spruce gum, and as useless as a shirt button without any button-hole.

He is az lazy az a bread-pill, and has no more hope than a last year's grasshopper.

He is a man without any gaul, and a woman without any gizzard.

He goes thru life on his tiptose, and dies like cologne water spilt on the ground.

■　　　■　　　■

THE JEALOUS MAN.

The *Jealous Man* iz always a-hunting.

He is always a-hunting for sumthing that he don't expect tew find, and after he has found it then he iz mad becauze he has.

These fellers don't beleaf in spooks, and yet they are about the only folks who ever see any. A jealous man iz always happy, jist in proportion az he iz miserable.

Jealousy iz a disease, and it iz a good deal like sea sickness—dreadful sick and can't vomit.

■   ■   ■

I notiss that when a man runs hiz head against a post, he cusses the post fust, all creation next, and sumthing else last, and never thinks ov cussing himself.

■   ■   ■

It iz az hard work tew make a weak man upright az it iz an empty bag.

■   ■   ■

God save the phools! and don't let them run out, for if it want for them, wise men couldn't get a livin.

■   ■   ■

THE STIFF MAN.

The *Stiff Man* looks down, when he walks, upon folks. He don't seem tew hav but one limber joint in him, and that iz located in hiz noze.

He is a kind of masculine turkey, on parade in a barn-yard.

He is generally loaded with wisdum clear up tew the muzzle, and when he goes off, makes a noise like a cannon, but don't dew any damage.

I hav seen him fire into a crowd, and miss evry man.

This kind ov *stiff man* iz very handy tew flatter. They seem tew know they ain't entitled tu a good article, and, therefore, are satisfied with hard soap.

Thare ain't but few men who git stiff on what they actually know, but most all ov them git stiff on what they actually feel.

Stiff men are called aristokrats, but this ain't so. There ain't no such thing as aristokrats in this country.

The country ain't long enough yet, unless a man haz got sum Indian in him.

Az a gen'ral thing, stiff men git mad dreadful easy, and have tew git over it dreadful easy, bekause folks aint apt tew git a big scare at what they ain't afraid ov.

Stiff man had a grandfather once, who went tew Congress from our district, and there ain't one in the whole family that have been able tew git limber since.

■   ■   ■

The two richest men now living in America that i kno of, iz the one who haz got the most money and the other who wants the least; and the last one iz the happiest ov the two.

■   ■   ■

If yu want to find out a man's real disposition, take him when he iz wet and hungry. If he iz aimiable then, dry him and fill him up, and you have got an angel.

■   ■   ■

The man whom yu kan hire to work on a farm for nothing, and board himself, will just about earn hiz wages.

■   ■   ■

I never knew, in all mi life,
Any man tew go crazy,
Who alwuss took things setting down,
And cultivated hiz lazy.

■   ■   ■

Hope claims the most, and iz satisfied with the least, ov any passion ov the heart.

■   ■   ■

Wiskey friends are the most unprofitable ones i know ov, they are always reddy tew drink with yu but when yu git reddy tew drink with them, they ain't dry.

■   ■   ■

Thar iz no limit tew the vanity of this world, each spoke in the wheel thinks the whole strength ov the wheel depends upon it.

■   ■   ■

I don't never hav enny trouble in regulating mi own conduct, but tew keep other pholks straight iz what bothers me.

■   ■   ■

Convince a phool ov hiz errors, and you make him your enemy.

■   ■   ■

Mules are like summen, very cornupt at harte,— I hav known them to be good mules for 6 months, just to git a good chance to kik sumboddy = Josh Billings =

■   ■   ■

THE GASSY MAN.

The gassy man iz a kind ov itinerant soda fountain, a sort ov hi-pressure reservoi ov soap-suds, who spouts bubbles and foam, whenever he opens his mouth.

These quacks in the small beer line, have but phew brains, but their brains are like yeast, they cant rise without running over every thing.

I have known them tew argy a point 3 hours and a half, and never offer one good reason in the whole time.

They mistake words for ideas, and their tongues travel tew just about az much purpose az a boy's wind mill duz, in the teeth ov a stiff nor wester.

They are the vainest ov all human beings that have yit bin discovered, and think, because people cant escape their furious effervescence, they are pleazed and convinced.

I never knew one ov theze windmills yet, but what thought Soloman waz almost an idiot compared tew them, and I never knew one to ever discover hiz mistake.

Yu mite az well undertake tew git the pride out ov a peacocks tail, bi laffing at it, az to convince theze phellows that what they say aint either wit or wisdom.

The gassy man iz not bi any means a bad man at heart, he iz often az good natured az he is phoolish, but hiz friendship aint worth much more tew you than the love ov a lost pup, who iz ready tew follow any one off who will pat him on the back.

■   ■   ■

THE SHARP MAN.

The sharp man iz often mistaken for the wise one, but he iz just az diffrent from a wize one az he iz from an honest one.

He trusts tew hiz cunning for success, and this iz the next thing to being a rogue.

The sharp man iz like a razor—generally too sharp for any thing but a shave.

These men are not tew be trusted—they are so constituted that they must cheat sumbody, and, rather than be idle or lose a good job, they will pitch onto their best friends.

They are not exactly outcasts, but live cluss on the borders ov criminality, and are liable tew step over at any time.

It iz but a step from cunning tew rascality, and it iz a step that iz alwuss inviting to take.

Sharp men hav but phew friends, and seldom a confidant. They hav learnt tew fear treachery by studying their own natures.

They are alwuss busy, but like the hornet, want a heap ov sharp watching.

The sharp man iz alwuss a vain one. He prides himself upon his cunning, and had rather do a shrewd thing than a kind one.

■   ■   ■

It is highly important, when a man makes up hiz mind tew become a rascal, that he should examine hisself closey, and see if he aint better constructed for a phool.

■   ■   ■

Man iz an enterprizing kritter, he haz lifted himself out ov barbarism bi the hair ov his own head, and in the mean time haz run the whole world so deeply in debt, that if it waz put up at auction to-morrow it wouldn't bring more than seventeen cents on the dollar.

■   ■   ■

A bigot iz a kind ov human ram, with a good deal ov wool over hiz eyes, but no horns.

■   ■   ■

THE WEAK MAN.

A weak man wants just about az much watching az a bad one, and haz done just about as much damage in the world.

He iz every body's friend, and therefore he iz no ones, and what he iz a going tew do next iz az unknown tew him as tew others.

He haint got enny more backbone than an angleworm haz, and wiggles in and wiggles out ov every thing.

He will talk to-day like a wise man, and to-morrow like a phool, on the same subject.

He alwuss sez "Yes," when he should say "No," and staggers thru life like a drunken man.

Heaven save us from the weak man, whose deceptions hav no fraud in them, and whoze friendships are the worst designs he can hav on us.

■   ■   ■

What chastity iz tew a woman, credit iz tew a man.

■   ■   ■

If you don't know how to lie, cheat and steal, turn yure attention to pollyticks, and learn how.

■　　　　　■　　　　　■

What iz happier tew meet than a good temper? It iz like the sun by day and the soft harvest moon by nite.

Give every one you meet, mi boy, the time ov day and haff the road, and if that dont make him civil dont waste anymore fragrance on the cuss.

■　　　　　■　　　　　■

I fully appreciate the proverb, "that speech iz silver, but silence iz golden," but i must say that sum ov the most discreet and dignified phools that i hav ever met hav been thoze who never ventured an opinyun on any subject.

■　　　　　■　　　　　■

I dont like tew speak disrespectfullness agin anybody's near relations, but i hav made up mi mind that Eve waz a phool, and that Adam waz a bigger one.

■　　　　　■　　　　　■

THE DIGNIFIED MAN.

It iz often the case that the dignified man iz nothing more than an owl among humans.

He dont alwus know but little, but when he duz he haz tew be careful ov that little and look wise even if he dont prove tew be so.

One good hoss laff would spoil him for life; if he lets go ov hiz dignity, hiz capital iz all gone and he iz ruined forever.

The dignified man that i am talking about, never takes enny chances, he weighs every word before it iz uttered, and measures every action before it iz expressed, and iz generally az free from blunders, or hits, az a toad stool iz. If he ever duz kick up and frolic he iz like the elastic elephant, and gay and cussid like the hippopotamus or wild sea hoss.

Dignity iz often substituted for wisdum, and iz quite often mistaken for it, but there iz az mutch diffrence between them az there iz between a pewter 10 cent piece and a genuine haff dollar.

I decided long ago not tew giv any man credit for being wise, just becauze he wouldn't bend hiz back or laff when he had a right tew be tickled.

Sum ov the most successful phools i hav ever met were az grave az a cut stone, and most all the truly wise that i have had the honor tew be introduced to, were alwuss a hunting for a good place tew roll on the grass.

Extreme gravity, in my lexicon, stands for an extreme phool.

The wust tyrant in the world iz the wife ov a henpecked husband.

The world all praise the philosophers, but toss their pennys into the caps ov the monkeys.

Employment iz the great boon ov life, a man with nothing to do, iz not haff so interesting, az a ripening turnip.

Sarcasm iz a keen weapon, but in handling it, many people take holt ov the blade, insted of the handle.

Men don't fall so often in this world from a want ov right motives, az they do from lack ov grip.

THE LAZY MAN.

Next tew the weak man the lazy man iz the wust one i know ov, without necessarily being a vicious one.

He iz too indolent tew practiss hiz virtue, if he haz got any, and therefore iz constantly open tew vice, which iz half-brother tew lazyness.

It iz hard work tew find lazyness and virtue mixt, but there iz such a thing.

Indolence iz one ov the worst mildews i know ov—it iz the great leak that haz let thousands ov men drizzle away.

Lazyness iz not positively a crime, but they look and act wonderfully alike.

Lazyness iz not ornamental even tew an old man, but tew a yung one it iz a shining disgrace.

I hav seen lazy men that i thought waz innocent, but i never felt like warranting one ov them for more than 90 days.

Thare iz nothing about a man that will outlast a nick name, it will stick to him, az long as a bobtail will to a dog.

■　　　■　　　■

Most people repent ov their sins bi thanking God they aint so wicked az their nabors.

■　　　■　　　■

I dont kno how it iz with other pholks, but with me, the fall ov the Roman empire iz a great deal easier tew bear than a fall on the ice.

■　　　■　　　■

Nobody really luvs to be cheated, but it duz seem az tho every one waz anxious to see how near they could come to it.

■　　　■　　　■

One ov the best temporary cures for pride and affectation that i hav ever seen tried iz sea sickness; a man who wants tew vomit never puts on airs.

■　　　■　　　■

The biggest phool in this world haint been born yet; there iz plenty ov time yet.

■　　　■　　　■

Thare iz az much flop in some ov our pollyticians, az there iz in a buckwheat slapjak, on a hot griddle.

■　　　■　　　■

Lasting reputations are ov a slow growth, the man who wakes up famous sum morning, iz very apt to go to bed sum night and sleep it all off.

■　　　■　　　■

Man waz created a little lower than the angells, and he haz been a gitting a little lower ever since.

■　　　■　　　■

I hav seen folks who I thought had too mutch propriety, it would be a relief to see them do some thing just a little phoolish, once in a while.

■　　　■　　　■

Virtew in a poor man iz looked upon az a jewel in a toad's noze.

■　　　■　　　■

THE JOLLY MAN.

Jolly men are most always good men.

It iz dreadful eazy tew mistake spasmodic hilarity for good nature.

I have seen men who were called jolly good fellows who were az treacherous in their joy az a cat iz.

Yu will alwus notice one thing, when a cat purrs the most, she haz just thought ov sum new kind ov deviltry.

I kno ov no vice in genuine jollity.

When a man iz jolly all over, he iz too happy and careless tew be vicious.

I hav seen people who could laff long and loud, but there was no more good nature in it than there iz grief in a hyena when they imitate the wail of an infant.

'Tis true we can't alwuss tell about theze things, but if we watch a man all summer, and hang around him all winter, when spring cums agin we ought tew be able tew guess whether the laff that iz in him iz the aroma ov his good nature, or iz only the aroma ov the hiccups.

■   ■   ■

Young man, set down, and keep still, yu will hav plenty ov chances yet to make a phool ov yourself before you die.

■   ■   ■

It iz a wise man who profits bi hiz own experience—but it iz a good deal wiser one, who lets the rattlesnaik bite the other fellow.

■   ■   ■

Take all the phools out ov this world, and there wouldn't be any phun, nor profit living in it.

■   ■   ■

Almost any phool can prove that the bible aint true, it takes a wize man to believe it.

■   ■   ■

Wize men sometimes build air castles just for the fun ov the thing, it iz only the phools who build them, and then undertake to live in them.

■   ■   ■

I hav seen folks who wuz violently oppozed to gambling, simply because they had found out that they couldn't win.

■   ■   ■

I notice one thing, when a man stubs his toe he cusses all

creashun fust, then the toe, but never himself.

■   ■   ■

Dont change your bait mi boy, if yu are ketching fish with angle worms—stick to the worms.

■   ■   ■

Let the yung rabbit go, mi son, and when he gits bigger, ketch him agin ;—the boy dun az he waz told, and he haz been looking for that rabbit ever since.

■   ■   ■

THE AUCKSHIONEER.

The auckshioneer iz an unfortunate individual who duz other peoples lying for 10 dollars a day, and boards himself. He haz got az much jaw az a wolf trap, and as much cheek az a 10 year old mule. He takes up the profession quite often on the same principle that a horse doctor does his, not because he iz fit for the bizzness, but just to have one in the naborhood. His greatest pride iz to mingle what he calls humor with hiz talk when he iz on the block, but hiz jokes are gennerally az level az a cold slapjax. He iz at the height ov hiz ambition when he haz worried a laff out ov the bystanders, and uses the same rhetoric, and similees, when he sells out a line ov bank securitys, that he duz, when he closes out an old one-eyed pelter, under a chattell mortgage, in front ov the court house.

A cuntry auckshioneer, and a cuntry horse jockey, are two won-derphull cusses, in the rural distrikts. I have been an auckshioneer and know what i am talking about.

■   ■   ■

Young ones and dogs?—thoze who are the least able to support them, generally hav the most ov them.

■   ■   ■

Poor human natur iz too full ov its own grievances tew have any pity to spare,—if yu show a man a big bile on your arm, he will tell yu he had one twice az big az that, on the same spot, last year.

■   ■   ■

There is some men who have so little backbone that you can't help them, you mite as well undertake to stand an angleworm up on end, and ask him to dance a jig.

■   ■   ■

If you give a beggar nine dollars, at different times, and then re-fuse him the tenth, he will swear you have cheated him out of it.

■   ■   ■

One half the troubles ov this life can be traced to saying "*Yes*" too quick, and not saying "*No*" soon enuff.

■   ■   ■

I dont beleave in the final salvation ov all men, because there are so many cases in which i cant see how it iz going tew be made tew pay.

■   ■   ■

ADVICE TEW YOUNG MEN.

Dont be discouraged if your mustache dont gro; it sumtimes happens whare a mustache duz the best, nothing else duz so well.

Dont be afraid ov anything that iz honorable, and dont forget that the best friend that God haz given any one iz hiz conscience.

Larn tew wait!—this iz a hard gait for a young man tew travel, but iz the surest way tew git there.

If you have got sum wild oats (and a few wont spoil yu) git them in early, and sow them deep, so they will rot in the ground.

■   ■   ■

I don't beleave in fighting; i am solemly against it; but if a man gits tew fighting, i am also solemnly aginst his gitting licked. After a fight iz once opened, all the virtue there iz in it iz tew lick the other party.

■   ■   ■

Nature seldom makes a phool, she simply furnishes the raw materials, and lets the fellow finish the job to suit himself.

■   ■   ■

I never knew a man yet whose name waz *George Washington Lafayette Goodrich,Esq.*, and who alwus signed his name. For the full amount, but what waz a bigger man on paper than he waz by nature.

■   ■   ■

Whenever i see a man anxious tew git into a fite that dont belong tew him, i am always anxious for him, for i kno he iz certain tew be the worst whipped man in the party.

■   ■   ■

I can tell exactly how my nabors young ones ought tew be fetched up, but i aint so clear about mi own.

■   ■   ■

Q: Who iz the best lawyer?
A: He who does the least bizzness.

■   ■   ■

AN EPISTOL.

Dear Snyder.—Yu tell me that yu hav got the blues, and want to kno how to git shut of them. The following resipees will heal yu in 90 days if yu stik to them klussly. To wit, marry sum delikate only dauter of 22 summers (more or less) and take yure mother in law home with yu to board, this will oil the pores of the system, and the blues will eskape like steam out of the noze of a tea kittle. Once more, hire out to keep a distrikt skool for 9 dollars per month, and hash around the naborhood, or take a 3 year old kiking heifer to brake to milk, this will open yure swareing valves, and so hurry the blood, that the blues will leave yu in disgust, and fasten their fangs on to sum other phellow. Againly, go down into sum marsh in the kingdum ov Nu Jersey fishing for frogs in the month ov August, and fish with one hand, and slap muskeeters with the other, and the blues will take the hint and vacate yure natur like a shooting-star. Try either ov the abuv alteratives, dear Snyder, and if they dont work, go into the bak yard of sum Irish woman and kut her clothes line when it iz filled with the weeks washing, and if yu dont git the blues taken out ov yu, and a good deal else besides, yu are a morbid kuss and wont pay for experimenting on.

■   ■   ■

Hero's are skarse, but the man who kan make poverty respektable, is one ov them.

■   ■   ■

If yu would eskape envy, abuse, and taxes, yu must live in a deep well, and only cum out in the nite time.

■   ■   ■

Q: Who is the dearest old aunt?
A: The one whoze bank account iz all right.

■   ■   ■

It don't do tew trust a man too mutch, who iz alwus in a hurry, he iz like a pissmire, whose heart and bones lays in his heels.

■   ■   ■

One man ov genius to 97 thousand four hundred and 42 ov talent iz just about the rite proportion for actual bizzness.

■   ■   ■

There iz nothing like a sick bed for repentance. A man becomes so virtuous that he will often repent ov sins that he never haz committed.

■   ■   ■

About the last thing a man duz tew correct hiz faults iz tew quit them.

■   ■   ■

Fool and drunken men always make this mistake, the one thinks they are sensible, and the other always think they are sober.

■   ■   ■

A man's reptashun iz something like hiz coat, thare iz certain chemicals that will take the stains and grease spots out ov it, but it always has a second-handed kind ov a look, and generally smells strong ov the chemicals.

■   ■   ■

HOW TO PIK OUT A WIFE

FIND a girl that iz 19 years old last May, about the right hight, with a blue eye, and dark-brown hair and white teeth.

Let the girl be good to look at, not too phond of musik, a firm disbeleaver in ghosts, and one ov six children in the same family.

Look well tew the karakter ov her father; see that he is not the member ov enny klub, don't bet on elekshuns, and gits shaved at least 3 times a week.

Find out all about her mother, see if she haz got a heap ov good common sense, studdy well her likes and dislikes, eat sum ov her hum-made bread and apple dumplins, notiss whether she abuzes all ov her nabors, and don't fail tew observe whether her dresses are last year's ones fixt over.

If you are satisfied that the mother would make the right kind ov a mother-in-law, yu kan safely konklude that the dauter would make the right kind of a wife.

After theze preliminarys are all settled, and yu have done a reazonable amount ov sparking, ask the yung lady for her heart and hand, and if she refuses, yu kan konsider yourself euchered.

If on the contrary, she should say yes, git married at once, without any fuss and feathers and proceed to take the chances.

I say take the chances, for thare aint no resipee for a perfekt wife, enny more than thare iz for a perfekt husband.

Thare iz just az menny good wifes az thare iz good husbands, and i never knew two people married or single, who were determined tew make themselfs agreeable to each other, but what they suckceeded.

Name yure oldest boy sum good stout name, not after sum hero, but should the first boy be a girl, i ask it az a favour to me that yu kaul her Rebekker.

I do want sum ov them good old-fashioned, tuff girl names revived and extended.

■   ■   ■

ON COURTING

COURTING is a luxory, it is sallad, it is ise water, it is a beveridge, it is the plaspell of the soul.

The man who has never courted haz lived in vain; he haz bin a blind man amung landskapes and waterskapes; he has bin a deff man in the land ov band organs, and by the side ov murmuring canals.

Courting iz like 2 little springs ov soft water that steal out from under a rock at the fut ov a mountain and run down the hill side by side singing and dansing and spatering each uther, eddying and frothing and kaskading, now hiding under bank, now full ov sun and full ov shadder, till bimeby tha jine and then tha go slow.

I am in favor ov long courting; it gives the parties a chance to find out each uther's trump kards, it iz good exercise, and is jist as innersent as 2 merino lambs.

Courting iz like strawberries and cream, wants tew be did slow, then yu git the flavor.

Az a ginral thing i wouldn't brag on uther gals mutch when i waz courting, it mite look az tho yu knu tew mutch.

If yu will court 3 years in this wa, awl the time on the square if yu don't sa it iz a leettle the slikest time in yure life, yu kan git measured for a hat at my expense, and pay for it.

Don't court for munny, nor buty, nor relashuns, theze things are jist about az onsartin as the kerosene ile refining bissness, liabel tew git out ov repair and bust at enny minnuit.

Court a gal for fun, for the luv yu bear her, for the vartur and bissness thare is in her; court her for a wife and for a mother, court her as yu wud court a farm—for the strength ov the sile and the parfeckshun ov the title; court her as tho she want a fool, and yu a nuther; court her in the kitchen, in the parlor, over the wash-tub, and at the pianner; court this way, yung man, and if yu don't git a good wife and she don't git a good husband, the falt won't be in the courting.

Yung man, yu kan rely upon Josh Billings, and if yu kant make these rules wurk jist send for him and he will sho yu how the thing is did, and it shant kost yu a cent.

■   ■   ■

If a man should happen tew reach perfeckshun in this world, he would hav tew die immediately tew enjoy himself.

■   ■   ■

We are told "that an honest man is the noblest *work* ov God"—but the demand for the *work* has been so limited that i hav thought a large share ov the fust edition must still be in the author's hands.

■   ■   ■

I don't believe in bad luck being sot for a man, like a trap, but i hav known lots ov folks, who if there was any fust rate bad luck lying around loose, would be sure tew git one foot in it any how.

If a man was completely virtuous, i doubt whether he would be happy here, he would be so lonesome.

The man whose only pleasure in this life, is making money weighs less on the moral scales than an angleworm.

White lies are said tew be innocent, but i am satisfied that any man who will lie for fun, after a while will lie for wages.

Success iz az hard tew define as falling from a log, a man cant alwuss tell exactly how he did it.

It iz very difficult tew calculate upon success, unless a man sets up for a phool—in this department, i hav known hundreds to succeed, contrary tew their expectations.

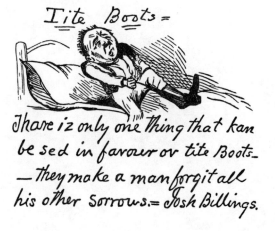

Tite Boots =

Thare iz only one thing that kan be sed in favour ov tite Boots— —they make a man forgit all his other sorrows.= Josh Billings.

CHAPTER III

CRITTERS—VARIOUS AND SUNDRY

Mice kan liv enny whare
fust rate ҩeept in a ɥhurch
— they fatt very slo in a
ɥhurch. — This shows that
they kant liv on religion,
enny more than a minister kan.
        Yures. Josh Billings

■   ■   ■

ESSAY ON SWINE.

HOGS generally are quadruped.

The extreme length ov their antiquity has never been fully discovered; they existed a long time before the flood, and have existed a long time since.

There iz a great deal ov internal revenue in a hog, there ain't much more waste in them than there iz in a oyster.

Even their tails can be worked up into whistles.

Hogs are good quiet boarders; they always eat what iz set before them, and don't ask any foolish questions.

They never have any disease but the measles, and they never have that but once; once seems to satisfy them.

There iz a great many breeds amongst them.

Some are a close corporation breed, and some are bilt more apart, like a hemlock slab.

Sum are full in the face, like a town clock, and some are az long and lean az a cow-catcher, with a steel-pointed noze on them.

They can all root well; a hog that cant root well, haz bin made in vain.

They are a short-lived animal, and generally die az soon az they git fat.

The hog can be learnt a great many cunning things, such az heisting the front gate off from the hinges, tipping over the swill barrells, and finding a hole in the fence to git into a cornfield, but there ain't any length tew their memory; it iz awful hard work for them tew find the same hole to git out at, especially if you are at all anxious they should.

Hogs are very contrary, and seldom drive well the same way you are going; they drive the most the other way; this haz never bin fully explained, but speaks volumes for the hog.

■   ■   ■

Money will buy a pretty good dog, but it wont buy the wag ov hiz tale.

■   ■   ■

I luv a Rooster for two things. One iz the crow that iz in him, and the other iz, the spurs that are on him, to back up the crow with.

■   ■   ■

THE GOAT

THE goat iz a coarse wollen sheep.

They have a split hoof and a whole tail.

They have a good appetite, and a sanguine digestion.

They swallo what they eat, and will eat anything they can bite.

Their moral characters are not polished, they had rather steal a rotten turnip, out ov a garbage-box, than tew cum honestly by a peck ov oats.

The male goat haz two horns on the ridge ov his head and a mustash on hiz bottom lip, and iz the plug ugly ov hiz neighborhood.

A masculine goat will fite anything, from an elephant down to his shadow on a deadwall.

They strike from their but-end, instead ov the shoulder, and are az likely tew hit, az a hammer iz a nailhead.

They are a hi seasoned animal, az much so az a pound ov assifidity.

They are faithful critters, and will stick tew a friend az long as he livs in a shanty.

They can clime anything but a greast pole, and know the way up a rock, az natural az a woodbine.

They are az certain tew raise az young ones, some familys have goats, and the other hav children. They are good eating when they are young, but they leave it off az they git stronger.

A fat gote would be a literary curiosity.

They use the same dialect az the sheep, and the young ones speak the language more fluently than the parents do.

There iz only two animals ov the earth that will eat tobacco - one iz a man and tother iz a goat, but the goat understands it the most, for he swallers the spit, chaw and all.

The male gote, when he iz pensive, iz a venerable and philosopher-looking old cuss, and wouldn't make a bad professor ov arithmetik in sum ov our colleges.

They are handy at living a long time, reaching an advanced age without arriving at any definite conclusion.

How long a goat lives without giving it up, there iz no man now old enough tew tell.

Methuzeler, if his memory waz bad at forgetting, mite give a good-sized guess, but unfortunately for science and this essay, Methuzeler aint here.

Goats will live in any climate, and on any vittles, except tanbark, and if they ever come to a square death, it iz a profound secret, in the hands of a few, to this day.

I wouldn't like tew believe any man under oath who had ever seen a masculine goat actually die, and stay so.

Speaking ov Methuzeler, puts me in mind ov the fact, if a man should live now days, as much az he did, and only have one eye tew see things with, he would have to have an addition put onto the back ov his head tew stow away things into.

The female goat iz either the mother, or sister, or cousin ov the male goat, according tew the prevailing circumstances in the case, or else i labour under a delusion, i forget which.

They give milk intuitively about a quart, before it iz watered, in twelve hours, which iz the subject ov nourishment in various ways.

This milk, which is extracted from the female goat, iz excellent tew finish up young ones on, but is apt to make them bellicose, and fightful.

It iz not uncommon for a babe, while inhaling this pugnative fluid, to let off hiz left collection or digit and catch the nurse on the pinnacle ov the smeller, and tap it for claret.

This iz a common fact among irish babes, and explains the reason why, in after life, these same babes make such brilliant hits.

In writing the history ov the male and female goat tew adorn the pages ov future times, i flatter miself that i have stuck tew the truth, and haven't allowed my imagination tew boss the job.

A great many ov our best bilt historians are apt tew mistake opinions for facts, this iz an easy mistake tew make, but when i strike a goose, or bed bugg, or goat, you notice one thing, i stay with them.—Finis.

■   ■   ■

THE CAT, AND THE KANGAROO.

THE cat, iz called a domestic animal,—but i never have bin able tew tell wherefore.

You cant trust one, any more than you can a case ov the gout. There iz only one mortal thing, that you can trust a cat with, and cum out even, and that iz, a bar ov hard soap.

They are az meak as Moses, but az full ov deviltry az Judas Iskaratt.

They will harvest a dozen ov young chickens for you, and then steal into the sitting room, az softly az an undertaker, and lay themselfs down on the rug, at your feet, full ov injured innocence, and chicken, and dream ov their childhood days.

All there iz sure about a cat, that iz domestic, that i kno ov, iz, that you cant lose one.

You cant lose a cat,—they are az hard to lose, az a bad reputation iz.

You may send one out ov the state, done up in a meal bag, and marked, "C.O.D.," and the next morning you will find him, or her, (according tew sex) in the same old spot, along side ov the kitchen stove, ready tew be stepped on.

Cats have got two good ears for melody, and often make the night atmosphere melodious, with their opera musik.

But the most wonderful thing, about a cat, that haz bin discovered yet, iz their fear ov death.

You cant induce one, by any ordinary means, to accept ov death,—they actually scorn tew die.

You may kill one, az much az you have a mind to, and they will begin life anew, in a few minnitts, with a more flattering prospectus.

Dogs i love, they carry their credentials in their faces, and cant hide them, but the bulk ov cats reputation lays buried in their stomach, az unknown tew themselfs, az tew any body else.

There iz only one thing, about, that i like, and that iz, they are very cheap,—a little money,—well invested,—will go a great ways, in cats.

Cats are very plenty in this world, just now, i counted 18 from my boarding house winder, one moon lite night, last summer, and it want a fust rate night for cats neither.

––––

The Kangaroo is an overgrown monkey. They are fellow citizens ov Afrika, and spend most ov their leisure moments on foot. They have four legs, but their fore legs aint ov much use to them; they do most ov their actual bizzness with their hind legs. They travel a good deal az a frog does—on the jump.

Kangaroos live upon roots, grass, and herbs, and can outjump anything in the wilderness. In the face they resemble the deer, but in the length ov their tails they resemble a whole herd ov deer.

A kangaroo's tail iz a living curiosity; in its general habits it looks and acts like a rat's tail, but in size you must multiply it by six thousand and upwards.

What on earth a kangaroo wants so much tail for has bothered the philosophers for ages, and i understand, that lately, at one ov their scientific meetings they have give it up.

The philosophers git beat oftener than anybody i know ov, but they seldom give a thing up; but the kangaroo's tail was too much for them.

But a kangaroo's tail don't bother me any more than a kite's tail does; a bob-tailed kangaroo on the jump would act just as a bob-tailed kite does in the air. Whenever i come across anything in nature that i cant explain, then i know at once that it iz all right for nature never made any blunders in the animals; if she has failed anywhere, it iz in man.

Nature gave man reason, and showed him how to use it, but man loves to open the throttle valve and let reason roam. This accounts for his running off from the track so often and getting bust up. I never knew a kangaroo tew bust up.

■   ■   ■

If i had 4 fust rate dogs i would name the best ov them "Doubtfull," and all the other 3 "Useless."

■   ■   ■

I thank the Lord that there iz one thing in this world that money kant buy, and that iz.— The wag ov a dogs tail.=
Yure Unkle, Josh Billings

■   ■   ■

THE POSSUM.

THE possum iz a fellow ov the Southern and Western States. He owns a sharp nose, a keen eye, a lean head, a fat body, and a poor tail.

He enjoys roots, chickens, grass, eggs, green korn, and little mice, and eats what he steals, and steals what he eats.

Hiz body is covered with a hairy kind of fur, ov a dirty white complexion; hiz feet and fingers resemble the racoon, hiz ears are a trifle smaller than the mules, and hiz tail iz az round az an eel, and az free from capilliaryness as the snake's stomach.

The possum's tail bothers me. I have looked at it by the hour; i have studied it, and tried tew parse it; i have figgered on it az close az i would a proposition in Euklid; i have hung over it az fondly az a chemist; i have fretted and wondered, have got mad, wept and swore, and cant tell to this day why a possum should have a hair-less caudel.

If some philosophic mind, out ov a present job, will explain this tail to me, and show me the mercy ov it, i will explain to him, free from cost, the pucker ov the persimmon, or the vital importance there iz in being bowlegged, two misterys which are only known to the Billings family.

The possum iz a lonesome and joyless vagabond, living just near enough to the smoke ov a chimney tew pick up a transient goslin or a ten dollar bill, or anything else that aint stuck fast.

The possum, in poor condition, is az full ov fat as a tallow can-dle in the month ov august, but having et possum myself, and boiled owl from necessity, i am full ov the opinion that between the two my choice would be never agin to take either.

Possums always have twins when they have anything, and sum-times an extra one, and they suckle their young on an entire differ-ent principal from the goose.

Their skins are a subject of traffic, and are worth in market from nine to ten cents a piece, provided the tail is amputated. A pos-sum's tail iz not only worthless, but iz a damage to any enterpriz-ing man.

These skins are colored and made into mink muffs, and sold for twenty-five dollars a head, tew those whose early education has bin neglected.

Thare iz only one thing about a possum's skin different from a hoss hide, they don't to shed their hair, every hair is drove in and clinched on tuther side.

Possums have beautiful white natural teeth; and their mouth iz az full ov them az a cow hide boot iz ov shoe pegs.

But say what you will about theze comic geniuses ov nature, they have got two things that they own and no other animul, feath-ered, or hairy, possesses them so much.

I mean toughness and cunning.

If a possum thinks he cant reach his hole, in the hollow ov the tree, tew escape a wandering dog, he lays himself down level on the opposite side ov his belly, and dies az dead az a two dollar watch.

I have often killed them with a club, sufficiently dead enough tew bury, and hiding behind a tree, for a few minutes have seen them born again, and sneak off into the underbrush.

If there iz any body who don't believe this i don't care, i only write what i know, and don't hold miself liable for other folks' ignorance.

If the possum only had hair on the tail i could account for him fully, but this lack ov the hirsute attachment bothers me.

I think now i would giv ten dollars tew be made well on this subject.

Altho the possum dies hard, he lives easy, and i might az well own it, forever, for i have spent a great quantity ov mi life surrounded by possums and other historic vermin, and never heard only of accident death in the possum family.

The muskrat and the possum have similar tails, but the muskrat steers himself with hiz while bathing, but the possum never bathes in anything but chicken blood.

The study ov nature iz a good risk to take, and will make some men az phull ov knowledge az an unabridged Webster's spellin book, while there iz others that nature nor anybody else haint bin able tew educate yet.

THE RABBIT.

THE rabbit iz a kind ov long-eared and short-tailed cat, and reside for a lving all over the United States ov Amerika. They are az harmless, so far az poison is consarned, az a young goslin.

They live in holes in the ground, holler logs, and under brush heaps, and can run faster and stop quicker than any 4 or 6 legged brute.

Their hind legs are twice az long and twice az fast az their fore ones, and they seem tew be bilt best for running up a hill, and backing down it. They are all colors known tew the trade, except green; green rabbits are out ov fashion.

Rabbits boil eazy, and eat soft, and are said tew be better vittles than the cat.

I don't know exactly how many rabbits thare are in the United States now, and never expect tew know, for thay can hatch out, and spred faster than the measles.

One pair ov healthy and industrious rabbits will settle a whole township in 18 months, and begin tew emigrate into the joining parts.

Rabbits are az eazy tew kill az a cucumber vine when it fust starts out ov the ground, and are az easy tew ketch az a bad cold.

Rabbits hav no cunning, and but little guile; i have kept them az pets, and consider them just about az safe az they are useless.

Their fur iz of sum value, but they are az tender tew skin without tearing az a biled potatoe.

■   ■   ■

THE POODLE.

THE poodle iz a small dog, with sore eyes, and hid amongst a good deal ov promiscuous hair.

They are sumtimes white for color, and their hair iz tangled all over them, like the head ov a young black.

They are kept az pets, and, like all other pets, are az stubborn az a setting hen.

A poodle iz a woman's pet, and that makes them kind ov sacred, for whatever a woman loves she worships.

I have seen poodles that i almost wanted tew swop places with, but the owners ov them didn't act to me az tho they wanted tew trade for anything.

There iz but few things on the face ov this earth more utterly worthless than a poodle, and yet i am glad there iz poodles, for if there wasn't there iz some people who wouldn't have any object in living, and have nothing tew love.

Thare iz nothing in this world made in vain, and poodles are good for fleas.

Fleas are also good for poodles, for they keep their minds employed scratching, and almost every bodys else's, too, about the house.

I never knew a man tew keep a poodle. Man's nature iz too coarse for poodles. A poodle would soon fade and die if a man waz tew nurse him.

I don't expect any poodle, but if any body duz give me one he must make up his mind tew be tied onto a long stick every Saturday, and be used for washing the windows on the outside.

This kind ov nursing would probably make the poodle mad, and probably he would quit, but i cant help it.

If i have got tew keep a poodle, he haz got tew help wash the windows every Saturday. I am solid on this point.

Bully for me.

■   ■   ■

THE MULE. *

THE mule is half hoss and half Jackass, and then comes tew a full stop, natur discovering her mistake.

They weigh more, accordin tu their heft, than any other creature, except a crowbar.

They cant hear any quicker, nor further than the hoss, yet their ears are big enough for snow shoes.

You can trust them with any one whose life aint worth any more than the mules. The only way tew keep the mules into a pasture is tew turn them into a meadow joining, and let them jump out.

They are ready for use, just as soon as they will do tew abuse.

They haint got any friends, and will live on huckle berry brush, with an occasional chance at Canada thistels.

They are a modern invention, i dont think the Bible deludes tew them at tall.

Tha sell for more money than any other domestic animile. You cant tell their age by looking into their mouth, any more than you could a Mexican cannons. They never have no disease that a good club wont heal.

If they ever die they must come rite tew life again, for i never heard nobody say "ded mule."

They are like some men, very corrupt at heart; ive known them tew be good mules for 6 months, just tew git a good chanse to kick somebody.

I never owned one, nor never mean to, unles there is a United Staits law passed, requiring it.

The only reason why they are patient, is because they are ashamed ov themselfs.

I have seen educated mules in a circus.

They could kick, and bite, tremenjis. I would not say what I am forced to say again the mule, if his birth want an outrage, and man want tew blame for it.

Any man who is willing tew drive a mule, ought to be exempt by law from running for the legislature.

---

* This is the first published article that Josh was paid for ($1.50). It was reprinted across the nation and brought him national publicity.

They are the strongest creatures on earth, and heaviest according tew their size; i heard tell ov one who fell off from the tow path, on the Erie kanawl, and sunk as soon as he touched bottom, but he kept rite on towing the boat tew the next station, breathing thru his ears, which stuck out ov the water about 2 feet 6 inches; i did'nt see this did, but an auctioneer told me ov it, and i never knew an auctioneer tu lie unless it was absolutely convenient.

■　　　■　　　■

KATS

A KAT iz sed to have 9 lives, but i believe they dont have but one square death.

It iz almost unpossible to tell when a kat iz dead without the aid ov a coroners jury.

I have only one way myself to judge ov a dead kat.

If a kat iz killed in the fall ov the year, and thrown over the stone wall into your neighbors lot, and lays there all winter under a snow bank, and dont thaw out in the spring, and keeps quiet during the summer months, and aint missing when winter sets in agin, I have always said, that '*that kat*,' was dead, or was playing the thing dreadful fine.

Speaking ov kats, mi opinion iz, and will continue to be, that the old-fashioned calico-colored kats iz the best breed for a man ov moderate means, who haint got but little money to put into kats.

They propugate the most intensely, and lay around the stove more regular than the Maltese, or the brindle kind.

The yeller kat iz a fair kat, but they ain't reliable; they are apt tew stay out late nights, and once in a while git on a bad bust.

Black kats have a way ov gitting on the top ov the wood-house when other folks have gone tew bed, and singing duets till their voices spoil and their tails swell till it seems az tho they must split.

■　　　■　　　■

THE PORKUPINE

The porkupine iz a kind ov thorny woodchuck.

They are bigger than a rat, and smaller than a calf.

They live in the ground, and are az prickly all over az a chesnutt burr, or a case ov the hives.

It iz said that they have the power ov throwing their prickers like a javelin, but this iz a smart falshood.

An old dog wont touch a porkupine any quicker than he would a fire brand, but young dogs pitch into them like urchins into a sugar hogshed.

The consequence ov this iz they git their mouths filled with prickers, which are bearded, and cant back out.

A porkupine's quill when it enters goes clean thru and comes out on the other side ov things. This iz a way they have got.

The porkupine iz not bad vittles, their meat tastes like pork and beans with the beans left out.

They have a cute way ov stealing apples known only to a few.

I hav seen them run under an apple tree, and rolling over on the fruit which had fallen from the tree, carry off on their prickers a dozen ov them.

I have often told this story to people, but never got any tew beleave it yet.

Porkupines have got a destiny tew fill, it may be only a hole in the ground, but they kan fill that az full az it will hold.

■   ■   ■

Mules are like sum men, to git them whare yu want them, turn them into the lot jineing, and let them jump out.

■   ■   ■

■   ■   ■

THE MINK.

THE mink iz about fourth cuzzin tew the musk rat, and haz sum things in common with him; they both smell alike.

He iz one ov yure land and water citizens, and kan dive deeper, do it quicker, and kum out dryer than enny thing i know ov.

His phur iz one ov the luxurys ov the present generashun and iz worth az mutch akording tew its size as one dollar bills are.

He haz no very strong pekuliarity ov karakter except hiz perfume, which iz about haff way in its smell between the beaver and the musk rat.

The mink haz 4 times the kunning that the musk rat haz, and iz bilt long and slim like a little girl's stocking.

They are not handy tew ketch, but when ketched are skinned whole.

I hav trapt a good deal for mink and hav kaught them mity little, for they are almost az hard tew ketch in a trap and keep thare as a ray ov light iz.

Thare iz sum people who hav et mink, and sed it waz good, but i wouldn't beleave sutch a man under oath, not bekauze he ment tew lie, but bekauze he didn't kno what the truth waz.

I et a piece ov biled wilekat once, and that haz lasted me ever since, but i never waz parshall tew wild meat ennyhow.

I lived 25 years ov mi life whare game ov all kinds waz plenty. We had bear, oppossum, buffalo and rattlesnaik, and then nights we had draw poker and hi lo Jak, just tew waste the time a leetle.

■   ■   ■

THE MUSK RAT.

THE musk rat iz bigger than a squirrell, and smaller than a woodchuk, and iz az unlike them az a Rokaway klam and a lobster are different from each other.

He iz amphibikuss, and kan liv on the land a good deal longer than he kan liv under the water.

He feeds upon roots, herbs, and soft klams, and smells like the wake of a fashionable woman out on parade.

He bilds houses in the winter, about az big az flour barrels, all over the marshes, and enters them from the cellar.

Hiz phur iz worth just about 25 cents, and aint lively in market at that.

Yu kan ketch them in allmoste enny kind ov a trap that haz got a way tew git into it. They are not kunning, and aint diffikult tew suit.

When i waz a boy i trapped every winter for musk rats, and bought the fust pare ov skates i ever owned with their skins.

I hav seen them in winter setting up on end on the ice, close beside their holes, az stiff az an exclamation point, and when they see me they change ends and point down, like a semicolon, and that was the last ov them.

The musk rat has a flat tail, with no more fur on it than a file has.

I dont despize musk rat—oh, no!—but i dont worship him.

He has but phew sins tew answer for; the chief one iz digging holes in the bank of the Erie Kanal, and letting the water brake out. He will have tew answer for this sumtime.

I luv all the animals, all the bugs, all the beasts, all the insex, all the katterpillars, bekause they are so natral. They are az mutch, if not more, an evidence tew me ov the existance, the power, and the luv, ov an overruling Providence, as man iz.

I can see az much fust klass natur in an angleworm, according tew the square inch, az i can see in an elephant.

I luv tew go phooling around amung the animiles ov all kinds in a warm day; i had rather set down bi the side ov an ant hill and see the whole swarm pitch onto a lazy kuss who won't work, and run him out ov the diggins, than tew set six hours at the opera and applaud what i don't understand, and weep at the spot whare the rest do, and pay 3 dollars for the privilege ov doing it.

■   ■   ■

HOW TEW PICK OUT A DOG.

DOGS are gitting dreadful skase, and if you dont pick one out putty soon, it will be forever too late.

I have written during my younger days, when I knew a good deal more than i do now, or ever shall know again, an essay onto dogs, and in that essay i claimed that the best kind ov a dog for all purposes for a man tew have was a wooden dog.

The experience ov years don't seem tew change my opinion, and i now, az then, recommend the wooden dog.

Dogs, az a genral thing, are ornamental, and the wooden dog can be made highly so, after any pattern or design that a cultivated taste may suggest.

If the wooden dog iz made with the bark on, so mutch the better; for we are told by those who study sich things that dogs which bark never bite.

Wooden dogs never stray away three or four times a year, like flesh and blood dogs do, and don't cost 5 or 10 dollars reward each time tew make them come home again.

Wooden dogs don't have the old hydrophobiskiousness; neither are they running round, and round, and round, and round after them selfs, trying tew catch up with a wicked flea, who iz bizzily engaged gnawing away at the dog's—continuation.

There ain't no better watch dog in the world than the wooden one. You set them tew watching any thing, they will watch it for 3 years, and they aint crazy, and want tew jump thru a window in a minute; if they just happen tew hear a boy out in the streets whistling *"Yankee Doodle"* or *"Sally Cum Up."*

Wooden dogs won't stretch themselfs out in front ov the fire place, taking up all the hot room, nor they won't fly at a harmless old beggar man, who only wants a crust, and tear him all tew little bits in a minute.

If you want tew pick out a good dog, pick out a wooden one, they range in price, all the way from 10 cents tew a dollar according tew the lumber in them, old age don't make them cross and useless, and if they do happen tew lose, a head, or a leg, in some scrimmage, a dose ov Spaldings glue taken at night, jist before they retire will fetch them out all straight, in the morning.

■   ■   ■

THE MOUSE.

EVER since natur waz discovered, mice have had a hole tew fill.

Paradise, az good a job az it was, would not have bin thoroughly fitted up without a mouse tew dart across the bowers like a shaddow, and Eve would never have known how tew scream pretty without one ov these little teachers.

Adam would never hav bin fit tew contend with the job ov gitting a living outside the garden if he hadn't trapped successfully for a mouse.

Catching a mouse iz the first cunning thing that every man does.

Mice are the epitome of shrewdness; their faces beam with sharp practice; their little noses smell ov cunning, and their little black-beaded eyes titter with pettit larceny.

They are az cheerful az the cricket on the hearth. i should be a-fraid tew buy a house that hadn't a mouse-hole in it.

I like tew see them shoot out ov their hole in the corner, like a wad out ov a pop-gun, and stream across the nursery, and to hear one nibble in the wainscot, in the midst ov the night, takes the death out ov silence.

Mice always move into a new house first, and are there ready tew receive and welcome the rest ov the family.

They are more ornamental than useful, according to the best information we have az yet; but this iz the case with most things

Mice cum into this world tew seek their fortune, four at a time, and lay in their little kradles ov cotton or wool, like bits ov rare-dun meat, for a month, with not a rag on them.

When they dine, they do it just az a family ov young piggs duz; each one at their own particular spot at the table, and it is seldom that you see better-behaved boarders, or them that understand their bizzness more thoroughly.

I have seen them at their meals, and i will take my oath that everything iz orderly, and az strictly on the square, as a checker-board.

When mice hav reached their manhood, their tails are just the same length az their bodys. This would seem at first sight tew be a great waste ov tail.

The philosophic mind, ever at work, applying means tew ends, might be a big fool enough tew want to know why a bob-tailed mouse wouldn't be a better finished job; but philosophy has no bizzness tew alter things to suit the market. It must take mouse-tails just az they come, and either glorify them, or shut up.

If there wasn't anybody in the natural philosophy trade, i hav thought it would be jist as well for nature because a man, if he cant orthodox a reason for the entire length ov a mouse's tail iz often willling tew tell his nabors that the whole critter iz a failure.

Such iz man; but a mouse iz a mouse.

The mouse can live anywhere tew advantage, except in a church. They fat very slow in a church. This goes tew show that they cant live on religion any more than a minister can. Religion iz excellent for digestion.

There aint a more prolific thing on earth (prolific ov fun i mean now) than a mouse in a district school-house. They are better than a fire-cracker tew stir up a school-marm with, and are just the things tew throw spellin books at when they are on the run.

One mouse will educate a parcel ov young ones more in ten min-nitts during school time than you can subtract out ov their heads in three days with arithmetic.

Now there iz many folks who cant see anything to write about in a mouse; but mice are full ov information. The only way that edu-kation was first discovered was bi going tew school to nature. Books, if they are sound on the goose, are only nature in type.

A great many contend that a mouse iz a useless critter; but can they prove it?

I am willing to give an opinion that too many mice might not pay; but this applies to musketoze, elephants, and side-wheel steamboats.

A mouse's tail iz az unhairy az a shoestring. This iz another thing that bothers the philosophers, and i aint agoing to explain it unless i am paid for it.

I have already explained a great many things in the newspapers that i never got a cent for.

There aint nothing on earth that will fit a hole so snug az a mouse will. You would think they waz made on purpose for it, and they will fill it quicker, too, than anything I ever saw. If you want to see a mouse enter hiz hole, you mustn't wink. If you do, you will have tew wait till next time.

I love mice. They seem tew belong to us.

Rats i dont love. They lack refinement.

■   ▩   ■

THE POLE KAT. [SKUNK]

M Y friend, did you ever examine the fragrant pole kat closely? I guess not, they are a critter who won't bear examining with a microscope.

They are beautiful beings, but oh! how deceptive.

Their habits are few, but unique.

They build their houses out ov earth and the houses have but one door tew them, and that iz a front door.

When they enter their houses they don't shut the door after them.

They are called pole kats bekause it iz not convenient tew

kill them with a club, but with a pole, and the longer the pole the more convenient.

Writers on natural history, disagree about the right length ov the pole tew be used, but i would suggest, that the pole be about 365 feet, especially if the wind iz in favor ov the pole kat.

When a pole kat iz suddently walloped with a long pole, the first thing he, she, or it duz, iz tew embalm the air, for many miles in diameter, with an acrimonious olfactory refreshment, which permeates the ethereal fluid, with an entirely original smell.

This smell iz less popular, in the fashionable world, than lubins extract, but the day may come when it will be bottled up like musk, and sold for 87 ½ cents per bottle; bottles small at that.

A pole kat will remove the filling from a hens egg, without breaking a hole in the shell, bigger than a marrow fat pea.

How this iz did historians have left us to doubt.

This iz vulgarily called "sucking eggs."

This iz an accomplishment known among humans, which it iz said they have learnt from the pole kats.

Pole kats also deal in chickens, young turkeys, and young goslins.

They won't touch an old goose, they are sound on that question.

Man iz the only fellow who will attempt tew bite into an old goose, and his teeth fly off a grate many times before he loosens any ov the meat.

A pole kat travels under an alias, which is called *skunk*. There iz a great many *aliases* that there iz no accounting for, and this iz one ov them.

I have caught skunks in a trap. They are eazier tew git into a trap than tew git out ov it.

In taking them out ov a trap great judgment must be had not tew shake them up; the more you shake them up the more ambrosial they am.

One pole kat in a township is enough, especially if the wind changes once in a while.

A pole kat skin iz worth 2 dollars, in market, after it iz skinned, but it iz worth 3 dollars and fifty cents tew skin him.

This iz one way tew make 12 shillings in a wet day.

SUM SNAIX.

THE ADDER.

THE adder iz az spotted az a checker-board, and are very beautiful tew admire at a proper distance off.

They hav a coal black eye, which revolves on its axis, and shines
like a glass bead.

They can be found in wet places, and are handy tew live, both
down in the water, and up on the top ov the land. They can slip
off from an old bridge, or a log, into a mill pond, az natural, and
az easy, az a pint ov turpentine, and know how tew swim, and
wave, on the breast ov some water like the shaddo ov the weeping willow.

They are harmless tew bite, but one adder, would spoil all the
bathing there was in a mill pond for me, when i was a boy.

■   ■   ■

*I don't take enny phoolish
chances, if i waz called upon
to mourn over a ded mule.
i should stand in front ov
him, and do mi weeping =
J. Billings Esq*

■   ■   ■

THE STRIPED SNAIK.

The striped snaix is one ov the garden varietys. They inhabit
door yards, and stone heaps down at the foot ov the garden, and
piles ov old boards, and weedy spots, and grass generally.

They are the domestic snaik, if there iz any such thing, and are really az harmless az an old garter, but az full ov fraid tew almost every body, az a torpedo.

The first snaix, we hav any account ov much, waz the devil, surnamed bellyzebubb, who wiggled his way into the Garden of Eden, and without a single trump in his hand, beat our two original ancestors, out ov joy ineffable, and glory halleluia forever, and gave them in exchange for it sorrow without stint, and woe unutterabel. This was an uncommon poor trade for the human family. All snaiks are sneaks, and steal around on their slippry stomachs, az still, and greasy, az lamp ile.

Snaix cant stand the encroachments ov civilization, the seed ov the woman iz always after them with a long pole, and a man, post haste for a doctor, will always dismount, and hitch hiz animule hoss, tew put an extra head onto a snaix.

This kind ov treatment has always made snaik raising a dreadful risky bizzness tew follow.

Out ov one thousand snaixs born annually, the statistics show 930 ov them die in a great hurry, especially where churches and school houses flourish.

I don't know ov a more unhealthy spot in the world for a snaix tew settle down and undertake tew bring up a family than near a district school house.

Let any body just holler "*striped snaix*" once, near a district school house, and you will see the snaix begin teu paddle, and the young ones begin tew boil out like hornets out ov their nest, and proceed for that snaix like a flock of young turkeys for a Junebug.

Striped snaiks are about two feet and one half in length, and about one inch in diameter, and "thereby hangs a tail."

THE MILK SNAIK.

The milk snaix hangs around pasture lots, and iz said tew fasten onto the udders ov the cows, and git his milk punch in this underhand way.

I don't believe this, but in writing the biography ov snaix no man iz obliged tew tell the whole truth about them any how.

Fish and snaix are two things that authors are apt tew consider the facts ov when they write onto them.

I never knew a man yet, not even of fust rate judgment, if he should catch a fish that weighed 4 pounds but would guess he weighed 6, and if he should kill a snaix that was 5 feet, and three inches long, would want tew swear he waz 14 foot long, without taking the crooks out ov him.

This iz human nature, and human nature is heavy on a marvel.

The Bible sez, *"marvel not,"* and altho i look upon all things in the Bible with the utmost veneration, I hav wondered if Joner's catching the whale just az he did, wasn't some kind ov authority for the fish storys ov the present days.

If a man in these times should catch a whale az Joner did, he would write an account ov it, and travel around the country and lecture onto it, and when he described the size ov that whale, if a man wasn't smart in figures, he would git a poor idea of the animal's dimensions.

I never have saw a milk snaix yet, and if i fool my *life* away, and don't never see one, I don't intend tew mourn inconsolably about it.

I have already seen all the snaix I want to, and wouldn't go a haff a mile from here to see all the snaix on the bosom ov the earth unless there was a bonfire ov them.

Snaix ov all kinds have got but one destiny tew fill, and Divine Providence has fixt that; it is tew git their heads squeezed by a suitable sized pebble.

THE HOOP SNAIK.

This remarkable snaix haz a funny way ov taking their tail in their mouth and making a hoop ov themselfs. They can travel a good gait.

There iz a tradition that the end ov their tail iz ov bone, and iz filled with poison, ov the most deadly dimentions, but I think this iz only a lie.

Az I said before, it iz so natural tew lie about snaix that it iz a great wonder to me that they don't leave this world entirely, and take up their abode somewhere else, where they can have a fair show.

I am about 7 eights ov a mind tew believe that the hoop snaix iz one ov P.T. Barnum kind ov critters, that you pay your money tew see in the menagarie, and then take your chances.

The only way tew git at the truth about snaix iz to believe all you hear, and more too.

THE ANAKONDY.

The anakondy iz the great original land snaix, 365 feet in length, 4 feet below the eyes, 19 feet in circumference, and can swallow an ox whole, if you will saw his horns off.

They can wind themselfs around the tallest oaks in the forest, and tear it up by the roots, and lay waist a whole village in their wrath.

The anakondy iz a resident ov the tropical climates. He would freeze up solid in Vermont the fust winter, and would be cut up into cord wood by the natives.

Anakondy would, i should think, if it waz green, would make a lazy fire.

THE GARTER SNAIX.

The garter snaik derives his name from the habit he has ov slipping up a gentlemen's leg, and tieing himself into an artistic bow knot about his stocking, just below the knee.

This iz more ornamental than pleasant, and has been known tew result in the death ov the snaix.

I can imagine several things more pleasant than a live snaix festooned around one ov my legs; but then I am a nervous individual, and when any thing begins tew crawl around on me promiskus, I am too apt tew inquire into it suddenly.

I suppose there iz plenty ov stoics would love tew have a snaix do this, but would pat him on the head, and chuck him under the chin, and sich like.

I give all snaix fair notice that they cant garter me, and if i couldn't git rid of them any other way, I would dissever myself from the leg, and stump it the rest ov my days.

But the more i reflect upon these things, the more i think the garter snaix iz a myth—a kind of inexplicable thing indiscribabel, full ov mistery, and iz a mere type or shadow ov the old, time-honored garter itself.

There iz a great deal ov dream-like mist and wonderment in the garter.

They live in poetry and song, and are seldom seen.

THE EEL SNAIK.

The eel snaix iz the only kind that iz valuable for food.

They will bite a hook az cheerfully az a snapping turtle, and hang on like a puppy tew an old cowhide boot.

They are much easier tew git onto a hook than to git off, for when you draw them out ov the water they will tie themselfs and the fish line into more than 7 hundred dilemmas.

I had just az leafs take a bumble bee off from a dandylion az an eel off from a hook.

Fried eels are said tew be good, but I always have tew shut at least one eye when I eat them.

I don't know az an eel iz the same az a snaix exactly, but they are near enough to suit me.

THE SEE SARPENT SNAIX.

The see sarpent snaik beats all the snaix that have ever put in an appearanse yet.

There ain't but one ov them, and he has only been seen 5 times az yet.

The fust time he was seen was off Nahant, on the American shore, and was seen there twice afterwards.

He has been seen twice at Newport, and we are told by the knowing ones, that he certainly may be expected there next season, and all judicious persons are urged tew engage their rooms at the hotels, in time tew witness the great moral show.

This snaix iz believed by naturalists tew be one thousand feet in length, with a head on him az big az a two story log-house.

He measures one hundred feet in diameter, and iz 90 feet from hiz mouth tew the base ov his fust fin.

He haz two rows ov teeth in his upper and lower jaws, each tooth being three foot in length, and requires 10 tons ov fish for his daily support.

He coils himself about the largest whale, and crushes him tew jelly, in about 15 minnitts.

He travels between the coast ov Labrador and the Gulf ov Mexico, and can make, against a head wind, one hundred and thirty-six knots an hour.

The crowned heads ov Europe would give almost anything if he would visit their shores, but he iz the *Great Amerikan Snaix*, and don't have tew leave home.

Snaix done a bad job for man in the garden ov Eden, and why they are still allowed tew hang around this world iz one ov thoze misterys which are a hard job for an uneducated man like me tew explain.

I abhor a snaix ov any kind, but when they have the power ov poisoning a fellow, added tew their ability tew stare him into fits, they are sublimely pestiverous.

THE KOPPER-HED SNAIX.

This poison cuss iz about 18 inches long, ov a dark yellow colour, and az full ov natural venom az a quart ov modern whiskey.

They live on the side hills among the rocks and stones, and are always ready tew bite at a minnitt's notice.

They are the meanest snaix that meanders for a living, and there iz poison enough in one ov them to kill off a whole tribe ov border injuns, if it was judiciously applied.

I have killed them myself in the month ov August, when they was so full ov deadly virus that it would make you seasick tew look at them.

I cant think ov a meaner death than tew be bit by a kopper-hed and then lay down and die; it iz almost az unpleasant az being hung.

■   ■   ■

SNAILS AND SNAIKS.

THE slowest gaited animal on the face ov the earth iz the snail. They are one ov the few who take their house with them, when they go away from home.

Snails are said tew be delicate eating, but if i can have all the hash i want, i will try and struggle along without any snail. You cant fool me with hash, I know how that iz made, but i don't know how snail are put together. Ignorance iz sed tew be bliss, and i hav often thought that it was, and if i don't never know how snails taste, i don't think now i shall repent ov it.

It has always been a source ov much doubt with me, in my hours ov contemplation, which was made first, the snail or his shell, but if i don't know even this, i don't mean tew git mad about it.

I have great faith in any job that nature turns out, and i had rather have faith than knowledge, it saves a great deal ov hard work. It costs a great deal to know all about things, and then you ain't certain, but faith iz cheap, and don't make any blunders.

Science iz smart, but she cant tell you what makes the flowers blush so many different colors, but faith can. Science on a death bed iz a pigmy, but faith iz a giant.

STRIPED SNAKE # 2.

The striped snake iz one ov the slipperiest jobs that nature ever turned loove.

They travel on the lower side ov themselfs, and can slip out ov sight like blowing out a candle. They were made for some good purpose, but i never have bin informed for what, unless it was tew have their heads smashed.

They are said tew be innocent, but they have got a bad reputation, and all the innocence in the world won't cure a bad reputation.

They live in the grass but seldom git stept on, because they don't stay long enough in the right place.

THE RATTLESNAIX.

The rattlesnaik iz ov a dull yellow color, from four to six feet in size, accordin tew length, and all the way ov a bigness.

They have a poison tooth, and a deadly nature.

On the further end ov their body they hav sum loose bones, which they can play a tune upon, which makes the noise from which they take their name from.

There iz only one remedy for the bite ov a rattlesnaik that i know ov, and that iz whisky.

I have seen a man that had bin bit by one, drink three quarts ov whisky, and be sober enough all the time tew join the sons ov temprance.

I hope I never shall be bit by a rattlesnaix, not so mutch on account ov the snaik az on account ov the wisky.

I think three quarts ov wiskey in my person at onct would keep me drunk forevermore.

The great mortal enemy ov the snaiks iz the hog.

I have seen a woods hog take after a rattlesnaix, and catch him in running 50 yards, and with 3 rips and a snatch, tear mister rattlesnaix into ribbons, and then swallow him whole without saying grace.

The woods, or wild hog, iz the great snakes eradicator. They will hunt for them like a setter dog for a woodcock and if the snaix bite them, they have a way ov laying down in a mud hole and soaking the poison all out ov them.

When i was a little boy, and wore naked feet, and was loafing around loose for strawberrys, i was often times just a going tew step on a striped snaik, but it always cured me ov strawberrys.

If a striped snaik got into a 10-acre lot before i did, i always considered that all the strawberrys in that lot belonged tew the snaik.

"Fust come, fust serve," was mi motto.

I am just az afraid ov snaiks now az i waz 40 years ago, and if i should live tew be az old az Nebudkennezer waz, and go tew grass as he did, one striped snaik would spile 50 acres ov good pasture for me.

Wimmin don't love snaiks any more than i do, and i respect her for this.

How on earth Eve was seduced by a snaik, iz a fust class mystery tew me, and if i hadn't read it in the bible, i would bet against it.

I believe everything there iz in the bible, the things i cant understand, I believe the most.

I would't swop off the faith i have got for any living man's knowledge.

Snaiks are all sorts, and all sizes, and the smaller they are, the more i am afraid ov them.

I wouldn't buy a farm half price that had a striped snaik on it.

Dead snaik are a weakness with me; i always respect them, and whenever i see a dead one in the road, i don't drop a tear on him, but i drop another stone on him, for fear he might alter his mind and come tew life again, for a snaik hates tew die just az much az a kat does.

I never could account for a snaik or a kat hateing tew die so bad, unless it was because they was so poorly prepared for death.

■   ■   ■

"THE CLAM."

THE clam iz a bulbous plant, and resides on the under side ov the water. He iz born az the birds are, but don't come out ov his shell. He iz deserted by his parents at a young and tender age, but don't become clamarous on this account, but sits still, and keeps watch with hiz mouth, for something tew come along.

His temper iz said tew be cold and clammy, but he must have a relish for something, for his mouth waters all the time.

There iz nothing more docile than the clam, and altho they sometimes git into a stew, they are az easy tew lay your hand on, and cetch, az s stone, but they are like an injun, not very talky; they have got an impediment in their noise; their lips open with too much titeness, and their mouth iz tew full ov tongue tew be glib.

Clams were first discovered, az the the measles was, by being caught. How long a clam can live I don't beleaf they can tell themselfs, probably 5 thousand years, but a large share ov this time iz wasted; a clam's time aint worth much, only tew grow tuff in; it is jiss so with some other folks I know ov.

■　　　■　　　■

The highest rate of interest that we pay iz for borrowed trouble. Things that are always a-going tew happen, never do happen.

■　　　■　　　■

I have known people who had so little character that they didn't even hav any phailing.

■　　　■　　　■

There iz no phun in gitting kikt bi a mule, but thare iz lots ov phun in knowing that he kant do it agin—
How is This, Josh Billings

■　　　■　　　■

"THE CRAB."

NATURE is fond ov a joke.
She must have felt full ov fun, when she made a soft shell crab. The strongest emotion the crab has iz tew bite. They aint a-

fraid tew bite a sawlog, or a black bear. They are born in the water, but they can live out doors on the land as long az they can find anything tew bite.

They have several leggs, which are all located on the starboard side ov their person. Crabs live under cover, like the mud turtles, but they move every fust ov May, into a new one.

They are said tew be good eating, but you wouldn't think so tew stand and look at them; it would bother a stranger tew tell where tew begin; it would be a good deal like trying tew make a sudden dinner out ov a cross-cut saw.

They are boiled in a pot, about 3 bushels ov them, until they stop biting, and then they are done, and are et by thowing away the body, and sucking the pith out ov the limbs. It is a good deal like trying tew get the meat out ov a grasshopper's leggs. It is considered a good day's work to git one dinner out of boiled crabs; I think perhaps a person mite sustain life on them, but he would have tew work nite and day to do it, and keep a smart man boiling crabs all the time. Crabs bite with their feet, and hang on like a country couzin.

■   ■   ■

THE BULL HEAD.

THIS remarkable beast of prey dwells in mill ponds and mud puddles close to the ground, and lives upon young lizzards and dirt.

They have no taste to their mouths, and never spit out anything that they can swallow.

They have two ugly black thorns sticking out on the sides ov their hed, and are az dangerous tew handle az a six-bladed penknife, with the blades all open to oncet.

They are like a cat, yu have got to skin them before they are fit to eat, and after they are thoroughly cooked, if yu set them away in the cupboard until they git cold, they will begin life anew, and become az raw az a live mule.

They will live after they are dead az long az striped snaik can.

I don't advise any man to fish for bull heads, but if yu feel az tho yu must, this iz the only best way to do it.

Take a dark, hot, drizzly night in the month ov june; steal out quietly from home; tell your folks yu are going tew the neighbors to borry a setting of hen's eggs; find a saw log on the banks ov a stagnant mill-pond, one end of which lays in the water; drive the mudturkles and water snakes off from the log; straddle the log, and let your leggs hand down in the water up tew your garters; bait your hook with a chunk ov old injun rubber shoe; az fast az yu pull up the bull heads, take them by the back ov the neck and stab their horns onto the saw log; when you have got the saw log stuck full, shoulder the saw log, and leave for home; git up the next morning early, skin the bull heads, and split up the saw log into kindling wood, let your wife cook them for brekfast, and sware the whole family to keep dark about it.

This iz the only respectabel way to have anything to do with bull heads.

■　　　■　　　■

THE MACKREL.

THE mackrel iz a game fish. They ought tew be well edukated, for they are always in schools.

They are very eazy to bite, and are caught with a peice ov old flannel pettycoat tied onto a hook.

They ain't the only kind ov fish that are caught by the same kind of bait.

Mackrel inhabit the sea, but thoze which inhabit the grocerys alwus taste to me az tho they had been born and fatted on salt.

They want a good deal ov freshning before they are eaten and want a good deal ov freshning afterward.

If I can hav plenty of mackrel for brekfasst i can generally make the other two meals out ov cold water.

Mackrel are considered by menny folks the best fish that swims, and are called "the salt of the earth."

■　　　■　　　■

THE POLLYWOGG.

THE plyywogg iz created bi the sides ov the road, out ov thick water, and spends hiz infancy in pollywogging.

After he haz got through pollywogging he makes up hiz mind that this world want made for pollywogs and "nothing venture nothing have," and then he turns hiz attenshun tew bigger things.

He looks out upon life with the eye ov wisdum, and studdying the various animals ov creashun, he cums tew the konklusion that the best thing he kan do iz tew bekum a frog.

This iz the way that frogs fust cum tew be made, and pollywoggs tew be lost.

The pollywogg now leaves the water and spends a part ov hiz summers upon land.

He haz tew fite hiz way through life, and generally goes on the jump.

Being better at diving then he iz at dodgeing, he often runs hiz hed aginst sticks and stuns that the boys throw at him, but hiz two mortal enemys ar the frenchman and striped snaik.

The frenchman iz satisfied with hiz hind leggs, but the snaik swallow him whole.

I have seen sum good time made by the frog, and the snake, the snake after the frog, and the frog after dear life.

If the frog kan only reach a tree, and klimb it, he iz safe, for a snake kant travel a tree.

I don't know az the pollwogg gains ennything by swopping himself oph for a frog, unless it iz experience, but i never hav bin able to dikover much ov enny happiness in experience.

If experience ever made a man happy, i should hav happiness to sell, for I am one ov them happy phellows who never found ennything (not even the bit ov a lobster) only through the kindness of experience.

■   ■   ■

I say to 2 thirds ov the rich people in this world — make the most ov yure money, for it makes the most ov yu = Happy Thought = Josh Billings

Chapter IV

OUR AMERICAN ECCLESIASTES
OFFERS WISDOM AND MORALITY.

■ ■ ■

The only way to tire a phool out, iz to listen to him. and agree to every thing he sez =

Affekshionately Josh Billings

■ ■ ■

JOSH BILLINGS being duly sworn, testifys as follers: Eight wont go into 6 and have much ov anything left over. Many a young fellow has found out this sum in arithmetics by trying tew git a number 8 foot into a number 6 boot.

Virteu, in one respect, iz like money. That which we have tew work the hardest for sticks tew us the best.

Men ov phew but active brains have the best executive abilitys. Their brains are like a bullet-compact, and go straight for the bull's eye.

I hav often herd there was men who knew more than they could tell, but i never met one. i have often met thoze who could tell a great deal more than they did know, and was willing tew swear to it besides.

To be proof agin flattery, a man must have no vanity, and such a man never existed; if he did, he iz now one ov the lost arts.

Sum people are good simply because they are too lazy tew be wicked, and others, because they haven't got a good chance.

In mony, interest follows the principal; in morals, principle often follows the interest.

You will notice one thing—the devil seldom offers tew go into partnership with a bizzy man, but you will often see him offer tew join the lazy man, and furnish all the capital.

Curiosity had twins—one waz *Invention* and the other waz *Stick Your Noze Into Things.*

Love iz about the only passion ov the heart, that i can think ov now, that never makes any mistakes that she can be held account-able for. If you was a going tew try pure love for a crime, what court would you take her before?

I dont know after all, but it iz jist about az well tew git above your bizzness as it iz tew have your bizzness git above you.

"In time ov peace prepare for war." This iz the way sum fami-lys live all the time.

Whenever you hear a man who always wants tew "bet hiz bot-tom dollar," you can make up your mind that that iz the size ov his pile.

The vices which a man contracts in his youth, however much he may shake them off, will often call on him thru life, and seek tew renew hiz acquaintance.

Prudery iz often like the chestnutt burr. It seems az tho it never would open, but by and by it does, and lets the fruit drop out.

Every man has his follys, but thare iz this difference—in the poor man, they look like crimes, while, in the rich man, they only appear tew be eccentricitys.

Old age increases us in wisdom, and also in rheumatism.

We never outgrow our follys—we only alter them.

There iz this difference between charity and a gift—charity comes from the heart; a gift, from the pocket.

When fortune pipes, we must dance. It aint always that she iz in tune.

I think the honesty ov men iz oftner the effect ov policy than principle.

There iz only one kind ov folks who can keep a secret good,

and they never take any tew keep.

The man who iz wicked enough tew be dreaded iz a safer man in community than the one who iz just virtuous enough not be suspected.

Gravity don't prove any thing. If a man iz really wise, he dont need it, and, if he aint wize, he shouldn't have it.

There iz no excuse whatever for the insolence ov wealth; there may possibly be for the insolence ov poverty.

Dont forget one thing, my boy—that when five men call you a success, and one man calls you a failure, that the one man's testimony iz what fetches the jury.

Lazyness iz the fust law ov nature; self-preservation iz the second.

You cant convert sinners by preaching the gospel tew them at haff price. Any sinner who iz anxious tew git his religion in that way, iz satisfied with a poor article.

■   ■   ■

The man who haz got nothing to recommend him but robust health, and an excessive flow ov animal spirits, iz az unpleasant an associate az a 4 year old colt.

■   ■   ■

Health is like money—we never have a true idea ov its value until we lose it.

■   ■   ■

The most dangerous person in this world, iz the one with the most talent, and the least virtew.

■   ■   ■

I have made up my mind that human happiness consists in having a good deal to do, and then keep a doing it.

■   ■   ■

Vanity iz az common to the human family, az fleas iz to a dog, and makes them just about az uneasy.

■   ■   ■

The man who can't enjoy anything but flattery, iz az bad off az the one who cant drink anything but whiskey.

■   ■   ■

RAMRODS.

THE higher up we git, the more we are watched—the rooster on the top ov the church-steeple, is ov more importance, altho' he is tin, than two roosters in a barn-yard.

Take all the pride out ov this world, and mankind would be like a bob-tailed peacock, anxious to hide under sumbody's barn.

I think the heft ov people take az much comfort in bragging ov their misfortunes, az they do ov their good luck.

A secret ceases tew be a secret if it iz once confided—it iz like a dollar bill, once broken, it iz never a dollar again.

If a man iz full ov himself, don't tap him, but rather plugg him up, and let him choke tew death or bust.

The man who cant find any virtew in the human heart haz probably given us a faithful synopsis ov his own.

I don't think that Fortune haz got any favourites, she was born blind, and i notice them who win the oftenest, go it blind, too.

It iz a safer thing any time, to follow a man's advice, than his example.

The heart is wife ov the head, and we who have tried it, all know how persuasive the wife iz—especially when she wants sumthing.

I have noticed one thing, that the most virtuous and discreet folks we have amongst us, are those who have either no passions at all, or very tame ones—it iz a great deal easier tew be a good dove, than a decent serpent.

The man who takes a dollar iz a thief, but if he steals a million he iz a genius.

He who duz a good thing secretly, steals a march on heaven.

Hunting after health, iz like hunting after fleas, the more you hunt them, the more they flea.

Take the selfishness out ov this world, and there would be more happiness than we should know what to do with.

■   ■   ■

AFFURISMS.

Thare seems to be affectation in every thing; even sin has its imposters.

It is a fact (known to us doctors) that you can catch the little pox ov a man before it breaks out on him eazier than you can after it has broke out. Tis thus with wickedness; the openly so are less dangerous than those who have it under the skin.

It don't show good judgment to be surprised at anything in this world, for there is nothing more certain than uncertainty.

Every human physical lump on the face ov this earth iz susceptible tew flattery; sum you can daub it on with a whitewash brush, while others must have it sprinkled on them, like the dew from flowers.

Every man has a perfect right tew hiz opinion, provided it agrees with ours.

Our continual desire for praise ought tew satisfy us ov our mortality, if nothing else will.

Confession iz not the whole ov repentance, but it iz the butt end ov it.

If virtue did not so often manage tew make herself repulsive, vice would not be half so attractive.

Cunning iz not an evidence ov wisdom, but iz prima facie evidence ov the want of it. If we were wize enough tew ketch a fox by argument, we shouldn't have to set a trap for him.

Prosperity makes us all honest.

Love iz a child ov the heart; and it iz lucky if the head iz the father ov it.

A coquette in love iz az silly az a mouse in a wire-trap; he don't seem tew know exactly how he got in, nor exactly how he iz going to get out.

Every man thinks hiz nabor happier than he iz, but if he swops places with him he will want tew trade back next morning.

Love iz like the measles; we cant have it bad but once, and the later in life we have it the tougher it goes with us.

There is nothing so easy to learn az experience, and nothing so hard to apply.

■   ■   ■

The man who iz always trying to create a sensashun, will git so pretty soon, that he cant create even a disturbance.

■   ■   ■

If you want to git a fust class situation in sum alms house, give all your property to your children before you die.

■   ■   ■

There's lots ov men in this world that are like a rooster, take the cockade and spurs off from them, and you couldn't hardly tell them from a hen.

■   ■   ■

He who elevates hiz profession iz the best mechanic, whether he preaches the gospel, peddles phisic, or skins eels for a living.

■   ■   ■

It aint no disgrace for a man to fall, but to lay there and grunt, iz.

■   ■   ■

The diffrence between a mistake, and a blunder.

When a man sets down a poor umbreller, And takes up a good one, he makes a mistake. but when he sets down a good umbreller, and takes up a poor one, he makes a blunder. Excuse haste. Josh Billings.

■   ■   ■

I serpose that why advice is such a drug in the market iz because the supply always exceeds demand.

■   ■   ■

I had much rather *always* look forward tew the time when i am goin tew ride in a carriage, than tew look back once tew the time when i used to do it.

■   ■   ■

Modesty weighs a pound, impudence only 6 ounces, this accounts for the diffidence ov the one, and the vivacity ov the other.

■   ■   ■

Knowledge is like money, the more a man gits the more he hankers for.

■   ■   ■

In a world like this, whare there iz at least five false things to one that iz true, guessing iz poor bizzness.

■   ■   ■

I never have seen a bigot yet but what had a small and apparently brainless head—but i hain't seen all the bigots, you know.

■   ■   ■

I dont want any better proof ov a good hod-carrier than tew hear another hod-carrier say, ''He iz a cussed fool and dont understand hiz bizzness.

■   ■   ■

Flattery iz just like cheese, or anything else we deal in, the supply is always regulated by the demand.

■   ■   ■

I never bet any stamps on the man who iz always telling what he would have did if he had bin there; I have noticed that this kind never git there.

■   ■   ■

Lazyness weighs eighteen ounces to the pound.

■   ■   ■

It iz a good thing tew be headstrong, but it iz a better thing tew understand that a stone wall iz a hard thing tew buck against.

■   ■   ■

Them folks who are sudden, aint apt tew be solid; lively streams are always shallow.

■   ■   ■

A man has got about done going down hill when he gits where he brags on hiz lazyness; such a critter is ov no more use tew himself nor others than a frozen-tew-death rooster in a barnyard.

■   ■   ■

When eloquence and wisdom contend for the superiority in a man, he haz got about az far above the rest of us az he can git.

Take all the fools and good luck out ov this world, and it would bother the rest ov us tew git a living.

Slander iz like the tin kettle tied to a dorg's tale—a very good kind ov kettle so long az it ain't our dorg's tale.

I like them kind of folks, who, if they do once in a while weigh out a pound with only 13 ounces in it, are just az apt tew make the next pound weigh 19 ounces.

Secrets are a burden, and that iz one reason why we are anxious to have somebody help us carry them.

I dont know how it iz with other folks, but with me, the fall ov the Roman empire iz a great deal easier tew bear than a fall on the ice.

There iz just az much difference between precept and example, az there iz between a horn that blows a noise, and one that blows a tune.

Politeness iz the science ov gitting down on your knees before folks without getting your pantaloons dirty.

Virtue iz like strength, no man can tell how much he has got ov it till he comes across something he can't lift.

Take the humbug out ov this world, and you wont have much left tew do bizzness with.

The most miserable people i know ov are those who make pleasure bizzness; it iz like sliding down a hill 25 miles long.

It ain't much trouble tew bear the pain of somebody else's lame back, but tew have the lame back oneself ain't so stylish.

Flattery iz like Colone water, tew be smelt ov, not swallowed.

■　　　■　　　■

Bare necessitys will support life no doubt, so will the works support a watch, but they both want greasing once in a while jist a lee-tle.

■　　　■　　　■

I have always noticed that he iz the best talker whose thoughts agree with our own.

■　　　■　　　■

There iz "many a slip between cup and lip," but not half az many az thare ought tew be.

■　　　■　　　■

Pretty much all the philosophy in this world iz contained in the following bracket—*grin and bear it*.

■　　　■　　　■

"Misery luvs company," but cant bear competition, there aint no body but what thinks there boil iz the sorest boil in the market.

■　　　■　　　■

Blessed iz he who haz a big pile, and knows how to spread it.

■　　　■　　　■

Rumor iz like a swarm ov bees, the more you fite them the less you git rid ov them.

■　　　■　　　■

Genius after all ain't anything more than elegant common sense.

■　　　■　　　■

It iz the little things ov this life that plague us—Muskeeters are plenty, elephants scarse.

■　　　■　　　■

Every time a man laffs harty, he takes a kink out ov the chain that binds him to life, and thus lengthens it.

■　　　■　　　■

I never knew a profound fool yet, who did not affect gravity, nor a truly wize man, whoze face was not always cocked and primed for a laugh.

■　　　■　　　■

How common it iz tew see folks laff vividly without meaning

any thing; this i call heat lightning.

■   ■   ■

Thare iz nothing the wurld will pay so mutch for az fust rate nonsense, and there iz nothing in the market so scarse.

■   ■   ■

Thare iz not only phun but thare is virtew in a harty laff; animals kant laff and devils won't.

■   ■   ■

Laffing devils are the most dangerous. If i had a mule that wouldn't neither kik nor bite, i should watch him dredful spry till i found out whare hiz malice lay.

■   ■   ■

I have lived in this world jist long enuff tew look carefully the second time into things that i am the most certain ov the fust time.

■   ■   ■

Fools are telling us (confidentially) "*that time is short;*" but the difficulty lies not in the shortness ov time so mutch az it duz in the length ov the fools.

■   ■   ■

There iz no medicine like a good joke; it iz a silver-coated pill that frolics and phisicks on the run.

■   ■   ■

It iz a great art tew be superior tew others without letting them know it.

■   ■   ■

Wit, without sense, iz like a razor without a handle.

■   ■   ■

I have larn't one thing, by great experience, and that iz, I want as much watching az mi neighbors do.

■   ■   ■

I have noticed one thing, that just about in proportion that the passions are weak, men are seemingly virtuous.

■   ■   ■

Thare iz a grate deal ov speculation that spends its time trieing to untwist the untwistable, this iz like setting down in a wash tub, and trieing to lift up the unliftable.

■   ■   ■

Virtew, backed up by courage, iz the perfection ov human natur. I don't reckon mercy nor pity always among the virtews; they are often only amiable weaknesses. Justice iz the square root ov all the virtews. I wouldn't have any mercy nor pity hove out for rubbish; neither would i have a man think, because he melts at the anguish ov the viscious, that it iz virtew that ails him.

■   ■   ■

Thare iz a grate deal ov bad luk lieing around loose in this world, but it iz publick property, it dont belong tew anybody in pertikular.

■   ■   ■

What a blessed thing it iz that we cant "see ourselfs az other see us,"—the sight would take all the starch out ov us.

■   ■   ■

Human happiness iz a dreadful hard thing tew define. I have seen a man, perfectly happy without any shirt tew hiz back, bekum suddenly furious becauze sumboddy had given him one, the collar ov which wasn't starched stiff enuff.

■   ■   ■

The best philosophers and moralists i have ever met, have been thoze who had plenty to eat, and drink, and had money at interest.

■   ■   ■

We have bin told that the best way to overcome misfortunes iz tew fight with them — I have tried both ways, and recomment a successful dodge.

■   ■   ■

Blessed iz them who have no eye for a keyhole, nor ear for a knot-hole.

■   ■   ■

Error will slip thru a crack, while truth will git stuck in a door-way.

■   ■   ■

There iz only one thing that i can think ov now, that i like to see idleness in, and that iz in mollassiss — i want mi mollassiss slow and easy.

■   ■   ■

I know plenty ov folks who are so condem contrary, that if they should fall into the river, they would insist upon floating up stream.

■   ■   ■

Advertising iz sed tew be a certain means of success; sum folks are so impressed with this truth, that it sticks out ov their tombstone.

■   ■   ■

Fust impretions are sed tew be lasting. Any man who has only been stung bi a hornet once will swear to this.

■   ■   ■

I never knew ennybody yet to get stung by hornets, who kept away from whare they was — it iz jist so with bad-luck.

■   ■   ■

Experience has the same effect on most folks that age has on a goose, it makes them tuffer.

■   ■   ■

The safest way for most folks to do iz to do az the rest do. Thare aint but phew who can navigate without a compass.

■   ■   ■

The time tew be carefullest iz when we hav a hand full ov trumps.

■   ■   ■

Those persons who spend all ov their spare time watching their simptoms, are the kind who enjoy poor health.

■   ■   ■

I have always noticed one thing, when a person bekums disgusted with this world, and concludes to withdraw from it, the world very kindly lets the person went.

■   ■   ■

There iz a grate deal ov bad luck lieing around loose in this world, but it iz public property, it dont belong tew any body in pertikular.

■   ■   ■

A person with a little smattering ov learning, iz a good deal like a hen's egg that haz been sot on for a short time, and then deserted by the hen, it iz spoilt for hatching out anything.

■   ■   ■

Adversity iz a poultice which reduces our vanity and strengthens our virtew—even a boy never feels half so good az when he haz just bin spanked and sot away tew cool.

■   ■   ■

The tongue iz really a verry fast member ov the body politick, he duz all the talking, and two-thirds ov the thinking.

■   ■   ■

We are told that riches takes wings and flies out ov sight, and i hav known them tew take the proprietor along with them.

■   ■   ■

He who spends hiz younger days in disapation iz mortgaging himself tew disseaze and poverty, two inexorable creditors, who are certain tew foreclose at last, and take possession ov the premises.

■   ■   ■

Blessed iz he who always carrys a big stone in hiz hand but never heaves her.

■   ■   ■

I beleave in sugar coated pills.—I also beleave that virtue and wisdom can be smuggled into a man's soul by a good natured proverb, better and deeper than tew be mortised into it with a wormwood mallet and chissell.

■   ■   ■

There are but dredful phew people who can talk ten minnits tew you without lugging into the conversation their back or stummuk aches.

■   ■   ■

Dangers are sum like a cold bath, very dangerous while you stand stripped on the bank, but often not only harmless, but invigorating, if you pitch into them.

■   ■   ■

Virtew iz like strength, no man can tell how mutch he has got ov it till he cums across sumthing he can't lift.

■   ■   ■

Patience, if it iz merely constitutional, don't appear tew me to be any more ov a virtue than cold feet are.

■   ■   ■

The gay are alwus looking ahead, and the sad are always looking back; it iz a great pity they don't change works with each other.

■   ■   ■

Genuine happiness iz like a genuine ghost, everybody talks about them and seems tew beleaf in them, but i guess nobody hain't seen one yet.

■   ■   ■

i have cum tew the conclusion that what every body praizes wants close watching.

■   ■   ■

The way tew *Fame* iz like climbing a greast pole; there aint but phew can do it, and even then it don't pay.

■   ■   ■

Hunting after fame iz like hunting after fleas, hard tew cetch, and sure tew make yu uneazy if yu do or don't cetch them.

■   ■   ■

Success iz a coquet, and a bashful lover never wins her.

■   ■   ■

White lies are sed tew be innocent, but i am satisfied that any man who will lie for phun, after a while will lie for wages.

■   ■   ■

About the best thing that experiense can do for us iz tew learn us how tew enjoy mizery.

■   ■   ■

Virtew that can't whip Vice, in a fair stand up fite, any time, aint worth having.

■   ■   ■

There iz one witness that never iz guilty ov perjury, and that iz the conscience.

■   ■   ■

"If you are looking after happiness don't take the turnpike, take one ov the byroads, you will avoid the tollgates, and find it less crowded and dusty."

■   ■   ■

Faith and curiosity are the gin cocktails ov success.

■   ■   ■

Debt iz like any other kind ov a trap, eazy enough tew git into, but hard enough tew git out ov.

■   ■   ■

How can we ever expect tew find a perfect person in this world when we can't even find one who iz haff az good az he can be.

■   ■   ■

I have finally come tu the conclusion, that a good reliable sett ov bowels, iz wurth more tew a man, than any quantity ov brains.

■   ■   ■

Wise men go thru this world az boys go tew bed in the dark, whistling tew shorten the distance.

■   ■   ■

"Do unto others az yu would have them do unto yu." Praize in others what you would like to hav praized in you, iz the very sublimity ov blowing your own trumpet.

■   ■   ■

A kicking cow never lets drive untill jist az the pail iz full, and seldom misses the mark; it iz jist so with sum men's blunders.

■   ■   ■

What an agreeable world this would be tew live in if we could pump all the pride and selfishness out ov it! It would improve it az much az taking the fire and brimstone out ov the other world.

■   ■   ■

Genius after all ain't anything more than elegant common sense.

■   ■   ■

It iz a lucky thing that epitaffs dont appear on a man's tombstone untill he has gone dead. If they were published while he waz living, what an insult most ov them would be tew his reputation.

■   ■   ■

"*People ov good sense*" are those whoze opinyuns agree with ours.

■   ■   ■

TRUTH iz like the burdocks a cow gits into the end ov her tail, the more she shakes them off, the less she gits rid ov them.

■   ■   ■

Going tew law, iz like skinning a new milk cow for the hide, and giving the meat tew the lawyers.

■   ■   ■

What iz the next worst thing tew lieing? Gitting catched at it.

■   ■   ■

"Familiarity breeds contempt." This only applies tew men, not tew hot buckwheat slapjacks, well-buttered and sugared.

■   ■   ■

It iz all important that fashion should be perfumed with az much morality az possible, for it controls more people than law or piety duz.

■   ■   ■

When yu strike ile stop boring ; menny a man haz bored klear thru, and let the ile run out at the bottom.

■   ■   ■

Chapter V

EATABLES, DRINKABLES,
AND SUCH-LIKE

■ ■ ■

Waiting for sumthing to turn up, iz like setting down in a 10 aker lot, with a pail between yure legs, expekting sum cow to bak up and be milkt.

■ ■ ■

A LETTER

Oct. 15th, 1880.

TO THE DEAR PUBLICK:

The Receipts for cooking whitch appear in this little volume are not to be considered arbitrary, they are the suggestions ov a man who never haz been able to cook his own goose just exackly right, but rest assured my dear friends, that they are submitted to your considerashun by one, who has but little malice in his nature, and less cunning. Should none ov them be found to work perfection, dont tear the hair out ov your head about it, baldness wont improve the matter; just thank the Lord they aint any wuss than they are, and you hav gained something by the experiment.

■   ■   ■

KORN.

KORN iz a serial, i am glad ov it.

It got its name from Series, a primitive woman, and in her day, the goddess ov oats, and such like.

Korn iz sometimes called *maize,* and it grows in some parts of the western country, very amazenly.

I have seen it out there 18 foot hi (i dont mean the actual korn itself, but the tree on which it grows.)

Korn haz ears, but never has but one ear, which iz az deaf az an adder.

Injun meal iz made out ov korn, and korn dodgers iz made out ov injun meal, and korn dodgers are the tuffest chunks, ov the bread persuasion, known tew man.

Korn dodgers are made out ov water, with injun meal mixed into it, and then baked on a hard board, in the presence ov a hot fire.

When yu can't drive a 10 penny nail into them, with a sledge hammer, they are said, by good judges, to be well done, and are ready tew be chawed upon.

I have gnawed two hours myself on one side of a korn dodger without produsing any result, and i think i could starve to death twice before i could seduce a korn dodger.

They git the name *dodger* from the immediate necessity ov dodgeing, if one iz hove horizontally at you in anger.

It iz far better tew be smote bi a 3-year-old steer, than a korn dodger, that iz only three hours old.

Korn was fust discoverd by the injuns, but where they found it i don't know, and i don't know as i care.

Whiskey (noble whiskey) is made out ov korn, and whiskey is one ov the greatest blessings known tew man.

We never should have bin able tew fill our state prisons with energetic men, and our poor-houses with good eaters, if it want for noble whiskey.

We never should have had any temperance sons ov society, nor democratic pollyticians, nor prize fights, nor good murders, nor phatt aldermen, nor whiskey rings, nor nothing, if it want for blessed whiskey.

If it want for korn, how could any boddy git korned?

And if it want for gitting korned, what would life be worth?

We should all sink down to the level ov the brutes if it want for gitting korned.

The brutes don't git korned, they haint got any reason nor soul.

We often hear ov *"drunken brutes,"* this is a compliment to oxen which dont belong tew them.

Korn also haz kernels, and kernels are often korned, so are brigadier-ginerals.

Johnny cake is made out ov korn, so iz hasty pudding.

Hasty pudding and milk is quick tew eat.

All you have got to do iz to gap, and swallow, and that iz the last ov the pudding.

Korn waz familiar tew antiquity. Joseph was sent down into Egypt after sum korn, but his brothers didn't want him to go, so they took pity on him and pitted him in a pit.

When his brothers got back home, and were asked where Joe waz, they didn't acknowledge the korn, but lied sum.

It has been proved, that it iz wicked to lie about korn, or any ov the other vegetables.

There iz this difference between lying, and sawing wood, it iz easier to lie, especially in the shade.

Korn has got one thing that nobody else has got, and that iz a kob.

This kob runs thru the middle ov the korn, and iz as phull ov korn as Job waz ov boils.

I always feel sorry when i think ov Job, and wonder how he managed tew set down in a chair.

Knowing how tew set down, square on a boil, without hurting the chair, iz one ov the lost arts.

Job was a card, he had more patience and boils, tew the square inch, than iz usual.

One hundred and twenty-five acres ov korn tew the bushel iz considered a good crop, but i have seen more.

I hav seen korn sold for 10 cents a bushel, and in some parts of the western country, it iz so much, that there aint no good law against stealing it.

In conclusion, if you want tew git a sure crop ov korn, and a good price for the crop, feed about 4 quarts ov it to a shanghi rooster, then murder the rooster immediately, and sell him for 17 cents a pound, crop and all.

■ ■ ■

Abuse is the logic of loafers.

■   ■   ■

The more rare a mans qualitys are, the more he will be found fault with,—dust on a dimond iz always more noticeable than dust on a brick.

■   ■   ■

Experience teaches a good many things, but dont learn us but a few.

■   ■   ■

I have seen old villains who were comparitively pure, they had either worn out their vices, or thier vices had wore out them, i dont know which.

■   ■   ■

It requires the greatest ov skill tew hide a weakness.

■   ■   ■

BEER.

I HAV finally cum tew the conclusion, that *lager beer* iz not intoxicatin.

I have been told so bi a german, who said he had drank it all nite long, just tew tri the experiment, and was obliged tew go home entirely sober in the morning. I have seen this same man drink sixteen glasses, and if he was drunk, he was drunk in german, and nobody could understand it. It iz proper enough tew state, that this man kept a lager-beer saloon, and could have no object in stating what wasn't strictly thus.

I beleaved him tew the full extent ov my ability. I never drank but 3 glasses ov lager beer in my life, and that made my head untwist, as tho it was hung on the end ov a string, but i was told that it was owing tew my bile being out ov place, and I guess that it was so, for I never biled over wuss than i did when I got home that nite. Mi wife was afraid i was agoing tew die, and i was almoste afraid i shouldn't, for it did seem az tho everything i had ever eaten in my life, was coming tew the surface, and i do really believe, if mi wife hadn't pulled off my boots, just az she did, they would have come thundering up too.

Oh, how sick i was! it was 14 years ago, and i can taste it now.

I never had so much experience, in so short a time.

If any man should tell me that lager beer was not intoxicating, i should believe him; but if he should tell me that i wasn't drunk that nite, but that my stummuk was only out ov order, i should ask him tew state over, in a few words, just how a man felt and acted when he was well set up.

If i want drunk that nite, i had sum ov the most natural symptoms a man ever had, and keep sober.

In the fust place, it was about 80 rods from where i drank the lager, tew my house, and i was over 2 hours on the road, and had a hole busted thru each one ov my pantaloon knees, and didn't have any hat, and tried tew open the door by the bell-pull, and hiccupped awfully, and saw evrything in the room tryin tew git round onto the back side ov me, and in setting down onto a chair, i didn't wait quite long enough for it tew git exactly under me, when it was going round, and i set down a little too soon, and missed the chair by about 12 inches, and couldn't git up quick enough tew take the next one when it come, and that ain't all; mi wife said i was az drunk az a beast, and az i said before, i begun tew spit up things freely.

If lager beer iz not intoxicating, it used me almighty mean, that i know.

Still i hardly think lager beer iz intoxicating, for i hav been told so, and i am probably the only man living, who ever drunk any when his bile wasn't plumb.

I don't want tew say anything against a harmless temperance beveridge, but if i ever drink any more it will be with my hands tied behind me, and my mouth pried open.

I don't think lager beer iz intoxicating, but if i remember right, i think it tastes to me like a glass with a handle on one side ov it, full ov soap suds that a pickle had bin put tew soak in.

■   ■   ■

Intellect without judgement iz what ails about one halff the smart people in this world.

■   ■   ■

A fanatic iz the worst man we have to contend with, reason has no effect on him, and it iz agin the law to club him.

■   ■   ■

HOW TEW PIK OUT A WATERMELLON.

SOMETIME about the 20th ov August, more or less, when the moon iz entering her second quarter, and the old kitchen clock has struck twelve midnite, git up and dress yourself without making any noise, and leave the house by the back door, and step lightly across the yard, out into the hiway, and turn tew your right.

After going about haff a mile, take your fust left hand road, and when you come tew a bridge, cross it, and go thru a pair ov bars on the right, walk about two hundred yards in a south-east direcshun, and you will come suddenly on a watermellon patch.

Pick out a good, dark-colored one, with the skin a leetle rough-ish; be careful not to injure any ov the vines by stepping on them; shoulder the watermellon, and retrace your steps, walking about twice az fast az you did when you come out.

Once in a while look over your shoulder too see if the moon is all right. When you reach home, bury the watermellon in the hay mow and slip into bed, just as tho nothing had happened.

This is an old-fashioned, time-honered way, tew pick out a good watermellon, just the way our fathers and grandfathers did it.

After you have et the watermellon tear up the recipee.

I am not anxious tew have this recipee preserved, but i dont want it forgotten.

One watermellon during your life is enough to pick out in this way.

Dont do it but jist once, and then be kind ov sorry for it after-wards.

Many people will wonder and worry whare the moral comes in, in this sketch, and it is hard tew tell; but i will venture to say that there aint a prominent moralist in America but has picked out his watermellon by this recipee, sometime during his life, and will tell you that he remembers favourably the spirit ov adventure that prompted the undertaking, and never can forgit the sober sense ov shame that followed it.

■　　　　■　　　　■

THE APPLE DUMPLIN.

The dumplin are about the natral size ov your fist made out ov dough, and filled with apples. They are served up hot, with sum sweet-tasting liniment on them, and are az eazy to struggle with az a sugar-plum. They aint so good cold az they ought to be. Cold dumplin, and raw potatoe, eat similar. I never et apple dumplin yet, without thanking the Lord for that one, and the Landlady for another one. Four apple dumplins, at one sitting, iz just about mi size. I wish i knew who invented these kind-hearted balls, i would like to weep over his memory. Punkin pi, and apple dumplin, have dun az much to civilize man az any two missionarys that have ever lived. Good vittles iz next to good morals any how. You may talk about virtew az mutch as you pleze, you cant never inoculate a man with virtew fust rate on an empty stummuk. Give a man four apple dumplin, with some good kind ov ointment on them, and after he has et them, and they have settled down to hard pan, you can crawl up to him on either side, with a dose of morality, or even some new kind of sope, for taking spots out ov clothes.

■   ■   ■

The role ov the politikal demagogue iz to induce others to beat the bush, while he coolly bags the rabbit.

■   ■   ■

PUNKIN PIE.

Punkin pie iz the sass ov Nu England. They are vittles and drink, they are joy on the haff-shell, they are glory enough for one day, and are good cold or warmed up. I would like to be a boy again, just for sixty minnitts, and eat myself full ov the blessed old mixture. Enny man who dont luv pumpkin pi, wants watching cluss, for he means to do somethin mean the fust good chance he can git. Give me all the punkin pi i could eat, when i was a boy, and i didn't care whether sunday-school kept that day or not. And now that i have grown up to manhood, and have run for the legislature once, and only got beat 856 votes, and am thoroly married, thare aint nothing i hanker for worss and can bury quicker, than two-thirds ov a good old-fashioned punkin pi, an inch and a half thick, and well smelt up, with ginger and nutmeg. Punkin pi iz the oldest Amerikan beverage i know ov, and ought to go down to posterity with the trade mark ov our grandmothers on it; but i am afraid it won't, for it iz tough even now to find one that tastes in the mouth at all az they did 40 years ago.

■   ■   ■

AGRIKULTIBUSS.

1st. Scarcity beets are the hardest kind ov beets to beat; their grate scarsity makes them beat all other kind ov beets.

■   ■   ■

2d. Turnips should be planted near the top ov the ground, if you want them tew turn up good.

■   ■   ■

3d. Egg plants iz good, but eggs sot under a steady hen will produce more chickens than they will tew plant them.

■   ■   ■

4th. Potatoes are generally a healthy crop, but they are liable tew hav weak eyes.

■   ■   ■

5th. Cowcumbers do the best in a lot by themselfs; it aint best tew cumber up a kitchen gardin with cows.

■   ■   ■

6th. Oats will grow on some warm land, but tew yield well they hav got tew be thrashed; it iz jist so with beans, only beans has got to be poled fust, and thrashed afterwards.

■   ■   ■

7th. Rye duz the best on a dry and thirsty soil, espeshily old rye; too much water will drown out old rye.

■   ■   ■

HOW TO CONCOCT CRANBERRY PI.

Roll out 2 thin covers ov dough, lay one ov them in an earthen dish, with the bottom down, deposit a pint ov cooked cranberrys on the top ov the bottom cover, spred the other cover on the top ov the cranberrys, lacerate a few holes in the upper side ov the top cover to let the steam meander, cast the Pi into the oven, let it stew for 27 minnits by the clock, then twitch it out, set it in a draft to chill, serve it up with sum Brandy or Rum-cheeze, cut the Pi acrost the top, into two haffs, give one ov the haffs to your wife and children, and Mother-in-Law, take the other haff yourself, observing, that poor Pa is sick, and cranberry Pi always did agree with him.

■   ■   ■

Prosperity iz the most dangerous kind ov flattery.

■   ■   ■

ROAST GOOSE.

Pick out a tender goose (if you can), dispel the feathers from his person carefully, amputate his head, and feet, remove him internally, make a filling ov hi seasoned dough, sew him up tite, lay him in an iron pan, face side up, insert him into a hot place, let him try it for 4 hours, flop him over once in a while, to git an average on him, jab him occasionally with a 3 tined fork, to see what he iz a doing, when you think he has got thru snatch him out, lay him on a platter, surround hiz person with dandylions, and sweet majorum, let two people eat him, one goose iz not quite enough for two people, but iz a leetle too much for one.

■   ■   ■

There are no weeds, that wilt so quick, as the weeds,—ov the widower.

■   ■   ■

HOW TO DEVIL CRABS.

The art ov Deviling crabs iz a joyfull one, but it iz yet in its infancy, and possibly ought to remain there, but we are in full posession ov the art, in all its primeval force, and beauty, and will send a knowledge ov the same, upon receipt ov 25 cents, and warrant the receipt, or return the money by the next mail, and throw in dozen crabs besides. For very full particulars address, Josh Billings, Paragrapher, care ov G. W. Carleton and Co., Publishers, Book and stationary dealers, corner ov 5th avenue and 23rd st., underneath 5th avenue Hotel, near Madison Park, city, and state of New York, United States ov Amerika, Western Hemisphere. Yours with delight, Josh Billings.

■   ■   ■

It takes a very smart man to be a successfull phool.

■   ■   ■

CORRESPONDENCE.

New York, August 9th, 1880.

MI DEAR MADAM:

You say you have tried my receipt, received bi mail, for "Deviling Krabs," and it wouldn't work. This astounds me, I never knew it to hesitate before. Pleaze state (at my expense) the exact size ov the crab you tried it on, the number ov claws he had, whether he waz a hard shell, or a soft shell, about how old he mite be, also, what your impressuns were, about the natureal disposition, ov the krab, whether he was particularly warlike, or docile in his manner, and any facts that may occur to you, an explicit answer to the above interrogatorys, will enable me to git at a diagnosis ov this particular krab's case.

Yours politely,
Josh Billings

■   ■   ■

A glowing epitaff costs but little, and no one dares dispute it.

■   ■   ■

TO MAKE A GOOD RUM SAUCE.

Take one quart ov good old Nu England rum, or brandy, or whisky, toss into it six ounces ov sweet Orange county butter, mingle slices ov lemon with it, dust it with nutmeg, chastise it severely with "A" number one white sugar, bring it to a mild boil on a hot stove, stir it resolutely while boiling, taste ov it often, to see if it has got the right idea to it, take it off carefully from the stove, let it drip slowly into a gilt-edge earthen bowl, set it away gently for two hours in an ice-box, to equalize, then use it freely on baked, boiled, or fried pudding, in quantitys to flatter the taste. A wine glass ov this elixir, taken before meals, as a brace, iz not a difficult thing to struggle with, but it iz dezigned principally for puddins.

■   ■   ■

MAIL MATTER.

Pine Grove, Indiana, *September 5th, 1880.*

Dear Josh:

I hav tried, in my household, your grate remedy for makeing

"Good Rum Sauce," and must say that nothing has ever entered our family, since it waz organized, that has given sutch distuingshed satisfaction. Joshua, you are a philosopher and philanthropister, may you never grow bald-headed. You won't need any tomb stun when you die; your epitaff will be a household word. "Rum Sauce" haz done the bizzness for you. Enclosed please find 10 dollars, and put it to the credit ov "Rum Sauce" on your books. My wife uses the sauce on all her pudding fixins, and I take it regular, before meals, az an alterative.

Yures sweetly.
BOB WAGSTAFF, Jun.

■   ■   ■

It iz a mighty mean trick to set an old grandpa to churning butter.—I am a grandpa miself, but I wont churn for no concern—not if I kno miself.

■   ■   ■

TO MAKE DOE NUTS.

Take one quart ov rye flower, and three pints ov korn meal, amalgamate well together, sift them thru a cane-bottomed chair, add six ounces ov pork fat, and jam well together, lay the jam on a table, and level it with an iron rolling pin untill you git tired, turn it over and roll it again on the other side, sprinkle with a little mollassis az you go along, cut it up into fractions, three inches and a haff long by 2 and a half wide, twist each fraction into the shape ov a cork-skrew, drop the fractions into some bileing tallow, and let them sputter for 9 minutes, take them out with a pair ov tongs, and lay them into a collender to drain, pack them down tite in a stun jar, and serve them up with cold water, when the minister and hiz wife make their annual winter evening visit.

■   ■   ■

A man can live on the bare necessarys ov life—so can a mud-turkle.

■   ■   ■

FRIED EELS.

Bait a hook with the toe ov an old injun rubber shoe, cast the hook into some mud hole where the eels congregate; when the eel bites, twitch az tho you had been stung bi a hornet, drag the eel home with the hook in his mouth, bile him in hot water for 60 min-nitts to loosen his skin, peal him az yu would a bannanner, then soak him in kerosene oil and turpentine, equal parts, for four days, to quell his muskular actions, then cast him into a brass kittle, put him onto a red hot stove, and let him fry untill he gits enough ov it, then coil him up in the bottom ov a porcelain dish, like a piece ov tarred rigging, then pour an ointment over him made ov sour milk scented with cinnamon oil, then set him out on the front steps ov your house, open the front gate wide, go to bed, and let sumbody steal him.

■   ■   ■

I don't know that civilation has increased the virtews so much, az it has hid the vices.

■   ■   ■

HOW TO COOK A SHAD.

Catch the shad fust, this iz all important—many a shad has been cooked and eaten before he was ketched—eradicate the scales from his adipose membrane, deftly remove the allimentary ar-rangements from his subteranean nature, banish all the bones from his being, stuff him with ground crackers lubricated with Scoharie county butter, perfume suitably with pepper and sault, straddle a gridiron with his person, over a golden mass ov hickory coals, for 28 minutes, lay him on a milk-white platter, his head to the windward, surround him with sliced lemon and tube roses, blow the horn for dinner and ask in some ov your poor relations to the feast. Shad eaten in this way will be blest, whether you ask grace or not.

■   ■   ■

GOOD RHY COFFEE.

Rhy coffee iz good, but Rhyo iz better. To make a good Rhy coffee, take one quart ov old Rhy (not liquid Rhy, but Rhy in the berry); if you cant git Rhy, beans will do, burn it in a spider over hot coals untill it iz burnt, drop in a lump ov possum fat, and agitate it lively, while it iz burning, with a pewter spoon, burn it untill it iz az black and shiny az pattent leather, let it cool off, and then spill it into a coffee mill, grind it untill it iz ground, take a tea cup ov the grindings and boil it untill it iz boiled, insert sugar to the taste, whiten with good Ayshire milk. This iz a dose for two, drink standing to the suckcess ov the American flag, and the everlasting perpetuashun ov the Union, one and inseperable.

■   ■   ■

Contentment iz not happiness,—if it iz, you cant beat a Rockaway clam.

■   ■   ■

HASTY PUDDING.

Hasty pudding iz made out ov injun meal and hot water, about haff and haff. It gits its name from the sudden manner in which it iz made. Hang a 4 gallon kittle on a crane, in an old-fashioned fireplace, fill it up to the waist with water, set her to boiling, then sift in the meal with one hand, and with a wooden ladle stir lively with the other; in twenty minutes it will be done; dip out into two quart bowls, haff pudding and haff milk, call the roll, and let the young ones pitch in. Two bowls full iz a dose for a young one; when they have finished, wipe their mouths with a crash towel, kiss them all around, hear their little prayer, and tuck them up in their little beds for the night.

■   ■   ■

KRONOLOGY.

Geese were fust roasted during the third century.
"Roast pig was discovered about the year 896.
"Boiled eggs were invented during the reign ov Trajan.
"Quails on toast appeared about the end ov the 9th century.

"The fust mention made ov baked shad waz in 1493.

"We hav no earlier record ov hash than the year 2.

"Oysters were found in 756, appeared later, on the haff shell, 804.

"There is no posative date when the fust Bologna sausage was seen; one historian says in the fore part ov the 6th century, others put it later. I am more interested when the last one will appear than I am when the fust one did.

■   ■   ■

PICKLED TOUNGE.

Take a good quiet tounge (there are a great many tounges that wont keep still long enough to pickle), thrust the tounge into boiling water for seven minutes, peal it az you would a boiled potato, prepare a fluid ov vinegar, spiced with cloves and kardamon seeds, put the tounge in a glass jar, with the round side ov the tounge up, pour the solution slowly over the tounge, set it away where the rats can't git at it; some lonesum nite, when the bleak winds ov November are mourning outside, eat the tounge all alone by yourself, wash it down with a cup ov strong coffee, then go to bed, and somewhere about the center ov nite you will see your late lamented mother-in-law prancing around the room, a 2:40 gait, on a cream colored nite-mare.

■   ■   ■

Opportunitys are game birds, and if they are got, must be got on the wing.

■   ■   ■

ROAST CLAM.

Roast clam iz joy on the haff shell, glory enuff for one day, az natural az an infant, and az luscious az honey in the comb. Take a Rockaway clam, lay it softly on the glittering coals, watch the bivalve with the solicitude ov a mother, when it opens its steaming mouth, and issues from its lips the exquisite aroma, lift it delicately to the platter, unhinge its upper cover, drop a wee lump ov butter on the liquid morsel, salt and pepper the dear viand gently, raise it up tenderly with the left hand, part your mustash with the right, throw your head back az tho you waz inspired, drop the juicy mass into your mouth, wink languidly, swallow slowly, and the joyful victory iz complete. Three cheers, for roast clam on the haff shell.

THE NOBLE CODPHISH BALL.

Come listen to my story, yee men and women all,
While I sing to you a ditty ov the *Noble Codfish Ball*. Korn beef and
cabbage has its friends, and so has suckertash,
And some there be who relish a plate ov mutton hash.
Baked beans and pork are well enough, but since poor Adam's fall,
Nothing has discounted yet, a boneless codfish ball.
Let Britons praise roast beef, and Frenchmen frogs hind leggs,
And Germans sing ov sausages, and beer in little kegs.
The universal Yanke nation, her lads and lasses all, Will ever shout
the praises ov, the *Noble Codfish Ball*.

*I kno lots ov people whose only reckomendashun iz that they
are helthy—so iz an onion.*

HASH.

Hash iz made out ov cast-off vittles, homogenius, abnormal,
and at times unequal in its nature. Hash has done more to push the

human family, than any other kind ov mixt food. It will be impossible to lay down any specifick rule, to create this abstruse, and at the same time, gentle food. Anything that will chop fluently will produce hash. No one has taken out a pattent yet, for the production ov this promiscuous viand. Hash requires but little cooking, but may be compared to a foundered horse—goes the best when it iz well warmed up. For the creashun ov hash, tallent iz ov more importance than genius. Finally, hash may be likened unto the human family—from some stand points it iz fair, from others it iz bad, and from all suspicious.

■　　　■　　　■

If there iz no hereafter, reason iz a fraud, and instinct a failure.

■　　　■　　　■

HOW TO MAKE SHADOW SOUP.

Pick out a good thin chicken (Shanghi breed iz the best), disrobe him ov his plumage, amputate his spurs, remove the comb from his head, confiscate his tail feathers, place him in a strong sunlight, let the shaddow reach across two gallons ov strained rain water in a shallow pan, let the shaddow remain on the water for 10 minnitts, then take him by the bill, and lead him gently backwards and forwards through the water, three or four times, bring the water to a sudden boil, season to suit the taste, and serve up with a raw onion, and a bunch ov wooden tooth-picks. This soup iz very popular with boarding-house keepers, and it iz said will cure the dispepsy, or kill the patient, I hav forgot which.

■　　　■　　　■

A woman never luvs the man she can govern.

■　　　■　　　■

PORK AND BEANS.

I sing ov Pork and Beans. All hail ! yee greasy, and health-inspiring bulbs. Heaven bless the hour that gave you birth and sent you joyous, singing thru the world this ditty,—"*Walk up ladies, and gents, here's your happy Pork, and Beans, only 10 cents a platter, here's where you git the worth ov your money, and the right change back.*" I have dove deep into the subsoil ov history, and find that one Barnabus Ignatius, a haberdasher ov the thirteenth century, on or about the 26th day ov April, in the old ov the moon, discovered Pork and Beans, while hunting for something else. Pork, and Beans, old boy! Give us your hand, you have many a time been the best friend i had on earth. I have bought a platter ov you, in a shabby stall, with the last dime i had, and then went into the world, too full for utterance, ready to fite stern fortune for a stake, at any range. Pork, and Beans, you dear, and nutritious old lubricator, you healthy, and cheerful conglomeration ov small ovals, and grease, my boyhoods refreshment, my refuge in the time ov manhood, and my alcohol in the cold hour ov penury and want, if the world ever turns a cold shoulder on you, with none to flatter you, no one to take you in, come to mi cupboard, and rest in peace, you will allways have one friend who knows your honesty.

Pork, and Beans, i love yu, i will sing your praises, i will pray for you, and if worse, comes to worse, i will shed mi coat, and plunge elbow deep into any man who iz sassy to you.

P.S. Pork and Beans, I shall lunch with you tomorrow at precisely haff past two, until then, mi dear old side partner, a fond adew.

■　　　■　　　■

THE KUNTRY SAUSAGE.

The kuntry sausage iz an oleagenous fruit. They measure about seven inches one way, and an inch the other, and a pound ov them fried will give 2 pounds ov grease. They are good for the dispepsy, and liver ailment, and enough of them, will bring on the salt rume, and the biles. They are az good cold, az they are het up, and if you eat hearty of them Monday morning for breakfast, you can taste them Saturday night of that week for supper. There is two breeds ov these oily vagrants, one iz balony, and the other iz Connecticut. The balony iz the biggest; and will keep oleaginous for 9 years, and not perish. I have seen balony so advanced in life that they was all covered with wrinkles, like an old cows horn, one wrinkle for each year. The only true way to git at the longevity ov a balony, iz to count the wrinkles. After the balony gets too old for chewing, they can be used for kindling wood, or be kept for plugging up rat holes. They make the best kind of plugs known to man, they will keep the rat gnawing away at the plug all the time, and it iz from 18 months, to 2 years, before he can see day light. The Connektikutt sausage iz az old az the American revolution, and our forefathers used them, after they got age enough, for cattridges, to fire into the pesky British. Many a British has had his earthly bizzness closed out by our Connektikutt sausage. I have seen a balony that was 2 feet long, and 4 inches around the waist, it had been bored out, and was used az a horn to play in the orchestra, and the German who owned it, said it was 13 years old, last March. This was 5 years ago, and i presume the sausage iz alive yet. The sausage iz born with a tite skin on them, and this skin iz tuff, and hard for the stomach to contend with!

■   ■   ■

LAGER BEER, AND SPRUCE GUM.

Lager beer iz a limber tonic. Five or six glasses ov it before breakfast makes the liver feel proud, accelerates the speed ov the blood, tones up the burial places of the body, and absorbs the wicked accumulations ov the system. Eight or nine tumblers ov it before dinner hurrys digestion, equalizes the morbid sap ov the natural man, arouses the dreaming energys, lubricates the bile, stimulates inaction, and pacifys the anxietys ov the nerves. Twelve, or fifteen pints in the afternoon awakens all the lethargys, starts perspiration, dissipates vertigo, scatters melancholy, and chases away all longings and apprehentions. Twenty-five, or thirty mugs ov it before supper clears the vision, stops all ringing in the ears, adds pride to the stomach, and acts like a charm on the lazy forces ov the constitution. Forty, or fifty cups ov it during the evening, permeates thru the entire subburbs ov the physical construction, ascends the spinal column, challenges the kidneys, makes the spleen laff, and finally sends the man to bed, about haff past eleven, az drunk az a phool.

■   ■   ■

SPRUCE GUM.

Spruce gum iz the blood ov a tree, boiled down to a chewable consistency. Every body chews gum in the State ov Maine, including the governor, and hiz wife, and while a horse jockey, down in Connektikut couldn't trade a horse without gitting badly cheated, if he didn't have a pine shingle to whittle, up in Maine, if you can manage to steal his gum, you can clean a jockey right out ov his horse. I have tended evening meetings up in Maine, and every body was chewing gum except the minister, and he seemed to be in a grate hurry to git thru, so that he could chew some. Chewing gum beats chewing tobacco, it costs less, and lasts longer, and when you git tired chewing, you can pass your gum to your nabor, and let him chew, you cant do this with tobacco.

■　　　　■　　　　■

Josh Billings, and The Bull.

Never take the Bull bi the horns Yung Man, but take him bi the tale. then yu kan let go when yu want to. = Yure warm friend, Josh Billings

■　　　　■　　　　■

HASH.

Hash has been abused more than any other ov the legitimate nourishments, and i guess it iz az able to stand it az well az any ov the rest ov them. The Duke ov Wellington used to call Hash, *"What's left over from the fight yesterday."* The Baron Rothchild said ov Hash, *"Hash haz no pedigree."* Tully, the Roman orator, on one ov hiz polished orations speaks thus beautifully and comprehensively, *"Hash has dun more to advance the human race than any other kind ov mixt phood."* Socrates the divine philosopher told ov hash, *"That it waz an end, without a means."* Mark Twain the innimitable calls it, *"Mystery,"* and Nasby the confederate autokrat ov the cross roads, informs us, that hash *"Iz like faith, the substance ov things hoped for, and the evidence ov things not seen."* Thomas Nast, the irrepressible man ov hidden meanings, represented *Hash* az a hydra-headed monster, in which pork, rooster, striped bass, sheep, roast beef, pickled clams, celery, cold potatose, broken napkin rings, orange peel, and bent hairpins, and many other contribushuns, stuck out in battle array. Gen. Jackson, the author ov *"By the Eternal,"* pronounced hash to be, *"The right Bower of economy.".* George Washington, the father ov us all, and the guardian ov the little axe, in one ov his festive moments, spoke ov hash az, *The Land-lady's best holts."* Hash iz a great fertilizer, and tho i often have seen hash, that i had my doubts about, i eat it manfully, and still live.

■   ■   ■

MISSELLANEOUS.
SOME VEGETABEL HISTORY.

THE strawberry is one ov nature's sweet pets.

She makes them worth fifty cents, the fust she makes, and never allows them tew be sold at a mean price.

The color ov the strawberry iz like the setting sun under a thin cloud, with a delicate dash of the rain bow in it; its fragrance iz like the breath ov a baby, when it fust begins tew eat wintergreen lozenges; its flavor is like the nectar which an old-fashioned goddess used tew leave in the bottom ov her tumbler, when Jupiter stood treat on Mount Ida.

There iz many breeds ov this delightful vegetable, but not a mean one in the whole lot.

I think i have stole them, laying around loose, without any pedigree, in somebody's tall grass, when I was a lazy schoolboy, that eat dredful easy, without any white sugar on them, and even a bug occasionally mixed with them in the hurry of the moment.

Cherrys are good, but they are too much like sucking a marble, with a handle tew it.

Peaches are good, if you don't git any ov the pin-feathers into your lips.

Watermelons will suit anybody who iz satisfied with halfsweetened drink; but the man who can eat strawberrys besprinkled with crushed sugar, and besmattered with sweet cream, (at sombody else's expense), and not lay hiz hand on hiz stomach, and thank the author ov strawberrys and stomachs, iz a man with a worn-out conscience—a man whose mouth tastes like a hole in the ground, that don't care what goes down it.

"Familiarity breeds contempt." This only applies tew men, not trew hot buckwheat slapcakes, well-buttered and sugared.

KONKLUSHUNS

Having examined closely all the diffrent kinds ov cooking, boiling, roasting and stewing, from quails on toast, all the way down to hash on a platter, having eaten in all the famous restaurants in the country, paying five dollars for the chance, and having dined in 10 cent saloons, on one kind ov meat and two kinds ov turnips, having studied bills of fare, untill I lost mi appetight in a labarinth ov miserable French, I feel like shouting, with the epicure ov old, "The Lord sends us meat, and the Devil sends us cooks."

To be charitable towards all things iz safe,—charity dont make any blunders.

Patience iz a good thing for a man to hav. but when he haz got so mutch ov it. that he kan fish all day long. withont enny bate on hiz hook,— Lazyness, iz whats the matter ov him = Josh Billings

Chapter VI

THE OLD, THE YOUNG
AND THE RELIGIOUS

Josh Billings, and the Yung Man:

Yung Man, don't kry for spilt milk, but pik up yure pail, and milking stool, and go for the next Cow. = Yures affekshionately, Josh Billings.

∎   ∎   ∎

FAITH.

FAITH iz the right bower ov Hope.

If it want for faith, thare would be no living in this world. We couldn't even eat hash with any safety, if it want for faith.

Human knowledge is very short, and don't reach but a little ways, and even that little ways iz twilite; but faith lengthens out the road, and makes it light, so that we can see tew read the letterings on the mile stones.

Faith has won more victorys than all the other passions or sentiments ov the heart and head put together.

Faith iz one ov them warriors who dont know when she iz whipped.

But Faith iz no milksop, but a live fighter. She don't set down and grow stupid with resignation, and git weak with the beauty ov her attributes; but she iz the heroine ov forlorn Hope—she feathers her arrows with reason, and fires rite at the bull's eye ov fate.

I think now if i couldn't have but one ov the moral attributes, i would take it all in faith—red hot faith I mean; and tho i mite make some fust rate blunders, i would do a rushing bizzness amung the various dry bones there iz laying around loose in this world.

■   ■   ■

Very old people often are free from all appearances ov sin, because they hav nothing left for either tew feed upon.

■   ■   ■

We have no more right to laff at a deformed person, than we have at a crooked tree—both ov them are God's arkitekture.

■   ■   ■

I wouldn't undertake tew correct a man's sectarian views any quicker than i would tell him which road tew take at a 4 corners, when i didn't know myself which was the right one.

■   ■   ■

It ought to be a fair trade to swop religions, but where will you find the christian party that iz willing to do it.

■   ■   ■

I find it iz a great deal easier for my philosophy to account for original sin, than for an attack ov the jumping tooth ache.

■   ■   ■

Temptations iz what tries a man's moral grip, Adam and Eve were very good plums until the devil shook their bush, then they let go their holt immediately.

■   ■   ■

One quart ov cheap whisky (the cheaper the better) judiciously applied, will do more bizzness for the devil than the smartest deason he has got.

■   ■   ■

There iz some folks in this world who spend their whole time hunting after righteousness and haint got any spare time tew practice it.

■   ■   ■

It dont require but a few brains tew make up an atheist, for the less a man knows the less he generally believes.

■   ■   ■

If I was a-going tew civilize a parcel of heathen on some distant isle by the job, i should debate some time in my mind which tew send, dancing-masters or missionarys.

■   ■   ■

Faith wont make a man virtuous, but it makes what virtue he has got red hot. Those who expect tew keep themselfs pure in this life, must keep their souls boiling all the time, like a pot, and keep all the time skimming the surface.

■   ■   ■

Religion in these days, iz composed ov vanity, and piety, and each man and woman iz a better judge ov the proportion than I am.

■   ■   ■

It iz hard work, at fust sight, tew see the wisdom ov a rattle snake bite, but there iz thousands ov folks who never think ov their sins untill they are bit by a rattle snake.

■   ■   ■

I often meet in my travels bigoted christians, who seem tew think, they are the guardian angels ov all the virtue in the world, such men would have us think, they are bills ov exchange, on the kingdom ov heaven, when in reality, they are only bogus postal currency.

■   ■   ■

You can judge ov a mans religion very well by hearing him talk, but you cant judge ov hiz piety by what he sez, any more than you can judge ov hiz amount ov linen by the stick out ov hiz collar and waistbands.

■   ■   ■

I have got a dreadful poor opinion ov all religious creeds; a man who depends upon a creed tew keep him pious, iz no better than he whom the penalty for stealing keeps out ov jail.

■   ■   ■

A LOOSE BILT EPISTLE.

DEAR Brigham:—
   Excuse this peripatetick letter.

I am a vagrant, and a wanderer on the trail ov literature, and write letters in a reckless, hap-hazard way. I wasn't harnessed young enough tew be kind in all harness.

If i had a boy now who had any symtoms ov any kind ov lawless, unfixed, and flux notions, and who didn't seem tew care whether he ever amounted tew any thing or not, and who couldn't tell where he waz last night till half past two this Morning, and who couldn't recognize hiz own washer-woman, and who wanted tew go into bizzness fur himself at 16 years old, with a capital ov two bottles ov Phalon's extract, and a mustache that resembled the mold on a pound ov limeberger cheese, I would say confidentially tu him:

"Son, i hav been tew blame thus far in frameing your timber, but yu can bet them patent leather boots yu hav got on, and witch haint bin paid for yet, that from now hereafter yu hav got tew begin again, and weed out your gardin sass, and sucker your grape vine, and plough up your wild oats, and underdrain your swamp land, and bush hook your briar patch, and fix your farm for a crop ov sum kind ov grain that will not disgrace both son and daddy, when it iz brought tew market."

This iz the way i would converse with the young Billings, and if he didn't begin, in ten minutes, tew take an account ov hiz bad debts, but begin tew argy the pint with me, and act young rooster up and down in front ov me, mi strong impression iz now, that i would retreat a step and let fly mi left persuader and land that boy sum 60 feet further off than he waz.

It would hav bin six hundred dollars in mi vest pocket if sum philanthropist, about thirty years ago, had got mi knob in chancery, and not given up the case till he had punched out ov my hed the fresh water notion that the best way tew foller a blind trail in the wilderness waz not tew take any compass.

This kind ov dead sure knowledge, among fresh yung men, haz landed four hundred out ov every five hundred ov them, before they had got half way thru life, into sum soft swamp, and the other hundred have sat out the close ov their lives on a fence, lamenting the hard work they did, in their younger days, tew make ! ⊘ X phools ov themselfs.

I kno it iz az eazy az chawing gum, for a young institution ov a boy, who haz got a burning-fluid nature, tew be anxious tew join all the torch-lite doings in the country, and tew holler "amen" before the prayer iz half through; but i feel it my duty tew tell these camphene children tew cork up their lightning.

I don't want any body's boy Billy tew be a dead head; a skim-milk cheeze; a colporter of water gruel; a pretty babling; a curl-papered nursery doll; an apron-tied anatomy blonde; a timid corpse amung hiz phellows, afraid ov a bug, and satisfied with a kitten.

I ain't voting for this breed ov boys; i only ask the virginity ov mi sex tew make up their minds, from the experiences ov those who have observed the elephant, that youth waz given them, not tew be boss, but apprentice; not tew lead, but tew foller; not tew harvest, but tew plant.

There iz no danger in turning a snaik loose; even before he gits fairly haired out, natur teaches him tew make his first wiggle a correct pattern for hiz last one. She makes him a snaik from the word "go," and nothing else, and if he takes a noshun tew go tew the devil—who cares?

But ov all the most deplorable luck that can be the inheritance ov a camphene boy, i don't kno ov a more dangerous one than tew be hiz own master, or the master ov hiz daddy.

I hav known sum ov theze eccentrics that Satan couldn't cetch, who hav dodged him successfully for the whole ov their lives, but i kan tell you, mi dear boys, it is no credit tew match yourselfs against the devil, even if you have a ded soft thing. This beating the devil at his own game, is like surviving the small pox, it may make you proof agin sum more small pox, but you are sure tew show sum ov the dents.

Dear Brigham, theze remakrs are not intended tew be personal, they wouldn't fit you any more than a side-saddle would fit the back stretch ov a trotting track for i know yu hav bin broke tew stand without tieing.

■　　　　■　　　　■

Humility iz a good thing tew have, provided a man iz sure he has got the right kind. There never iz a time in a cat's life when she iz so humble az just before she makes up her mind tew pounce onto a chicken, or just after she has caught and et it.

■　　　　■　　　　■

I like a wide-awake christian, one whose virtew has got some cayenne pepper in it.

■　　　　■　　　　■

Death iz the only thing in this life that iz certain; and even that ain't always a safe investment.

■   ■   ■

In bible times, when Balem's ass spoke, it waz a miracle; but the days ov miracles are over, and the greatest asses we have in these times are the gratest talkers.

■   ■   ■

Take all the prophecys that have come tew pass, and all that have caught on the center, and failed tew come tew time, and make them up into an average, and yu will find, that buying stock, on the Codfish Bank ov Nufoundland, at 50 percent, for a rise, iz in comparison, a good speculative bizziness.

■   ■   ■

I consider it a great compliment tew religion that there are only two substitutes for it; one is hipocrasy, and the other iz superstishun.

■   ■   ■

Thare iz a grate deal ov religion, in this world, that iz like a life Preserver,—only put on at the moment ov immediate danger,—and then, haff the time, put on, hind side before.

■   ■   ■

People are more apt tew make a shield ov their religion than they are a pruning-hook.

■   ■   ■

Just about az ceremonies creep into one end ov a church piety creeps out ov the other.

There iz a great deal ov religion in this world that iz like a life-preserver—only put on at the moment ov extreme danger, and put on then, half the time, hind side before.

■   ■   ■

One ov the best trades any man can make iz to sell out his religious creed and invest the proceeds in charity.

■   ■   ■

Faith beats both wisdom and learning.

■   ■   ■

Be merciful to all the dumb animals—no man can ride into heaven, on a sore-backed horse.

■   ■   ■

Some folks, az they grow older, grow wiser; but most folks simply grow stubbonner.

■   ■   ■

There iz two things about the devil which i admire, and which are worthy ov imitation, he iz always bizzy, and never was known to break an engagement.

■   ■   ■

It has been ascertained, by a learned professor, in Yale College, that the wicked work 50 per cent harder tew git to hell, than the righteous do to reach Heaven—what a waste of time and muscle!

■   ■   ■

Many people spend their time trying tew find the hole where sin got into this world—if two men break through the ice into a mill pond, they had better hunt for sum good hole tew git out, rather than git into a long argument about the hole they come tew fall in.

■   ■   ■

There iz no sects nor religious disputes amung the heathen, they all of them cook a missionary in the same way.

■   ■   ■

"Blessed are the meek and lowly" (and very lucky, too, if they don't git their noze pulled.)

■   ■   ■

There iz hipocrits in vice az well az in virtew; i have seen men affect the rake and the roue, whoze best holt waz the catechism.

■   ■   ■

Any man who can swop horses, or cetch fish, and not lie about it, is just about as pious az men ever git to be in this world.

■   ■   ■

The reason why so phew people are happy in this world iz becauze they mistake their bodies for their souls.

■   ■   ■

A good conscience iz a foretaste ov heaven.

■   ■   ■

BABYS.

Babys i love with all mi heart; they are mi sweetmeats, they warm up mi blood like a gin sling, they crawl into me and nestle by the side ov mi soul, like a kitten under a cook stove.

I have raized babys miself, and know what i am talking about.

I have got grandchildren, and they are wuss than the first crop tew riot among the feelings.

If i could have mi way, i would change all the human beings now on the face ov the earth back into babys at once, and keep them there, and make this footstool one grand nursery; but what i should do for wet nurses i don't know, nor don't care.

I would like tew have 15 babys now on mi lap, and mi lap ain't the handiest lap in the world for babys, neither.

My lap iz long enough, but not the widest kind ov a lap.

I am a good deal ov a man, but i consist ov length principally, and when i make a lap ov myself, it iz not a mattress but more like a couple ov rails with a joint in them.

I can hold more babys in mi lap at once, than any man in America, without spilling one, but it hurts the babys.

I never saw a baby in mi life that i didn't want tew kiss; i am worse than an old maid in this respect.

I have seen babys that i have refused tew kiss untill they had been washt; but the baby want tew blame for this, neither waz i.

There are folks in this world who say they don't luv babys, but yu can depend upon it, when they waz babys sumbody loved them.

Babys luv me, too. I can take them out ov their mothers' arms just az eazy az i can an unfledged bird out ov hiz nest. They luv me becauze i luv them.

And here let me say, for the comfort and consolation ov all mothers, that whenever they see me on the cars or on the steamboat, out ov a job they needn't hesitate a minute tew drop a clean, fat baby into mi lap; i will hold it, and kiss it, and be thankful besides.

Perhaps thare iz people who don't envy me all this, but it iz one ov the sharp-cut, well-defined joys ov mi life, mi love for babys and their love for me.

Perhaps there iz people who will call it a weakness, i don't care what they call it, bring on the babys. Uncle Josh haz always a kind word and a kiss for the babys.

I love babys for the truth there iz in them, i aint afraid their kiss will betray me, their iz no frauds, dead beats nor counterfits among them.

I wish i was a baby (not only once more) but forever-more.

■   ■   ■

HOROSKOPE FOR OCTOBER.

The male man usherd into existence this month will be ov an enquiring mind. The first thing he will enquire for will be sum good cider. He will study divinity at first, but will quit that and become a conductor on a hoss rale-rode; this pays better, and haz more perquisites. He will marry the woman ov his choice, which iz good, provided the choice is all right. His hair will turn grey before he dies, but after he dyes he will hav black hair the rest of hiz days.

■   ■   ■

Enny person having an easy pill to take, that will restore a shatterd reputashun, without change ov diet tew the patient, can hav this advertizing space highly reasonable.

■   ■   ■

The devil iz the father ov lies, but he failed tew git out a pattent for hiz invenshun, and hiz bizzness iz now suffering from competition.

■   ■   ■

Selfishness iz the alter which every man sets up in hiz soul and asks hiz conscience to be high priest ov the ceremonys.

■   ■   ■

I haven't much doubt that man sprung from the monkey, but what bothers me, iz, where the cussid monkey sprung from.

■   ■   ■

We are often ridiculed for telling old truths. The 10 commandments are old enough tew be wore out with truth; but who follers them?

■   ■   ■

The devil owes most ov his success tew the fact that he iz always on hand.

■   ■   ■

If there want no evil in this world, there wouldn't be much wisdom, i suppose.

■   ■   ■

There iz lots ov folks who are in sich a grate hurry tew git religion that they confess sins they aint guilty ov, and overlook those that they am.

■   ■   ■

The man who wrote, "I would not live always, I ask not tew stay," probably never had been urged sufficiently.

■   ■   ■

If I had the privilege ov making the Eleventh Commandment, it would be this—*owe no man*.

■   ■   ■

A sceptic iz one who knows too much tew be a good phool, and too little tew be wise.

■   ■   ■

Pure religion iz like good old hyson tea, it cheers, but don't intoxicate.

■   ■   ■

It iz hard tew quit play while we are winning. It iz just so in morals, men seldom undertake tew git religion az long az they can git any thing else.

■   ■   ■

Religion iz nothing more than a chattel mortgage, excepted, and recorded, az security for a man's morality, and virtew.

■   ■   ■

One ov the most reliable prophets i know ov iz an old hen, they don't prophesy any egg, until after the egg haz happened.

■   ■   ■

The genuine christians are the laffing ones, the man who haz tew watch hiz morality all the time for fear it will kick up its heels iz full ov the devil's oats.

■   ■   ■

The hardest thing that any man can do iz tew fall down on the ice when it iz wet, and get up and praise the Lord.

■   ■   ■

I hav known men so pious, that when they went out a fishing, on Sunday, they allwuss prayed for good luk a fakt. Josh Billings

■   ■   ■

The man who haint got any religion tew defend won't defend anything.

■   ■   ■

There iz lots ov folks who expect tew escape Hell jist because the crowd iz so great that are going there.

■   ■   ■

Thare iz lots ov folks in this world who can keep nine out ov ten ov the commandments, without any trouble at all, but the one that iz left they cant keep the small end ov.

■   ■   ■

He who simply repents ov a sin pays only 50 cents on a dollar, while he who forsakes it pays one hundred.

■   ■   ■

I look upon a pure joke with the same veneration that i do upon the 10 commandments.

■   ■   ■

Religion iz too often cut az the clothes are, according tew the prevailing fashun.

■   ■   ■

Politeness looks well to me in every man, except an undertaker.

■   ■   ■

All the good men in this world have got the same kind ov religion, it iz only the dead-beats, frauds, and hypocrits, whose religion differs.

■   ■   ■

I wouldn't give a shilling a pound for religion that you cant take anywhere out into the world with you, even tew a hoss race, if you have a mind tew, without losing it.

■   ■   ■

Heaven iz ever kind tew us, she puts our humps on our backs, so that we can't see them.

■   ■   ■

There iz a time for all things, there is a time tew pray, and there iz a time to say *amen,* roll up your sleeves and pitch in.

■   ■   ■

THE SKOOL BOY.

The skool boy iz the victim ov circumstances. If he lives in the country he haz got to git up early enough to punch the chickens off the roost, then start the fire in the kitchen stove, then put on the tea kettle, and then go for the cows. After the cows hav been milkt, he hurrys down his hash, and buckwheat cakes, and then thrashes beans two hours, with the old man, out in the corn cirb. Now he walks three miles in a snow path to the district skool house, and gits there just in time to help split up sum wood for the days fire. Skool opens, and he takes his seat on the flat side ov a slab bench and bends double over a Websters spelling book, dogeared, and without any covers. For variety, he stands up in a row and spells three syllable words, or scratches on a greasy slate a long sum in addition. Noon cums at last, and he eats, up in a corner, his two slices of stale rye bread, and hiz piece ov pie crust, and drowns the dry dinner, with a pint ov lukewarm water, out ov a pine pail, behind the stove. The only fun he haz, is to slide down hill, on a barrel stave, back ov the skool house and git thrashed when he goes home, if he happens to wear the toes ov hiz boots any, or rends the base ov hiz pantaloons. Night comes, and he haz had a days skooling, and plods bak home to saw wood enough to last next day, before he eats hiz pudding and milk supper, and slinks off up into the wood house chamber, to hiz corn husk bed, without any candel, only the light ov the stars, shining thru the cracks in the clapboards ov the building. This waz skoolboy life in the country 40 years ago, but if the boys, now days, had to skool it in this way, they would sue the old man for damages, and any kind ov a decent jury, would bring in a verdict to their favor.

■   ■   ■

Yung man, dont be afrade to blo yure own horn, but dont blo it in front ov the prooeshun, go to the rear and do it.=
yure uncle, Josh Billings.=

■   ■   ■

■   ■   ■

There iz few, if any, more suggestive sights tew a philosopher, than tew lean agin the side ov the wall, and peruse a clean, phatt, and well disciplined baby, spread out on the floor, trying tew smash a hammer all tew pieces with a looking glass.

■   ■   ■

Yung man, learn tew listen!—i don't mean at a key-hole. There iz plenty ov happiness in this life if we only knew it: and one way tew find it iz, when we have got the rumatiz tew thank Heaven that it aint the gout.

■   ■   ■

Give every one you meet my boy, the time of day and half the road, and if that dont make him civil dont waste any more fragrance on the cuss.

■   ■   ■

YOUNG man, when you have tew search Webster's Dickshionary tew find words big enough tew convey your meaning you can make up your mind that you don't mean much.

■   ■   ■

Men, if they ain't too lazy, live sumtimes till they are 80, and destroy the time a good deal az follows: the fust 30 years they spend throwing stones at a mark, the second 30 they spend in examining the mark tew see whare the stones hit, and the remainder iz divided, in cussing the stone-throwing bizzness, and nursing the rumatizz.

■   ■   ■

This seems to be about the way it iz did: When we are young, we *run* into difficultys, and when we git old, we *fall* into them.

■   ■   ■

My young friend, don't forgit one thing—however cunning you may be, the eaziest man in all the world for yu tew cheat iz yourself.

■   ■   ■

Children are like vines; they will climb the pole yu set up for them, be it crooked or strate.

■   ■   ■

It iz a dredful fine thing to whip a young one jist enough and not any more. I take it that the spot iz located jist whare their pride ends, and their mad begins.

■　　　　■　　　　■

Go slow, yung man, if yu tap both ends ov your cider barrel at once, and draw out of the bung hole besides; your cider aint a going to hold out long.

■　　　　■　　　　■

About the most we can hope in our old age iz tew endure the thoughts ov what we enjoyed when we waz young.

■　　　　■　　　　■

One ov the most diffikult, and at the same time one ov the most necessary things for us old fellows to know, iz that we aint ov so much account now az we waz.

■　　　　■　　　　■

The fust intimation i had that i waz gitting old waz, i found myself telling to mi friends the same storys over again.

■　　　　■　　　　■

In youth we run into difficultys, in old age, diffikultys runs into us.

■　　　　■　　　　■

A man don't alwus grow wise az he grows old, but alwus grows old az he grows wise.

■　　　　■　　　　■

When i see an old man marry a young wife, i consider him starting out on a bust, for i am reminded ov the parable in the Bible, about new wine, and old bottles.

■　　　　■　　　　■

A cheerful old man, or old woman, iz like the sunny side ov a wood-shed, in the last ov winter.

■　　　　■　　　　■

It iz hard work to be an old fellow and do the subject justice, if you are very cheerful, the world will call you frisky, if you are quite sedate, they will call you illnatured,—perhaps the best way iz to die off in good season.

■　　　　■　　　　■

About the most we can hope in our old age iz tew endure the thoughts ov what we enjoyed when we waz young.

■　　　　■　　　　■

A day in the life ov an old man iz like one ov the last days in the fall ov the year, every hour brings a change in the weather.

I love tew see an old person joyfull, but not kickupthe heels-full.

■ ■ ■

Three score year and ten iz the time allotted to man, and it iz enuff. If a man can't suffer all the misery he wants in that time, he must be numb.

■ ■ ■

Old age haz its priviliges—one iz tew find fault with everything.

■ ■ ■

Love seems tew hav this effekt, it makes a young man sober, and an old man gay.

■ ■ ■

When vice leaves an old man, it iz no ways certain that virtue takes the place ov it, for sin sumtimes quits us because it haz nothing to feed on.

LUKE BILLINGS.
HIZ MEMORANDUM.

Luke Billings was a skool-master ov the Nu England type and shadow. He waz an uprite and an austere man, az uprite az a sperm candle, and az austere as horse-radish. I look back onto Luke's memoirs and pity him, for i pity awl district-skool masters, all mothers-in-law, and all grass widders. Luke Billings spent hiz whole life in the district-skool speculation, and died az poor az a salt codfish. His assetts consisted ov a pocket-comb and a nu testament. He used tew board round the naborhood, and was always az hungry az pickrel. He never had any friends, nor any enemys; he waz like a guide board in this respect. Luke Billings never got married, he hadn't the time tew spare. He waz severely engaged, for 26 years, tew Nancy Burbanks, but they both died intestate. They sleep close together, in the old grave-yard, at lower Podunk. Sleep on! sleep on! dear old virgin couple, and pay no attention tew noboddy. Lukey wore hiz hair long behind, and kept a district-skool 34 years 6 months and 17 daze. Oh, dear! oh, dear! Luke i pity you, Luke Billings iz an ancestor that i look back upon every now and then with my memory, and want tew fite sumbody on hiz account. Fairwell, luvely Luke. Fairwell Lukey. Fairwell. Enuff sed.

■ ■ ■

MORAL.

From keeping skool, and the pay,
Two things pestiverous,
I feel az tho' I'd like to say,
Good Lord! deliver us.

■   ■   ■

Learning iz a good deal like strength, it requires good hoss sense tew know how tew apply it.

■   ■   ■

Life iz like a mountain—after climbing up one side and sliding down the other, put up the sled.

Whoever iz a sedate old man at 20, will be apt tew be a frivilous young one at 60.

■   ■   ■

The minds ov the young are eazily trained; it iz hard work to git an old hop vine to travel a new pole.

■   ■   ■

The longer i live the more i am convinced that mankind grows *different* not *worse*. Us old folks are apt to confound the terms.

■   ■   ■

Old dorgs nurse their grudges, but yung pups fight and then frolic.

■   ■   ■

Sum folks, az they gro older, gro wizer; but most folks simply gro stubborner.

■   ■   ■

The close intimacy ov old age seem tew consist in comparing gouts and rumatizz.

■   ■   ■

One ov the surest signs ov an intelligent civilization iz tew see amung the masses a becuming respect and reverence for the aged.

■   ■   ■

Old age iz covetous, becauze it haz larnt bi experience, that the best friend a man haz in this world, iz hiz pocket-book.

■   ■   ■

Thare are az many old phools in this world az young ones, and the old ones are the sillyest.

■   ■   ■

Pitch in yung man, head fust, and recolect this, the world dont owe yu but one thing, until you hav earned it, and that iz, a square phuneral.

■   ■   ■

I have often known the toe ov a cowhide boot, located in the rite spot, to be ov more value to a young man, than the legacy ov a rich unkle.

■   ■   ■

The eaziest thing for our friends to discover in us, and the hardest thing for us to discover in ourselfs, iz that we are growing old.

■   ■   ■

Don't forgit, yung man, that excesses in youth are a mortgage in favor ov diseaze by and by, which will not fail to forclose and enter on the premises.

■   ■   ■

If mankind were obliged tew giv their gifts secretly, they would look upon it az a great hardship.

■   ■   ■

It iz a good thing for those who have bin sinful tew turn over a new leaf, but it often happens that, in doing this, they turn over two leaves at onst, and become so suddenly virtewous that they freeze up stiff.

■   ■   ■

Misplaced charity iz a good blunder tew make.

■   ■   ■

When a man has done a charitable thing without letting the world know it, he haz done all that an angel could do in the premises.

■   ■   ■

The best invewstment I know ov, iz charity, you git your principle back immediately, and draw a dividend every time you think ov it.

■   ■   ■

"Blessed are the meek and lowly" (and very lucky, too, if they don't git their nose pulled.)

The devil iz the father ov lies, but he failed tew git out a patent for his invention, and hiz bizznezz iz now suffering from the competition.

I consider it a great compliment tew religion that there are only two substitutes for it; one is hipokrasy, and the other iz superstishun.

Whenever a minister has preached a sermon that pleazes the whole congregation, he probably has preached one that the Lord wont endorse.

I always advise short sermons, espeshily on a hot Sunday. If a minister cant strike ile in boring 40 minutes, he has either got a poor gimblet, or else he is boring in the wrong place.

Piety, like beans, duz the best on a poor soil.

A good wife iz a sweet smile from heaven.

Confess your sins tew the Lord, and you will be forgiven, confess them tew men, and you will be laffed at.

Those people who are trying to git to heaven on their creed will find out at last that they didn't have a thru ticket.

It iz all important that fashion should be perfumed with az mutch morality az possible, for it controls more people than law or piety duz.

Religion iz too often cut az the clothes are, according tew the prevailing fashun.

The best investment I know ov, iz charity, you git your principle back immediately, and draw a dividend every time you think ov it.

He who spends all his substance in charity will undoubtedly git his reward here and hereafter; but hiz reward here will be the poor-house.

■   ■   ■

He that desires tew be rich only to be charitable, iz not only a wise man, but a good one.

■   ■   ■

It iz human to err, but devlish to brag on it.

■   ■   ■

Blessed iz he who has a big pile and knows how to spread it.

■   ■   ■

Money iz like grain—it iz never so well invested az when it iz well sown.

■   ■   ■

Charity is like a mule, a good servant but a bad master. When charity gits entire control ov a man's affairs, it runs the affairs and the man both into the ground.

■   ■   ■

There iz a grate deal ov charity in this world so coldly rendered that it fairly hurts, it iz like lifting a drowning man out ov the water by the hair ov the head, and then letting him drop on the ground.

■   ■   ■

Tew enjoy a good reputashun, give publicly, and steal privately.

The infidel argys just az a
Bull duz chained to a
post. he bellows. and paws.
but he dont git loose from
the post i notiss.—
        not mutch, Josh Billings

Chapter VII

FEATHERED FRIENDS
FOR ALL SEASONS

If yu trade horses with a jockey yu kant git cheated but once.— but if yu trade with a 'deakon yu may git cheated twice.— once in the horse, and once in the deakon = Perhaps. Josh Billings

■　　■　　■

THE BAT.

THE bat is a winged mouse.

They live very retired during the day, but at nite come out for a frolic.

They fly very much unsartin, and act az tho they had taken a little too much gin.

They look out ov their face like a young owl, and will bite like a snappin turtle.

What they are good for i cant tell, and dont believe they can tell neither.

They dont seem tew be bird, beast, nor insect, but a kind of live hash, made out ov all three.

If thare want any bats in this world, i dont suppose the earth would refuse tew revolve on its axis, once in a while, just for fun.

But when we come to think, that thare aint on the face ov the earth, even one bat too much, and that thare haint been, since the days ov adam, a single surpluss muskeeters egg, laid by accident, we can form sum kind ov an idea, how little we know, and what a poor job we should make ov it, running the machinery of creation.

Man iz a fool any how, and the best ov the joke iz, he don't seem tew know it.

Bats have a destiny tew fill, and i will bet 4 dollars, they fill it better than we do ours.

Bats liv on flies, and hawks live on bats, but who lives on the hawks, i cant tell.

Biled hawk may be good, i never heard any body say it wasn't, but i dont hope i shall ever be called upon tew decide it.

Tew save life, i would eat biled hawk, but if it tastes az i think it does, i wouldn't ask for a second plate ov it.

■   ■   ■

THE HAWK.

THE hawk iz a carniverous foul, and a chickiniverous one too, every good chance he can git.

I have seen them shut up their wings, and drop down out ov the sky, like a destroying angel, and pick up a young goslin in each hand, and sore aloft agin pretty quick.

They bild their nests out ov the reach ov civilization, so that no mishionary can git to them, unless he can climb well.

Powder and double B shot, iz the only thing that will civilize a hawk clear through, so that he will stay so, and it takes a big charge ov this too.

I have fired a double-barrelled gun into them, loaded with fine shot, and it had the same exilirating effect on them, that 4 quarts ov oats would have, on an old hoss, it made them more lively for a few minnits.

I have seen dead hawks, but i never shed any tears over them.

I dont surpose that even hen hawks are made in vain, but i hav wondered, if just enough ov them, tew preserve an assortment, wouldn't answer.

■   ■   ■

I dont know az i want to bet any money, and give odds, on

the man who iz alwus anxious tew pray out loud every chance he can git.

■   ■   ■

When a man duz a good turn just for the fun ov the thing, he haz got a great deal more virtew in him than he iz aware ov.

■   ■   ■

Next tew the man who iz worth a million, in point ov wealth, iz the man who don't care a cuss for it.

■   ■   ■

Self-made men are most always apt tew be a leetle too proud ov the job.

■   ■   ■

THE PARTRIDGE.

THE partridge iz a kind ov wild hen, and live in the swamps, and on the hill sides that are woody.

They are very eazy tew cetch with the hand, if you can git near enough tew them tew put salt on their tail, but this iz always difficult for new beginners.

In the spring ov the year they will drum a tune with their wings on some deserted old log, and if you draw ni unto them tew observe the music, they will rise up, and cut a hole thru the air with a hum like a bullet.

Thare iz no burd can beat a partridge on the wing for one hundred yards, i am authorized tew bet on this.

The partridge are a game burd, and are shot on the wing, if they are not missed.

It iz dreadful natural tew miss a partridge on the fly, especially if a tree gets in the way.

I have hunted a grate deal for partridge, and lost a grate deal ov time at it.

The partridge lays 14 eggs, and iz az sure tew hatch all her eggs out az a cockroach iz who feels well.

When a brood ov young partridges fust begin tew toddle about with the old bird, they look like a lot ov last year's chestnut burs on legs.

Broiled partridge iz good if you can git one that waz born during the present century, but thare iz a grate many partridge around that waz with Noah in the ark, and they are az tuff tew git the meat off ov az a hoss shoe.

But broiled partridge iz better than broiled crow, and i had rather have broiled crow than broiled mule just for a change.

■　　　■　　　■

About all it takes tew make a wise man iz tew give other people's opinions az much weight as we do our own.

■　　　■　　　■

Take all the prophecys that have come tew pass, and all that have caught on the center, and failed tew come tew time, and make them up into an average, and yu will find, that buying stock on the Codfish Bank of Nufoundland, at 50 per cent, for a rise, iz, in comparison, a good speculative bizzness.

■　　　■　　　■

THE SNIPE.

THE snipe iz a gray, misterious bird, who git up out ov low, wet places quick, and git back again quick.

They are pure game, and are shot on the move.

They are az tender tew broil az a saddle rock oyster, and eat az easy az sweetmeats.

The snipe haz a long bill (about the length ov a doktor's) and get a living by thrusting it down into the fat earth, and then pumping the juices out with their tongue.

I hav seen snipe so phatt that when they was shot 50 feet in the air and phell on to the hard ground, they would split open like an egg.

This will sound like a lie to a man who never haz seen it did, but after he haz seen it did, he will feel different about it.

■　　　■　　　■

Whenever you see a young man hanging around a corner grosery, and drinking 3 cent gin every time he can git any body tew ask him, yu can make up yure mind that he haz bin unanimously nominated for the state prizon, and will probbly git his election.

■　　　■　　　■

Whenever you see an old goose setting on a post hole, and trying tew hatch the hole out, you can cum tew the conclusion that she is strikly a one idee goose.

■　　　■　　　■

Whenever a forlorn cat gits under your window in a hot nite, and begins tew holler, you may know that cat wants some-thing—killing probberbly.

■   ■   ■

Whenever you see a dog stop suddintly, in the road, with a flea onto him, and begin tew flea round, and round, after himself, untill he falls down, and rolls over, you will say tew yureself, that dorg iz like the wicked, he fleas, when no man perseweth.

■   ■   ■

DUK. No. 1.

T HE duk is a foul. There aint no doubt about this—naturalists say so, and common sense teaches it.

They are built sumthing like a hen, and are an up-and-down, flat-footed job. They don't cackle like the hen, nor crow like the rooster, nor holler like the peacock, nor scream like the goose, nor turk like the turkey; but they quack like a root docter, and their bill resembles a veterinary surgeon's.

They have a woven foot, and can float on the water az natural az a soap bubble.

They are pretty much all feathers, and when the feathers are all removed, and their innards out, thare iz just about az much meat on them az there iz on a crook-necked squash that has gone tew seed.

Wild duks are very good shooting, and are very good to miss also, unless you understand the bizness.

You should aim about three foot ahead ov them, and let them fly up tew the shot.

I have shot at them all day, and got nothing but a tail-feather now and then; but this satisfied me, for i am crazy for all kind ov sport, you know.

There are sum kind ov duks that are very hard tew kill, even if you do hit them. I shot, one whole afternoon, three years ago, at some decoy duks, and never got one ov them. I hav never told ov this before, and hope no one will repeat it—this iz strictly con-fidenshall.

They are fust rate feeders, and always have a leetle more appe-tite left.

Their legs are located on their body like a pair ov hind legs, and i hav seen them eat till they tipped over forwards.

Duks ought to have a pair ov before legs, and then they couldn't eat themselfs off from their feet.

Duks lay eggs, but don't lay them around loose.

Hunting duks' eggs iz a mitey close transaction.

A man couldn't earn 30 cents a day and board himself, hunting duks' eggs.

The wild duk iz a game bird, and are shot on the wing.

They can fli next faster tew a wild pigeon, and it you aim right at them on the wing, your shot will hit whare the wild duk just was.

I have seen acres ov them git up oph from the water at once; they made az much noise az the breaking up ov a camp meeting.

I have often fired into them with a double barrelled gun, when they was rising, with both mi eyes shut, and never injured any duk, az i know ov.

I always waz first rate at missing wild duks on the move.

Sumtimes a duk gits lame, and, when they do, they lay rite down and give it up.

Thare ain't no 2 legged thing on the face ov this earth can out-limp a lame duk.

You often hear the term "*lame duk*" applied tew some men, and perhaps never knew what it meant.

Study nature and you will find out whare all the truth comes from.

■   ■   ■

I have lived in this world jist long enough tew look carefully the second time into things that i am the most certain ov the fust time.

■   ■   ■

Philosophy iz a very good kind ov a teacher, and you may be able tew liv *by* it, but you cant liv *on* it—hash will tell.

■   ■   ■

TURKEY

Roast turkey iz good, but turkey with cranberry sass iz better.

The turkey iz a sedate person, but seldom forgits herself by git-ting onto frolic.

They are ov various colors, and lay from 12 to 18 eggs, and they generally lay them whare nobody iz looking for them but themselfs.

Turkeys travel about nine miles a day, during pleasant weather, in search ov their daily bread, and are smart on a grasshopper, and red hot on a cricket.

Wet weather iz bad on a turkey—a good smart shower will

drown a young one, and make an old one look and act az tho they had just been pulled out ov a swill barrel with a pair of tongs.

The masculine turkey or gobler, as they are familiarly called, hav seasons ov strutting which are immense.

I have seen them blow themselfs up with sentiments of pride or anger, and travel around a red flannel petticoat hung onto a clothes line just az tho they was mad at the petticoat for something it had did, or said tew them.

■   ■   ■

I had rather be a boy again, than to be the autokrat ov the world.

■   ■   ■

The hen turkey always has a lonesome look tew me **az** tho she had been abused bi somebody.

Turkey can endure az much cold weather az the vane on a church steeple, i have known them tew roost all night on the top limb ov an oak tree, with the thermometer 20 degrees belo zero, and in the morning fly down and wade through the snow in a barn-yard to cool off.

P.S.—If you cant have cranberry with roast turkey, apple sass will do.

■   ■   ■

THE HOSSTRITCH

The hosstritch iz a citizen ov the desert, and lay an egg about the size ov a man's head the next day after he haz been on a bumming excursion.

They resemble in size, and figger about 15 shanghi roosters at once, and are chiefly important for the feathers which inhabit their tails.

The hosstritch are hunted on hossback, and they can trot a mile close to 3 minnitts.

They lay their eggs in the sand, and i think the heat ov the sand hatches them out.

They ain't built right for hatchin out eggs, any more than a large-sized figger 4 iz.

I don't know whether their eggs are good tew eat or not, but i guess not for i never have seen ham and hosstritch eggs advertised on any ov our fashionable bills ov fare.

Boiled hosstritch may be nourishing and may be not; I think this would depend a good deal upon who was called upon tew eat it.

I shan't never enquire for boiled hosstritch az long az i remain in mi right mind.

If the hosstritch iz a blessing tew the desert country I hope they will stay thare, for so long as we have the turkey buzzard, and the Sandy Hill Crane, I feel az tho we could git along, and endure life.

I am writing this essay on the hosstritch a good deal by guess, for i hav never seen them in their natiff land, not never mean to, for jist so long az i kan git 3 meals a day, and live whare grass grows, and water runs, i don't mean tew hanker for hot sand.

■   ■   ■

It takes an uncommon smart man, now-daze, tew make money by telling the truth—it iz actually an evidence ov genius.

■   ■   ■

Scandal iz az cetching az the small pox, and perhaps thare iz but one real preventative, and that iz—tew be vaccinated with a deaf and dumbness.

■   ■   ■

I prefer an open, and brass-mounted villain tew a soft, tumid, panting hypocrit, who iz az unsafe az a sleeping snake.

■   ■   ■

THE PARTIRDGE No. 2.

The partridge iz also a game bird. Their game iz tew drum on a log in the spring ov the year, and keep both eyes open, watching the sportsmen.

Partridges are shot on the wing, and are az easy to miss az a ghost iz.

It iz fun enough to see the old bird hide her young brood when danger iz near. This must be seen, it cant be described and make any body beleave it.

The partridge, grouse, and pheasant are cousins, and either one ov them straddle a fry-pan natural enough tew have bin born thare.

Take a couple ov young partridges and pot them down, and serve up with the right kind ov a chorus, and they beat the ham sandwich you buy in the Camden and Amboy Railroad 87 1/2 per cent.

I have eat theze lamentable Nu Jersey ham sandwich, and must say that i prefer a couple ov bass wood chips, soaked in mustard water, and stuck together with Spalding's glue.

■   ■   ■

THE WOODKOK.

The woodkok iz one ov them kind ov birds who can git up from the ground with about az much whizz, and about az busy az a firecracker, and fly away az crooked az a cork-screw.

They feed on low, wet lands, and only eat the most delicate things.

They run their tongues down into the soft earth, and gather tender juices and tiny food.   They have a long, slender bill, and a rich brown plumage, and when they lite on the ground you lose sight ov them az quick az you do ov a drop ov water when it falls into a mill pond.

The fust thing you generally see ov a woodcock iz a *whizz*, and the last thing a *whurr*.

How so many ov them are killed on the wing iz a mistery to me, for it iz a quicker job than snatching pennys off a red-hot stove.

I have shot at them often, but i never heard ov my killing one ov them yet.

They are one ov the game birds, and many good judges think they are the most elegant vittles that wear feathers.

■   ■   ■

Silence iz one ov the hardest kind ov arguments tew refute.

■   ■   ■

The Devil iz said tew be the father ov lies, if this iz so, he has got a large family, and a grate many promising children among them.

■   ■   ■

THE GUINA HEN.

The guina hen iz a speckled critter, smaller than the goose, and bigger than the wild pigeon.

They have a keen eye, and a red kokade on their heads, and always walk on the run.

They lay eggs in great profusion, but they lay them so much on the sly, that they often can't find them themselfs.

They are az freckled az a coach dog, and just about az tough tew eat az a half-boiled crow.

They have a voice like a piccallo flute, and for racket, two ov them can make a saw that iz being filed ashamed ov itself.

They are a very shy bird, and the nearer you git tew them the further they git oph.

They are more ornamental than useful, but are chiefly good tew frighten away hawks.

They will see a hawk up in the sky three miles and a-half off, and will begin at once tew holler and make a fuss about it.

■   ■   ■

I think that a hen who undertakes tew lay 2 eggs a day must necessarily neglect some other branch ov bizzness.

■   ■   ■

Dame Barker had a yerling hen,
Who swore she'd set, or raise the dickens;
The dame sot her on an ear of corn,
And raised a bushel and a half ov chickens.

■   ■   ■

THE BLUEJAY.

T HE Bluejay iz the dandy among birds, a feathered fop, a jackanapes by nature and ov no use only tew steal corn and eat it on a rail.

They are a misterious bird, for I have seen them solitary and alone in the wooded wilderness, one hundred miles from any sighns ov civilizashun.

Az a means ov diet, they are just about az luxurious az a boiled indigo bag would be, such az the washwimmin use tew blue their clothes with.

The blujay haz no song—they can't sing even ''From Greenland's Icy Mountains;'' but i must say that a flock ov them, flying among the evergreens on a cold winter's morning, are hi colored and easy tew look at.

It iz hard work for me to say a harsh word aginst the birds but when i write their history it iz a duty i owe tew posterity not to lie.

■　　　　■　　　　■

I can't tell which iz the worse off, the man who iz all head and no heart, or the one who iz all heart and no head.

■　　　　■　　　　■

THE BOBALINK.

The bobalink iz a black bird with white spots on him.

They make their appearanse in the northern states about the 10th ov June, and commence bobalinking at once.

They inhabit the open land, and luv a meadow that iz a leetle damp.

The female bird don't sing, for the male makes noise enough for the whole family.

They have but one song, but they understand that perfectly well.

When they sing their mouths git az full ov music az a man's does ov bones who eats fried herring for breakfast.

Bobolinks are kept in cages, and three or four ov them in one room make just about as much noise az an infant class repeating the multiplikashun table all at once.

■　　　　■　　　　■

THE SWALLO.

THE swallo iz a lively bird.

Swallos make their appearance late in the spring, and always in a twitter about sumthing.

They have az much twitter, as a boarding school miss.

They can fli az swift az an arrow, and a great deal crookeder.

I have seen them skim a mill pond, close enough tew take the cream off from it, and even make the frogs dodge, and not touch the water.

When the swallo cums, spring has come sure, but there iz an old proverb, (one ov Solomans, i presume,) which sez, ''one swallo dont make a spring.''

This may be so, but i have seen a spring (ov water), that would make a great many swallows.

Swallos never have the dispepshy, they live upon nothing, and take a great deal ov exercise in the open air.

They dont set up nites busting, and never chat a tailor out ov his bill.

They dont waste any time in the morning making their toilet; but like the flowers, shake the dew from their heads, and are ready for bizzness.

I cant think ov any thing God has made, more harmless than a swallo, they are as innocent az a daisy, and az pure as the air they swim in, they wont live, shut up in a cage, much longer, than a trout will.

■   ■   ■

about the hardest thing a fellow kan do, iz to spark 2 girls at one time. and preserve a good average =
Try it, Josh Billings

■   ■   ■

■ ■ ■

The true definition ov a luxury iz something that another feller haint got the stamps to buy.

■ ■ ■

THE EAGLE.

There iz a great deal ov poetry in eagles; they can look at the sun without winking; they can split the clouds with their flashing speed; they can pierce the blu etherial away up ever so fur; they can plunge into midnight's black space like a falling star; they can set on a giddy crag four thousand miles hi, and looking down onto a green pasture can tell whether a lamb iz fat enough tew steal or not.

Jupiter, the Peterfunk, god ov the ancients, had a great taste for eagles, if we can beleave what the poets sing.

I hav seen the bald-headed eagle and shot them in all their native majesty, and look upon them with the same kind ov veneration that i do upon all sheep stealers.

■ ■ ■

THE PARROT.

The parrot iz a bird ov many colors, and inclined tew talk.

They take holt ov things with their foot, and hang on like a pair ov pinchers.

They are the only bird i know ov who can converse in the inglish language, but like many other nu beginners, they can learn tew swear the easiest.

They are kept az pets, and like all other pets, are useless.

In a wild state ov nature, they may be ov some use, but they lose about 90 per cent ov their value by civilization.

They resemble the border injun in this respect.

When you come tew take 90 per cent off from most any thing, except the striped snaik, it seems tew injure the profits.

I owned a parrot once, for about a year, and then gave him away, i haven't seen the man I give him to since, but i presume he looks upon me az a mean cuss.

If i owned all the parrotts thare iz in the United States, I would banish them immejiately tew their native land, with the proviso that they should stay thare.

I don't make theze remarks tew injure the feelings ov those who hav sot their feelings on parrotts, or pets ov any kind, for i cant help but think that a person who gives up their time and tallents tew pets, even a sore-eyed lap dorg, displays great nobility of character. (This last remark wants tew be took different from what it reads.)

■   ■   ■

There iz newmerous individuals in the land who look upon what they hain't got az the only things worth having.

■   ■   ■

THE DUK. No. 2

THE Duk iz a kind ov short legged hen.
When cooked they are very good means ov nourishment, in fact, it will do to call roast duk and apple sass easy tew contend with.

The duk has a big foot for the size ov their body, but their foot iz not the right kind ov a foot for digging in the garden.

Their foot iz like a small spider's web, only more substantial bilt.

They are amphibicuss, and can sail on the water az natural and easy az a grease spot.

They can dive in the water az handy az a bull frog, and never git water-soaked.

Water won't stay quiet on a duk's back no longer than quicksilver will where it iz down hill.

Duks hav a broad bill which enables them tew eat their food without any spoon.

They are more proffitable tew keep than a hen, because they can eat so much faster.

Duks are addicted tew a wild state ov nature, but civilizashun has did sumthing handsome for duks, and made them the companions ov man and old wimmin.

Next tew her grand children, an old woman thinks most ov her duks.

The duk iz a good hand tew raise feathers, which grows all over their person simultanously without any order.

There aint any room on the outside ov a duk for any more feathers.

They shed their feathers by having them pulled out, and these feathers make a good, tuff bed.

A duk's feather bed iz a good place tew raise nite mares on.

Men often call their wifes their "*dear duks,*" this is on account ov their big bills.

The duk don't crow like a rooster, but quacks like a duk.

They do a good deal ov quacking that don't amount tew much.

Sometimes doktors are called quacks, but i never have bin told why.

The duk iz not the most profitable bird extant for vittles; for, when you hav got off all the feathers, and pull out their stommuk, thare aint any more left on them, than there iz on the outside ov an eg shell.

■   ■   ■

THE SANDY HILL CRANE.

THE crane iz neither flesh, beast, nor fowl, but a sad mixture ov all those things.

He mopes along the brinks ov creeks and wet places, looking for sumthing he has lost.

He has a long bill, long wings, long legs, and iz long all over.

He iz born ov one egg and goes thru life az lonesome az a lasts year's bird's nest.

He lives upon lizzards and frogs, and picks up things with hiz bill az he would with a pair ov tongs.

He sleeps standing like a guide board, and sometimes tips over in hiz dreams, and then hiz bill enters the ground like a pick ax.

When he flies thru the air, he iz az graceful ax a wind-mill, broke loose from its fastenings.

Cranes are not very plenty in this world, but the supply, up tew this date, just about equals the demand.

The crane iz not a good bird for diet; the meat tastes like injun rubber stretched tight over a clothes hoss.

I never have et any crane, nor don't mean to, untill all the boiled owl in the country gives out.

I cant tell what the Sandy Hill crane was made for, and it aint none ov mi bizzness—even a crane from Sandy Hill can fill hiz destiny, and praise God loafing along the banks ov a creek and spearing frogs for his dinner.

I have spent much time among the birds, beasts, and fishes, and expect tew spend more, and tho i couldn't never tell exactly what comfort a musketo was tew the bulk ov mankind, or what credit he was tew himself, i am forced tew admit that any thing so perfectly and delicately made iz, to say the least, a dreadful smart job.

Cranes are very long-lived, and are az free from guile az a bread pill iz.

Cranes seldom git shot. There iz two reasons for this; one iz, they always keep gitting a little further off; and the other iz, there would be no more credit for a hunter in bringing a ded crane home for game than thare would be a yeller dog.

■   ■   ■

I honestly believe it iz better tew know nothing than tew know what ain't so.

■   ■   ■

We have bin told that the best way to overcome misfortunes iz tew fight with them—I hav tried both ways, and recommend a successful dodge.

■   ■   ■

THE DUV.

THE duv iz the lamb among birds.

They are az harmless az a dandy lion.

They don't do any hard work, but eat oats and bill and coo.

They love each other like a new married couple.

The duv always haz a good appetight; they will eat from dalite tew dark and seem tew be sorry they didn't eat some more.

They are a long lived bird, and like the bumble bee, are the biggest when they are born.

I never knew a duv tew lay down, and die ov old age.

They are very thrifty, they will increase faster than the multiplikashun table.

They are like the meazles, if you have them at all, you have got tew have a good many ov them.

The duv haz existed a long time, and was one ov Noahs pets, when he sailed.

The first duv he sent out ov the ark, brought back an olive branch, and the next time he sent her out, she didn't bring back anything.

She even forgot tew come back herself.

Noah had but one pair ov each breed ov duvs in the ark, and the one he sent out, and the one he had on hand, must have found each other, this explains the love, and effekshun, ov the duv.

The duv iz more ornamental than useful.

They are too innocent tew be very useful.

Sometimes too much innocence interferes with bizzness.

I hav known haff a dozen duvs tew git into a pie together, and make thenselves useful for a few minutes.

I don't hate duv pies.

The duv have always been a card tew define innocence.

The bible tells us, "to be az wize az a sarpent, *but harmless* as a duv."

This iz fust rate advice, but it means live bizzness.

Any body who iz az wise az a sarpent, can afford tew be az harmless az a duv.

The rite mixture ov duv and sarpent in a man's nature iz a good dose.

If a man has got too much snake in him, he iz liable tew overdo things, and if he haz got too much duv in him, he aint apt tew cook things enough.

The duv iz a homemade critter; they are as effeckshionate as a cockroach iz.

The nearer they can live tew where man does, the more they are apt tew do it.

Lambs and duvs have a great many weak points; but i wouldn't like any better fun than tew live where there want anything else but duvs and lambs. But this place aint laid down on any of the maps in this world.

Hawks and wolfs have made the duv and lamb trade dreadful unsartin.

I guess, afterall, that the evil things in this life help make the good things more desirable, and all things natural must be right, be they lamb, duv, wolf or sarpent.

■　　　■　　　■

Hope iz a hen that lays more eggs than she can hatch out.

■　　　■　　　■

THE ROBBING.

T HE robin has a red breast.

They have a plaintiff song, and sing az tho they waz sorry for sum thing.

They are natiffs ov the northern states, but go south to winter.

They git their name from their great ability for robbing a cherry tree.

They can also robin a currant bush fust rate, and are smart on a goose berry.

If a robin cant find any thing else tew eat, they aint tew fastidious tew eat a ripe strawberry.

They build their nest out ov mud, and straw, and lay 4 eggs, that are speckled.

Four yung robbings, in a nest, that are just hatched out, and still on the half-shell, are always az ready for dinner, az a newsboy iz.

If any body goes near their nest, their mouths all fly open at once, so that you can see clear down tew their palates.

If it wasn't for the birds, I suppose, ov course, we should all be et up by the catterpillars, and snakes, but i have thought, it wouldn't be any thing more than common politeness, for the robbings, tew let us have, now, and then, just one ov our own cherries, tew see how they did taste.

■ ■ ■

A Man with a very small hed, iz like a Pin, without enny, —very apt to git into things beyond his depth.

■ ■ ■

A HEN.

A HEN is a darn fool, they was born so by natur.

When natur undertakes tew make a fool, she hits the mark the fust time.

Most all the animal critters have instinct, which is wuth more to them than reason would be, for instinct don't make any blunders.

If the animals had reason, they would act just as ridiculous as we men folks do.

But a hen don't seem tew have even instinct, and was made expressly for a fool.

I have seen a hen fly out ov a good warm shelter, on the 15th ov January, when the snow was 3 foot high, and lite on the top ov a stone wall, and coolly set there, and freeze tew death.

Nobody but a darn fool would do this, unless it was tew save a bet.

I have saw a human being do similar things, but they did it tew win a bet.

To save a bet, is self-preservashun, and self-preservashun, is the fust law ov nature, so sez Blackstone, and he is the best judge ov law now living.

If i couldn't be Josh Billings, i would like, next in suit tew be Blackstone, and compose sum law.

But notwithstanding all this, a hen continues tew be a darn fool.

I like all kinds ov fools, they come nearer tew filling their destiny than anybody i know ov.

They don't never make any blunders, but tend rite tew bizzness.

The principal bizzness, ov an able bodied hen, iz tew lay eggs, and when she haz laid 36 ov them, then she iz ordained tew set still on them, until they are born, this iz the way young hens fust see life.

The hen has tew spread herself pretty well tew cover 36 eggs, but i hav seen her do it, and hatch out 36 young hens.

When a hen fust walks out, with 36 young hens supporting her, the party looks like a swarm ov bumble bees.

There aint nothing foolish in all this, but you put 36 white stones, under this same hen, and she will set there till she hatches out the stones.

I have seen them do this too—i dont wish tew say, that i have seen them *hatch out the stones*, but i hav seen them set on the stones, untill i left that naberhood, which waz two years ago, and i dont hesitate tew say, the hen iz still at work, on that same job.

Noboddy but a phool would stick tew bizzness az close as this.

Hens are older than Methuseler, and grow older till they die.

Now I dont want it understood, that any one hen can commense life, with the usual capital, and live 999 years.

This waz the exact age ov Methuseler, if I have been informed correctly.

I simply want tew be understood, that hens (az a speciality) laid, cackled, and sot a long time before Methuseler did.

After reading this last statement over again, i dont know az i make myself fluently understood yet.

I dont undertake tew say, that Mr. Mewthuseler, *cackled*, and *sot*, what i want tew prove, iz the fact that hens were here, and doing bizzness in their line, before Mewthussler waz.

Now I have got it.

There iz one thing about a hen that looks like wisdom, they don't cackle much untill after they have laid their egg.

Some folks are always a bragging, and a cackling, what they are going tew do before-hand.

A hen will set on one egg just az honest az she will set on 36 eggs, but a hen with one chicken iz always a painful sight tew me.

I never knew an only chicken do first rate, the old hen spoils them waiting on them, and then it tires out the old hen, more than 36 chickens would.

I think this rule works both ways, among poultry, and among other folks.

I have seen a hen set on 36 *duck eggs*, and hatch the whole ov them out, and then try tew learn them tew scratch in the garden.

But a ducks foot aint built right for scratching in the ground, it iz better composed for scratching in the water.

When the young ducks takes tew the water, it iz melancholy, and heart-breaking, tew see the old hen, stand on the brim ov the mill pond, and wring her hands, and holler tew the ducks, tew come right straight out ov that water, or they will all git drowned.

I have seen this did too, but i never see the ducks come out till they got ready, nor never see a young duck git drowned.

You cant drown a young duck, they will stand az much water az a sponge will.

Az an article ov diet, there is but few things that surpass cooked hen, if eaten in the days ov their youth and innosense, but after they git old, and cross, they contrakt a habit ov eating tuff.

After thinking the thing over, and over, and over, I am still prepared tew say, that a hen is a darn fool, anyhow you can fix it.

I don't speak of this as any disgrace two the hen, it only shows that nature dont ever make a fool without a destiny.

■   ■   ■

I think that a hen who undertakes tew lay 2 eggs a day must necessarily neglect sum other branch ov bizzness.

■   ■   ■

I hav seen men load a dubble barrell gun klear up to the muzzell, to kill a shipping bird mith, and git knokt hed over heels, when the gun went off.—and miss the bird besides.— a literal fakt, Josh Billings

■   ■   ■

CHAPTER VIII

PAEANS ON
OUR INSECT NEIGHBORS

The musketo iz born ov poor
but industrious parents,—
but haz in hiz veins, sum
ov the best blood in the Cauntry=
Yures for 90 Days. Josh Billings=

■   ■   ■

THE COCKROACH.

T HE cockroach iz a bug at large.
     He iz one ov the luxurys ov civilization.

He iz eazy to domesticate, yielding gracefully to ordinary kindness, and never deserting those who show him proper acts ov courtesy.

We are led to believe, upon a close examination ov the outward crust ov these fashionable insects, that they are a highly successful intermarriage between the brunette pissmire, and the "*artikilus bevo*," or common American grasshopper.

Naturalists however differ, which iz to be lamented, for a diversity ov sentiment, upon matters so important to the peace ov mind and moral advancement ov mankind in the lump, creates distrust, and tends to sap the substrata ov all bug ethics.

But let the learned and polite pull hair az much az they please about the ancestral claims ov the cockroach, it iz our bizzness and duty, az bug scrutinizer, tew show the critter up az we find him, without caring a single, solitary cuss, who hiz grandfather or grandmother actually waz.

Thare iz no mistaking the fact that he iz one ov a numerous family, and that hiz attachment tew the home ov hiz boyhood, speaks louder than thunder for hiz affectionate and unadulterated nature.

He dont leave the place he waz born at upon the slightest provocation, like the giddy and vagrant flea, or the ferocious bed bug, and until death, (or sum vile powder, the invention ov man) knocks at his front door, he and his brothers and sisters may be seen with the naked eye, ever and anon calmly climbing the white sugar bowl or running foot races between the butter plates.

How strange it iz that man, made out ov dirt, the cheapest material in market, and the most plenty, should be so determined to rid the world ov every living bug but himself.

I don't doubt if he could have hiz own way for six years, evry personal cockroach would be knocked off from the bosom ov the footstool, and not even a pair ov them left to repair damages with.

Such iz man!

The cockroach is born on the first ov May and the first ov November semiannually, and is ready for use in fifteen days from date.

They are born from an egg, four from each egg, and consequently they are all ov them twins. There is no such thing in the annuls ov nature as a single cockroach.

The maternal bug don't set upon the egg as the goose doth, but leaves them lie around loose, like a pint ov spilt mustard seed, and don't seem tew care a darn whether they get ripe or not.

But I never knew a cockroach egg fail tew put in an appearance. They are as sure tew hatch out and run as Canada thistles, or a bad cold.

The cockroach is ov two colours, sorrel and black. They are always on the move, and can trot, I should say, on a good track, and a good day, close tew a mile in three minutes.

Their food seems tew consist, not so much in what they eat as what they travel, and often finding them dead in my soup at the boarding-house, I hav come to the conclusion that a cockroach can't swim, but they can float.

Naturalists have also declared that the cockroach has no double teeth. This is an important fact, and ought tew be introduced into all the primary school books ov America.

But the most interesting feature ov this remarkable bug is the lovelyness ov their natures. They can't bite, nor sting, nor scratch, nor even jaw back. They are so amiable that I have even known them tew get stuck in the butter, and lay there all day, and not holler for help, and actually die at last with a broken heart.

To realize the meekness ov theze uncomplaining little cusses, let the philosophic mind just for one moment compare them to the pesky flea, who light upon man in hiz strength and woman in her weakness like a red hot shot, or to the warbling musketo, wild from a New Jersey cat-tail marsh, with his dagger in hiz mouth acheing for blood; or, horror ov horrors! to the midnight bed bug, who creeps out ov a crack az still and az lean az a shadow and hitches on to the bosom ov beauty like a starved leech.

Every man haz a right to pick his playmates, but az for me, i had rather visit knee deep among cockroaches than to hear the dieing embers ov a single muskeeter's song in the room joining, or to know that there waz just one bedbug left in the world and he waz waiting for mi kandle to go out and for me to pitch into bed.

In conclusion, to show that I aint fooling, i would be willing, if I had them to swap ten first class fleas any time for a small sized cockroach, and if the fellow complained that I had shaved him in the trade, I would return the cockroach and swear that we waz even.

■   ■   ■

BED BUGS.

I NEVER see anybody yet but what despised *Bed Bugs*.

They are the meanest ov all crawling, creeping, hopping, or biteing things.

They dassant tackle a man by daylight, but sneak in, after dark, and chaw him while he iz fast asleep.

A musketo will fight you in broad daylight, at short range, and give you a chance tew knock in his sides—the flea iz a game bug, and will make a dash at you even in Broadway—but the bed-bug iz a garroter, who waits till you strip, and then picks out a mellow place tew eat you.

If i was ever in the habit ov swearing, i wouldn't hesitate to damn a bed bug right tew his face.

Bed bugs are uncommon smart in a *small* way; one pair ov them will stock a hair mattrass in 2 weeks, with bugs enough tew last a small family a whole year.

It don't do any good to pray when bed bugs are in season; the only way tew git rid ov them iz tew boil up the whole bed in aqua fortis, and then heave it away and buy a new one.

Bed bugs, when they hav grown all they intend to, are about the size ov a bluejay's eye, and have a brown complexion, and when they start out to garrot are az thin az a grease spot, but when they git thru garroting they are swelled up like a blister.

It takes them 3 days tew git the swelling out ov them.

If bed bugs have any destiny to fill, it must be their stomachs, but it seems tew me that they must have bin made by accident, just az slivvers are, tew stick into somebody.

If they was got up for some wise purpose, they must have took the wrong road, for there cant be any wisdom in chawing a man all night long, and raising a family, besides, tew foller the same trade.

If there iz sum wisdum in all this, I hope the bed bugs will chaw them folks who can see it, and leave me be, because i am one ov the heretics.

Most ov the animals and insects (az well az the men) live on each other, but the spider iz the meanest in the whole lot, for they set traps for their victims, and dont even bait the traps.

I don't want any better evidence that a man iz a fool—than tew see him cultivate eccentricitys.

Advertising iz said tew be a certain means of success; some folks are so impressed with this truth, that it sticks out ov their tombstone.

THE FLEA.

THE smallest animal ov the brute creation, and the most pesky, iz the *Flea*.

They are about the bigness ov an onion seed, and shine like a brand new shot.

They spring from low places, and can spring further and faster than any ov the bug-brutes.

They bite wuss than the musketoze, for they bite on a run; one flea will go all over a man's suburbs in 2 minutes and leave him az freckled az the measels.

It iz impossible to do anything well with a flea on you, except swear, and fleas aint afraid ov that; the only way iz tew quit bizzness ov all kinds and hunt for the flea, and when you have found him, he ain't there. This is one ov the flea mysterys, the faculty they have ov being entirely lost jist as soon as you have found them.

I don't suppose there iz ever killed, on an average, during any one year, more than 16 fleas, in the whole ov the United States ov America, unless there iz a casualty ov sum kind. Once in a while there iz a dog gits drowned sudden, and then there may be a few fleas lost.

They are about as hard to kill as a flaxseed iz, and if you don't mash them up as fine as ground pepper they will start bizzness again, on a smaller capital, just as pestiverous az ever.

There iz lots ov people who have never seen a flea, and it takes a pretty smart man tew see one anyhow; they don't stay long in a place.

If you ever catch a flea, kill him before you do anything else; for if you put it off 2 minnits, it may be too late.

Many a flea has past away forever in less than 2 minnits.

■　　　■　　　■

About one half the pity in this world iz not the result ov sorrow, but satisfaction that it aint our hoss that has had his leg broke.

■　　　■　　　■

About the only difference between the poor and the rich, is this, the poor *suffer* misery, while the rich have tu *enjoy* it.

■　　　■　　　■

A secret iz like an acheing tooth, it keeps us uneasy until it iz out.

■   ■   ■

THE AUNTS.

T**he** ant iz a many footed insect.

They live about one thousand five hundred and fifty of them (more or less), in the same hole in the ground, and hold their property in common.

They have no holidays, no eight-hour system, nor never strike for any higher wages.

They are cheerful little toilers, and have no malice, nor back door to their hearts.

There iz no sedentary loafers amung them, and you never see one out ov a job.

They git up early, go tew bed late, work all the time, and eat on the run.

Yu never see two aunts argueing some foolish question that neither ov them didn't understand; they don't care whether the moon iz inhabited, or not; nor whether a fish weighing two pounds, put into a pail ov water already full, will make the pail slop over, or weigh more.

They ain't a-hunting after the philosopher's stone, nor gitting crazy over the cause of the sudden earthquakes.

They don't care whether Jupiter iz 30 or 31 millions ov miles up in the air, nor whether the earth bobs around on its axes or not, so long az it don't bob over their corn crib and spill their barley.

They are simple, little, busy aunts, full ov faith, working hard, living prudently, committing no sin, praising God by minding their own bizzness, and dying when their time cums, tew make room for the next crop ov aunts.

They are a reproach to the lazy, an encouragement tew the industrious, a rebuke tew the viscious, and a study to the Christian.

If yu want tew take a lesson in architecture, go and set down by the side ov their hole in the ground, and wonder how so many can live so thick.

If your patience needs consolation, watch the aunts, and be strengthened.

If man had (added tew his capacity) the patience and grit ov theze little atoms ov animated nature, every mountain on the bosom ov the earth would, before this, have bin levelled, and

every inch ov surface would scream with fruitfulness, and count-
less lots ov human critters would have bin added to the inhabitants
ov the universe, and bin fed on corn and other sass.

I have set by the hour and a half down near an aunt-hill and mar-
velled; have wondered at their instincts, and hav thought how big
must be the jackass who waz satisfied to believe that even an aunt,
the least ov the bugs, could have been created, made bizzy, and sat
to work by *chance*.

Oh, how i do pity the individual who believes that all things here
are the work ov an accident! He robs himself ov all pleasure on
earth, and all right in Heaven.

I had rather be an aunt (even a humbly, bandy-legged, profane
swearing ant), than to look upon the things ov this world az i would
on the throw ov the dice.

Aunts are older than Adam.

Man *(for very wise reasons)* wasn't bilt until all other things
were finished, and pronounced good.

If man had bin made first he would hav insisted upon bossing the
rest ov the job.

He probably would hav objected to having any little bizzy
aunts at all, and various other objections would hav bin offered,
equally green.

I am glad that man waz the last thing made.

If man hadn't have bin made at all, you would never have heard
me find any fault about it.

I haven't much faith in man, not becauze he cant do well but becauze he wont.

Aunts hav bye-laws, and a constitution, and they mean something.

Their laws aint like our laws, made with a hole in them, so that
a man can steal a hoss and ride thru them on a walk.

They don't have any whisky ring, that iz virtuous, simply, because it hooks bi the million, and then legalizes its own acts.

They don't have any legislators that you can buy, nor any
judges, laying around on the half shell, ready tew be swallered.

I rather like the aunts, and think now I shall sell out mi money
and real estate, and join them.

I had rather join them than the bulls or the bears, i like their morals better.

The bulls and the bears handle more money, it iz true, and make a great deal more noise in Wall street, one ov them sticking his horn into a flabby piece ov Erie and tossing it up into the air, and the other cetching it when it comes down, and trampling it under his paws.

This may be fun for the bulls and the bears, but it iz worse than the cholera morbust for poor Erie.

Aunts are a honest, hard-tugging little people, but whether they marry, and give in marriage, iz beyond my strength; but if they don't they are no worse off than they are out west (near the city of Chicago), where they marry to-day and apply for an injunction to-morrow; and are ready the next day to fight it out agin on some other line.

Wedlock out west (near the great grain mart Chicago) iz one ov them kind ov locks that almost any body can pick.

■   ■   ■

Nature never half-finishes a job, nor underlets a contract.

■   ■   ■

Take all the dangers out ov this world and it would be a coward's paradise.

■   ■   ■

The philosophers tell us that "nature abhors a vacuum." This accounts for the sawdust in sum mens heads.

■   ■   ■

If we give up our minds tew little things we never shall be fit for big ones. I knew a man once who could cetch more flies with one swoop ov his hand than any body else could, and he want good at anythin else.

■   ■   ■

What iz man?
Live dirt.

■   ■   ■

THE MUSKEETER.

Muskeeters are a game bug, but they wont bite at a hook. Thare iz millions ov them caught every year, but not with a hook, this makes the market for them unstiddy, the supply always exceeds the demand. The muskeeto iz born on the sly, and comes to maturity quicker than any other ov the domestic animiles. A muskeeter at 3 hours old iz just az reddy, and anxious to go into bizzness for himself, az ever he iz, and bites the first time az sharp, and natural, az red pepper does. The muskeeter has a good ear for music, and sings without notes. The song ov the musketo iz monotonous to some folks, but in me it stirs up the memorys ov other days. I have laid awake, all nite long, many a time and listened to the sweet anthems ov the muskeeter. I am satisfied that there wasn't nothing made in vain, but i cant help thinking how mighty close the musketoze come to it. The muskeeter haz inhabited this world since its creation, and will probably hang around here until bizzness closes. Whare the muskeeter goes to in the winter iz a standing conumdrum, which all the naturalists hav give up, but we know he dont go far, for he iz on hand early each year with hiz probe fresh ground, and polished. Muskeeters must be one ov the luxurys ov life, they certainly aint one ov the necessarys, not if we know ourselves.

■ ■ ■

The cockroach dont liv on what he eats, but what he kan git into. and often finding him ded in mi soup. i hav cum to the konklushun, that he kant swim, but that he kan float for a long time — Josh Billings

■ ■ ■

THE HUM BUGG.

The most vain and impudent bug known to naturalists (or any

other private individual) iz the hum bugg.

They have no very particular parents nor birth place, are born a good deal az toadstools are, wherever they can find a good soft spot.

It has been sed by commontaters that Satan himself iz the father ov hum buggs—if this iz a fact he has got more children than he can watch, and sum very fast young ones amongst them.

The hum buggs don't generally live a great while at once, but have the faculty ov dieing in one place, and being suddenly born in another.

They are ov all genders, including the masculine, feminine and neutral, and can live and grow phatt whare an honest bugg would starve to death begging.

The hum bugg will eat any thing that they can bite, and rather than loose a good meal will swaller a thing whole.

Every one says they despise the hum bugg and yet every body iz anxious tew make their acquaintance.

They have the entry to all circles ov sosiety without knocking, from the highest tew the lowest, and tho often kicked out, are welcomed again and flattered more than ever.

The hum bugg has more friends than he knows what to do with, but he manages tew give general satisfaction by cheating the whole of them.

The Bible sez "the grasshopper iz a burden"—and i believe it—but i think the hum bugg iz the heaviest bug ov the two.

But the world cant well spare the hum bugg; take them all out ov the world, and it would bother even an honest man tew git a living, for there doesn't seem, jist now, to be honesty enough on hand to do our immense dry good bizzness with.

Honesty iz undoubtedly the best policy for a long run, but for a short race, hum bugg has made some excellent time.

I hav been bit bad bi this bugg myself several times, but not twice in the same spot—i follow the Skriptures when i am where the hum bugg is plenty, if one bites me on one cheek, i turn him the other cheek also, but i don't let him bite the other cheek also.

There ain't any body, i suppose, who actually pines tew be bit by this celebrated bugg, they only luv tew see how near they can come tew it without missing.

Human nature iz chuck full ov curiosity, curiosity iz jist what hum bugg makes manny a warm meal off ov.

Some ov theze buggs are not so sharp bitten and poison az others, but this iz not so much owing tew their disposition az it iz tew their nature; they all ov them bite the full length ov their teeth.

If there iz any body who hain't never been bit bi a hum bugg yet, he must be somebody who has always stayed at home with his uncle, and, lived on bread and milk, or was born numb all the way through, and couldn't feel any kind ov a bite.

■   ■   ■

If i should hear a man brag that one ov these bugs *couldn't* bite him, I should set him down at once for a man who wan't a good judge ov the truth. The bite of a hum bugg iz wuss than a hornet's, and always different from a dog's, for the dog growls, and then bites, but the hum bugg bites, and lets you do the growling.

■   ■   ■

Credit iz like chastity; they both ov them kan stand temptashun better than they kan suspicion.

■   ■   ■

Contentment is the vittles, and drink ov the soul.

■   ■   ■

THE BUGG BEAR.

NATURAL History has its myths and its ghosts, az well az enny boddy else, and foremost among these iz—the bugg bear.

The bugg bear iz born from an imaginary egg, and iz hatched by an imaginary process.

They are like a shadow in the afternoon, always a good deal bigger than the thing that casts it.

They are compozed ov two entirely different animals, the *bugg* and the *bear*, but generally turn out to be pretty much all bugg.

They are like the assetts on a bankrupt broker, the more you examine them, the smaller they grow.

I have known them tew cum out ov a hole like a mice, and grow in tew minnits az big az an elephant, and then run back agin into the same hole they cum out ov.

They are like a young wild pigeon in their habits, and biggest when they are first born.

They are common to all countrys and all peoples, the

philosophers hav seen them az often az the children hav, and ben as badly skared by them.

They are az innocent az a rag doll, but are az full ov deviltry az a jack lantern.

Bugg bears are az plenty in this world az pins on the side walks, but noboddy ever sees them but those folks who are alwus hunting for them.

■   ■   ■

Punishments, tew hit the spot, should be few, but red-hot.

■   ■   ■

THE BUMBLE BEE.

THE Bumble Bee is one ov nature's secrets.

They probably have a destiny to fill, and are probably necessary, if a fellow only knew how.

They live apart from the rest ov mankind, in little circles numbering about 75 or 80 souls.

They are born about haying time, and are different from any bug i know of; they are the biggest when they are first born. They resemble some men in this respect.

Their principle bizziness iz making poor honey, but they don't make any to sell.

Boys sometimes rob them out ov a whole summer's work; but there is one thing about a bumble bee that boys always watch dreadful close, and that iz their *helm*.

I had rather not have all the bumble bee honey that is between here and the city ov Jerusalem, than tew hav a bumble bee hit me with his helm when he comes round suddin.

■   ■   ■

Fun iz the best phisick i know ov; it iz both cheap and durable.

■   ■   ■

SMALL SIZED VERMIN.
THE GRUB.

THE grub iz all the fashionable colors, except checkered, i never hav saw a checkered grub so far.

I would give ten cents tew see a checkered grub.

The grub (that i am talking about) boards in old rotten logs, and decayed stumps, and grubs for a living.

They are about one inch in size, and are bilt like a screw.

They look for all the world like a short strip ov fat pork.

They enter rotten wood, like an inch screw, pursued by a screwdriver.

They are very much retired in their habits, and are az free from anger az a toadstool.

Sum folks cant see any money in a grub, but i can

I hav chopt them out ov an old stump, the further end ov April, and then put them onto a hook, and crept down behind a bunch of willows, in the meadow, and dropt them, kind a natural, into the swift water, and in less then forty seconds have jerked out ov the silvery flood twelve ounces ov trout, and while he turned purple, and gold summersetts on the grass, i hav had mi heart swell up in me, like a halleluyer.

I had rather ketch a trout in this way than tew be president ov the United States for the same length ov time.

Thare may not be az much ambition in it, but there iz a glory in it, az crazy, and az safe, az soda water.

It don't take much tew make me happy, but it will take more money than any man on this futtstool, has got, tew buy out the little stock I always keep on hand.

■　　　■　　　■

THE LADY BUG.

The lady bug iz the most genteel vermin in market.

They are spotted red and black for color, are about the size ov a double B shot, and don't look unlike a drop ov red sealing wax.

They hang around gardens in the spring ov the year, and are worse and quicker, on cucumber vines, than a district schoolmaster iz on a kittle ov warm pork and beans.

The lady bug iz the pet ov little children, who catch them in their hands, and then sing to them the old nursery rime

"Lady bug, lady bug, fly away home,

Your house iz on fire, and your children will roam."

Let them go, and sure enough the lady bug does put for home in a great hurry.

The lady bug iz probably useful, but Webster's unabridged don't tell us for what.

Whenever i come across any bug, that i dont know what they waz built for, i dont blame the bug.

I hav great faith in anything that creeps, crawls, or even wiggles, and tho i haint been able tew satisfy myself all about the usefulness ov bed bugs, musketoze, and striped snakes, i hav faith that Divine Providence did not make them in vain.

A faith iz knowledge ov the highest order.

■   ■   ■

Every body seems tew be willing to be a fool himself, but he cant bear tew have anybody else one.

■   ■   ■

THE CURSID MUSKETO NO. 2

DEAR —— : — Your letter came safe unto hand last nite bi mail, and i hurry tew reply.

The best musketers now in market are raised near Bergen point, in the dominion ov New Jersey.

They grow there very spontaneous, and the market for them iz very unstiddy—the great supply injures the demand.

Two hundred and fifty to the square inch iz considered a paying crop, altho they often beat that.

They don't require any nursing, and the poorer the land the bigger the yield.

If it want for musketers i dont know what some people would do there tew git a living, for there iz a great deal ov cultivated land there that wont raise anything else at a profit.

The musketer iz a short lived bug, but don't waste any time; they are always az ready for bizzness az pepper sass iz, and can bite 10 minutes after they are born just az fluently az ever.

There iz people in this world so contrary at heart, and so ignorant, that they wont see any wisdom in having musketers around; i always pity such folks—their education haz been sorely neglected and aint level.

Wisdom iz like ducks eggs—if you git them, you have got tew search for them—there aint no ducks in these benighted days that will come and lay eggs in your hand—not a duck, Mr. —, not a duck.

The musketo is a social insect; they live very thick amongst each other, and love the society ov man also, but don't contract any ov hiz vices.

You never see a musketer that was a defaulter; they never fail to come to time, altho thousands lose their lives in the effort.

The philosophers tell us that the muskeeters who can't sing won't bite; this information may be ov great use to science, but aint worth much to a fellow in a hot nite where muskeeters are plenty.

If there ain't but one musketer out ov ten that can bite good, that iz enough to sustain their reputation.

The philosophers are always a telling us something that iz right smart, but the only plan they can offer us tew get rid ov our sorrows iz to grin and bear them.

They cant rob one single musketer ov his stinger by argument. I say bully for the muskeeter!

The muskeeter iz the child ov circumstances in one respect—he can be born, or not, and live, and die a square death in a lonesome marsh, 1600 miles from the nearest neighbor without ever tasting blood, and be happy all the time; or he can git into sumboddy's bed-room thru the key-hole, and take hiz rations regular, and sing psalms ov praise and glorification.

It don't cost a muskeeter much for his board in this world; if he cant find any boddy to eat he can set on a blade ov swamp meadow grass and live himself to death on the damp fog.

The musketo is a gray bug and has 6 legs, a bright eye, a fine bust, a sharp tooth and a ready wit.

He dont waste any time hunting up his customers, and always lights onto a baby first if there iz one on the premises.

I positively fear a musketo.

In the dark, still nite, when every thing iz az noiseless az a pair ov empty slippers, to hear one at the further end ov the room slowly but surely working his way up to you, singing that same hot old sissing tune ov theirs, and harking to feel the exact spot on your face where they intend tew locate, iz simply premeditated sorrow tew me; i had rather look forward to the time when an elephant was going tew step onto me.

The musketo has no friends, and but few associates; even a mule dispises them.

But i hav seen human beings who wasn't actually afraid ov them; i hav seen folks who had rather have a muskeeter lite onto them than to have a tract peddler lite onto them; i hav seen folks who were so tough against anguish that a muskeeter might lite onto them any where and plunge their dagger in up tew the hilt in vain.

I envy these people their moral stamina, for next tew being virtuous i would like tew be tough.

This life iz full ov pesky muskeetos, who are always looking for a job, always ready tew stick a thistle into you sum whare, and sing while they are doing it.

Dear Mr. ——, pardon me for saying so much about the cursid muskeeto, but ov all things on this earth that travel, or set still, for deviltry, there aint any bug, any beast, or any beastess, that i dred more, and love less, than i do this same little gray wretch, called cursid muskeeter.

■   ■   ■

Success iz quite often like falling off from a log, a man cant alwus tell how he kum to did it.

■   ■   ■

Most any body thinks they can be a good fool, and, they can, but to play the fool successfully, aint so natural.

■   ■   ■

THE HORNET.

T HE hornet is an inflamable bugger, sudden in his impressions and hasty in his conclusion, or end.

Hiz natural disposition iz a warm cross between red pepper in the pod and fusil oil, and hiz moral bias iz, "git out ov my way."

They have a long, black body, divided in the middle by a weak spot, but their physical importance lays at the terminus ov their suburb, in the shape ov a javelin.

This javelin iz always loaded, and stands ready to unload at a minute's warning, and enters a man az still az thought, az spry az litening, and az full ov melancholy az the toothake.

Hornets never argue a case; they settle all ov their differences ov opinion by letting their javelin fly, and are az certain tew hit az a mule iz.

This testy critter lives in congregations numbering about one hundred souls, but whether they are male and female, or conservative, or matched in bonds ov wedlock, or whether they are Mormons, and a good many ov them club together and keep one husband tew save expense, i dont know nor don't care.

I never have examined their habits much, i never considered it healthy.

Hornets build their nests whenever they take a notion to, and seldom are disturbed, for what would it profit a man tew kill 99 hornets and have the one hundredth one hit him with his javelin?

They build their nests ov paper, without any windows to them or back doors. They have but one place ov admission, and the nest iz the shape ov an overgrown pine-apple, and iz cut up into just az many bedrooms az there iz hornets.

It iz very simple tew make a hornet's nest, if you can, but i will argue any man 300 dollars he cant build one that he could sell tew a hornet for half price.

Hornets are az busy az their second cousins, the bee, but what they are about the lord only knows, they dont lay up any honey, nor any money, they seem tew be busy only jist for the sake ov working all the time, they are always in az much ov a hurry az tho they was going for a doctor.

I suppose this uneasy world would grind around on its axletree onst in 24 hours, even if there wasn't any hornets, but hornets must be good for something; but i cant think now what it iz.

There aint been a bug made yet in vain, nor one that wasn't a good job, there iz ever lots ov human men loafing around black smith shops, and cider mills, all over the country, that don't seem tew be necessary for anything but tew beg plug tobacco and swear, and steal water-melons, but you let the cholera break out once, and then you will see the wisdom ov having jist sich men laying around loose, they help count.

Next tew the cockroach, who stands tew the head, the hornet has got the most waste stommuk, in reference tew the rest ov his body, than any ov the insect population, and here iz another mistery: what on earth duz a hornet want so much reserve corps for.

I have just thought—tew carry his javelin in, thus you see, the more we discover about things the more we are apt to know.

It iz always good purchase tew pay out our last surviving dollar for wisdom, and wisdom iz like the misterious hen's egg; it aint laid in your hand, but iz laid away under the barn, and you hav got tew search for it.

The hornet iz an unsocial cuss, he iz more haughty than he iz proud, he iz a thorough-bred bug, but his breeding and refinement haz made him like some other folks i know ov, dissatisfied with himself, and everybody else, too much good breeding acts this way sometimes.

Hornets are long-lived—i can't state jist how long their lives are, but i know, from instinct and observation, that any critter, be he bug or be he devil, who is mad all the time, and stings every good chance he can git, generally outlives all his neighbors.

The only way tew git at the exact fighting weight ov the hornet, is tew touch him, let him hit you once with his javelin, and you will be willing tew testify in court that somebody run a one-tined pitchfork into you; and az for grit, i will state for the information ov those who haven't had a chance tew lay in their vermin wisdom az freely az i have, that one single hornet, who feels well, will break up a large camp meeting!

What the hornets do for amusement iz another question i can't answer, but some ov the best read, and heavyest thinkers among the naturalists say they have target excursions, and heave their javelins at a mark; but i don't imbibe this assertion raw, for i never knew anybody, so bitter at heart az the hornets are, to waste a blow.

There iz one thing that a hornet duz that i will give him credit for on my books—he always attends tew hiz own bizzness, and wont allow any body else tew attend tew it, and what he duz iz always a good job, you never see them altering any thing, if they make any mistakes, it iz after dark, and aint seen.

If the hornets made half az many blunders az the men do, even with their javelins, everybody would laugh at them.

Hornets are clear in another way, they have found out, bi trying it, that all they can git in this world, and brag on, iz their vittles, and clothes, and you never see one, standing at the corner ov a street, with a twenty-six inch face on, becauze some bank had run off, and took their money with him.

In ending off this essay, i will come tew a stop, by concluding, that if hornets waz a leetle more pensive, and not so darned peremptory with their javelins, they might be guilty ov less wisdom, but more charity.

But you cant alter bug nature without spoiling it for any thing else, any more than you kan an elephant's egg.

■   ■   ■

It iz a grate deal eazier tew be a philosopher after a man has had his dinner, than it iz when he dont know where he iz a going tew git it.

■   ■   ■

Wit without wisdom iz like a song without sense, it dont please long.

■   ■   ■

■   ■   ■

I dont bet on precocious children, the huckelberry that ripens the soonest iz always the first tew decay.

■   ■   ■

The Hornet iz a red hot
Child ov natur, and haz
a fizzness end to him.—
        Respektfully, Josh Billings

■   ■   ■

THE FLY.

THE fly iz not only a domestik, but a friendly insek, with out branes, but happily without guile.

They make their appearance amung mankind, a good deal az the wind duz, "whare it listeth."

How they are exactly born, i haven't been able yet tew investigate, but they are so universal at times, that i hav thought, they didn't wait tew be born, but took the fust good chance that was offered, and cum just az they am.

They are sed tew be male and femail, but i dont think they konsider the marriage tie binding, for they look so mutch alike, that it would be a grate waste ov time, finding out wich was who, and this would lead tew never ending fites, which iz the rhubarb ov domestik life.

They make their annual visit about the first ov May, but don't git tew buzzing good till the center ov August.

They stay with uz untill kold weather puts in an appearance, and then leave, a good deal az they cum, jist az they am.

Menny ov them are kut oph in the flower ov their yuth, and usefullness, but this don't interfere with their census, for their iz another steps right into their place, and heirs their property.

Sum looze their lives bi lighting too near the rim ov a toad's noze, and fall in, when the toad gaps, and others git badly stuck by phooling with mollassis.

Sum visit the spiders, and are induced tew remain, and thousands find a watery grave, bi gitting drowned in milk cans.

The fly iz no respekter ov pussuns, he lights onto the pouting lips ov a sleeping darkey, jist az easy az he duz onto the buzzum ov the queen ov buty, and will buzz an Alderman, or a hod-carrier, if they git in his way.

Flys, moraly konsidered, are like a large share ov the rest ov human folks, they wont settle on a good healthy spot in a man, not if they kan find a spot that iz a leetle raw.

Their principal food iz every thing, they will pitch into a ded snaik, or a quarter ov beef, with the same anxiety, and will eat from sun rise, till seven o'clock in the evening, without getting more than haff phull.

They will eat more, and hold less, than enny bug we kno ov.

The fly haz a remarkable impoverished memory, yu may drive him out ov yure ear; and he will land on yure forhed, hit him aginly, and he enters yure noze, the oftner yu git rid ov him on one spot, the more he gets onto another; the only way tew inculcate him with yure meaning, iz tew smash him up fine.

Naturalists dont tell us all about the soshull habits ov the fly, but i beleave they hav temprate habits, and altho they hang around grocerys a good deal, I never saw a fly the wuss for liquor, but i hav often seen liquor the wuss for flies.

They hav a big appetight for gitting into things, they are the fust at the dinner table, and alwus take soup, and dont leave untill the cloth is removed.

Flys see a grate deal ov good sosiety, they are admitted into all circles, and if they remember one haff that they see and hear, what a world ov phunny sekrets they could unfold; but flys are perfekly honarable, and never betray a konfidence.

What would sum lovers giv, if they could only git a fly tew blab, but a fly iz a perfek gentleman, he eats oph from your plate, enjoys yure conversashun, sees sights, and haz more phun, and privilege, than a prime minister, or a dressing maid, but when yu cum tew pump him, he iz az dry in the mouth, az a salt codfish.

Thare iz sumthing a fly will blow, but he wont blow a sekret.

Flys i think, must be born whole, for i never saw a haff born fly, they are all ov a size when yu fust see them, like a paper ov pins, and never git enny smaller.

I dont kno ov a more happy, whole souled, honest critter, among the bug dispensation, than a hansum, quare bilt fly, taking a free ride in central park, with the Mayor and hiz wife, or a free lunch at Delmonico's, with the minister from England, and then finishing up the bizzness ov the day, by sleeping upside down, on the ceiling ov my ladys bed chamber.

But thare iz plenty of pholks who kant see enny phun, or religion in a fly, whoze whole aim iz tew set molasses traps for them, tew chase them out ov the house with a sled stake, and then clear across a ploughed lot onto the next farm, tew git up nights in their stocking feet, tew worry them with the tongs, to drive them tew the brink ov despair, and finally ruin them, with deth.

I thank the Lord i ain't one ov thoze, i don't luv a fly enuff, to leave mi vittles, and fall down flatt on mi stummuk, and worship them, but a fly may cum and sit on mi noze, all day, and chaw hiz cud in slience, if he will only sit still.

Flys tickle me, but they don't make me sware, it takes a bedd bug, at the hollow ov night, a mean, loafing bed bugg, who steals out ov a krack in the wall, az silently az the swet on a dog's noze, and then creeps az soft az a shadder, on tew mi tenderest spot, and begins tew bore for my ile, it takes one ov theze foul fiends ov blood, and midnite, tew make me sware, a word ov two sillables.

A fly, the dear,little social innocent, kant make me sware, not even an abreviated dam.

I dispize enny men who sware, it iz not only wicked, but always smells ov whiskey.

This essa, on the little fly, who vist us, in the spring ov the year, just az they am, will not interest the exceeding literary, or thoze who think they hav discovered poetry in their sile, it takes the essa on the life, and deth, ov an orphan rosebud, or the golden sheen ov a sassy moonbeam, dancing in a budoir tew the dreams ov a restive beauty, it takes sumthing ov this breed, tew fetch them.

■   ■   ■

DEVIL'S DARNING NEEDLE.

This floating animal iz a fly about twenty times az big az a hornet, with a pair ov wings on him az much out ov proportion tew hiz body az a pair ov oars are to a shell boat.

They hang around mill ponds in hot weather, and when i was a boy if one ov them cum and sot on the further end ov the log where i waz a setting i always arose and gave him the whole of the log.

They have a body like a piece ov wire, sharp at the end, and look az tho they mite sting a fellow cheerfully, but i beleave there iz no more sting in them than there iz in cold water.

All children are afraid ov them, and i know ov one man now who had rather encounter a wild cat (provided the cat waz up in the top ov a tree and likely to stay there) than tew intersect a devil's darning needle.

They derive their name from the shape ov their bodys and their devilish appearance generally. (See Webster's unabridged on this subjekt.)

■   ■   ■

The fly iz a friendly kritter,
tho i never see him the muss
for liquor,— but i hav often
seen liquor, that waz a
good deal the muss for flys.
         less so *Josh Billings*

■   ■   ■

Chapter IX

WOMEN IN THEIR VARIETIES

Josh Billings, and the Twins.=

Thare iz 2 things in This world for which we are never fully prepared, and That iz,— twins.= Jess so, Jess so, Josh Billings.

■   ■   ■

FEMALE REMARKS.

DEAR Girls, are you in search ov a husband?

This is a pumper, and you are not required tew say "Yes" out loud, but are expected tew throw your eyes down onto the earth, az tho you was looking for a pin, and reply tew the inter-rogatory, with a kind ov drawed-in sigh, az tho you was eating an oyster, juice and all, off from the half shell.

Not tew press so tender a theme untill it becomes a thorn in the flesh, we will presume (tew avoid argument) that you are on the look-out for something in the male line tew boost you in the up-hill ov life, and tew keep his eye on the britching when yu begin tew go down the other side of the mountain. Let me give you some small chunks ov advice how tew spot your future husband:

1. The man who iz jealous ov every little attention which you git from some other fellow, yu will find, after you are married tu him, luvs himself more than he does yu, and what you mistook for solitude, you will discover, has changed into indifference. Jealousy isn't a heart-diseaze; it is a liver-complaint.

2. A mustache is not indispensible; it iz only a little more hair, and iz a good deal like moss and other excrescences—often duz the best on soil that won't raise anything else. Don't forgit that thoze things which yu admire in a phellow before marriage, you will probably have tew admire in a husband after, and a mustache will git tew be very weak diet after a long time.

3. If husbands could be took on trial, as irish-cooks are, two-thirds ov them would probably be returned; but there don't seem tew be any law for this. Therefore, girls, you will see that after you git a man, yu hav got tew keep him, even if yu lose on him. Consequently, if you have got any cold vitles in the house, try him on them, once in a while, during courting season, and if he swallers them well, and sez he will take sum more, he is a man who, when blue Monday comes will wash well.

4. Don't marry a pheller who iz always a-telling how hiz mother does things. It iz az hard tew suit these men as it iz tew wean a young one.

5. If a young man can beat you playing on a pianner, and cant hear a fish-horn playing in the street without turning a back summersett on account ov the musik that iz in him, i say, skip him; he might answer tew tend babe, but if yu set him tew hoeing out the garden, you will find that you hav got tew do it yourself. A man whoze whole heft lies in musik (and not very hefty at that), ain't no better for a husband than a seadlitz powder; but if he luvs tew listen while you sing some gentle ballad, you will find him mellow, and not soft. But don't marry any body for jist one virtew any quicker than you would flop a man for jist one fault.

6. It iz one of the most tuffest things for a female tew be an old maid successfully. A great many haz tried it, and made a bad job ov it. Evrybody seems tew look upon old maids jist az they do upon dried herbs—in the attic, handy for sickness—and therefore, girls, it aint a mistake that you should be willing tew swop yourself off with some true phellow, for a hussband. The swop iz a good one; but don't swop for any man who iz respectabel jist because his father iz. You had better be an old maid for 4 thousand years, and

then join the Shakers, than tew buy repentance at this price. No woman ever made this trade who didn't git either a phool, a mean cuss, or a clown for a husband.

7. In digging down into this subject, i find the digging grows harder the further i git. It iz much easier tew inform you who not tew marry, than who tew, for the reason there iz more ov them.

I don't think you will foller mi advice, if i giv it; and, therefore, i will keep it; for i look upon advise as i do upon castor oil—a mean dose tew give, and a mean dose tew take.

But i must say one thing, girls, or spoil. If you can find a bright-eyed, healthy, and well-ballasted boy, who looks upon poverty az sassy az a child looks upon wealth—who had rather sit down on the curb-stone in front ov the 5th avenue hotel, and eat a ham sandwitch, than tew go inside, and run in debt for hiz dinner and toothpick—one who iz armed with that kind ov pluck, that mistakes a defeat for a victory, mi advise is tew take him body and soul—snare him at onst, for he iz a stray trout, or a breed very scarce in our waters.

Take him i say, and bild onto him, az hornets build on to a tree.

■   ■   ■

BEAUTY

B EUTY iz a very handy thing tew have, especially for a woman who aint handsome.

Thare iz not much ov any thing more difficult tew define than beuty.

It iz a blessed thing that there ain't no rules for it, for the way it iz now, every man gits a handsome woman for a wife.

Thare iz great power in female beuty; its victories reach clear from the Garden ov Eden down to yesterday.

Adam was the fust man that saw a beutiful woman, and was the fust man tew acknowledge it.

But beauty in itself iz but a very short-lived victory—a mere perspective to the background.

Thare aint noboddy but a butterfly can live on beuty, and git fat.

When beuty and good sense jine each other, you hav got a mixture that will stand both wet and dry weather.

I have never seen a woman with good sense but what had beuty enough tew make herself highly agreeable; but i have seen 3 or 4 wimmin in my day who hadn't sense enough tew make a good deal ov beuty the least bit charming.

But, az i sed before, there ain't no positive rule for beuty, and i am dreadful glad ov it, for every body would be after that rule, and sumbody wouldn't git any rule, besides running a great risk ov gitting jammed in the rush.

Man beauty iz a awful weak complaint—it iz worse, if possible, than the nosegay dissease.

If there iz such a thing az a beutiful man on earth, he has my simpathy. Even mythology had but one Adonis, and the only accomplishment he had was tew bleat like a lamb.

■   ■   ■

Thare is only one good substitute for the endearments of a sister, and that iz the endearments ov sum other phellows sister.

■   ■   ■

If a dog falls in love with you at first sight, it will do to trust him—not so with a man.

■   ■   ■

Cheerful old girls, are the bridesmaids ov sosiety.

■   ■   ■

JOSH BILLINGS ADDRESSES THE
"FEMAIL PORDUNK SOWING SOCIETY."

FELLER SISTERS:—When I caste my eye on a circle of lovely wimmin bizzy with their needles, my heart seems tew stretch clean across mi bozzum. And when i reflect for a minnit, that they are tew work for nothing, and fund themselfs, and that a young heathin stands ready yelping around the corner, for the very shirt they are working on, it does seem to me, that i could shout hozzanner for 3 weeks on a stretch.

Feller Sisters, you can count on Josh Billings az a friend—he loves charity, az a pup hankers for new milk; his very nature looks out onto the horizen ov the poor folks, jist as the lite ov a tin lantern shines across a bog meadow.

And he sees the little bare back young ones shivering for a crust ov bread, and hungry for a shirt; then he looks at the Sisters, a talking and sowing, and sowing and talking, and he counts a whole parcel ov little shirts on the table, and then he thinks ov the widders cruise, and the bread hove onto the waters, mentioned in the good Book, and he feels just az tho he would like tew own all the femail sowing societies in the world hisself, and put his whole fortune in the little ready-made cotton shirt bizziness.

Oh Charitee! Oh Charitee! When Josh Billings communes with you, he feels az tho he had just been tried out, and set away tew cool.

Feller Sisters, don't be skeered, let the rich and the haughty stick up their noses, and let the educated laff.

Josh would like no better fun than just to bet his 9 dollars, that any Sister, in full communion with this here sowing society, who puts in full time, and cuts the cotton tew advantage, will git her final reward.

Tew conclude, Feller Sisters, pitch in; remember Mr. Lots wife, she that was salted for looken back.

Come together early, and often, buy your cotton by the piece; be careful how you deal out your shirts, for there iz every now and then, a bogus heathin.

Stand by your constitushion, and by laws, do all this, and the "Femail Pordunk Sowing Society" will go down tew future posterity like a wide-awake torchlite possession.

I bid you tenderly ajew.

■　　■　　■

THE MERMAID.

The mermaid iz a fish woman, and lives in six fathom water, close by the side ov some big, green enameled rock. They come out ov the water once a day, and climb up on the rock, and set there, and sort their hair, and fix, and fuss generally. They are half-fish, and half-woman, but what the pedigree ov the fish is, i dont remember, but striped bass, i think. I may be wrong about this, but don't recommend anybody to bet on my memory, mi memory was always fragile. The upper works ov the mermaid iz woman, an old maid generally, who has bin beat in love, or the fit ov a bonnett, and who has took to the waters, to drown her sorrows. While i never have saw a ghost, close to, i hav been equally unhappy in the mermaid line, having never witnessed one, not az i know ov. The mermaid iz a luxury, but i dont know az i want one, i love woman, and i love fish, but i want them in two pieces, if you pleaze. This mixing up things, I never did like. The mermaid haz an hazel eye, long, yellow worsted hair, a classic brow, nose slightly pug, hi cheek bones, even teeth, but a little too small, fingers lengthy, complexion orange, and red, cheeks full, with down on them, chin obtuse, without any dimple, eyelashes limber, ears too small, eyebrows arched just right, two fins on the back, scales one size larger than the shad, with the dorsal finish a little forked.

I never saw her az i sed before, but an old fisherman, who lives at Sandy hook, told me these things, and sezs he will swear to them. I think he would swear to the truth, for I never heard a man swear worse than this same old crab fisherman, who lives at Sandy hook.

■   ■   ■

I describe a kiss, az the time, and spot, whare affection comes tew the surface.

■   ■   ■

The woman born this month will be short ov stature, and acquainted with grief. She will want a great many things, in this world, that aint handy tew be got. She will marry just about the right time, and undertake tew live with her mother-in-law, which iz a difficult contract tew fill. The wimmin born this month are like a Rhode Island greening, ripen slow, and are most delightful away long into the winter.

■   ■   ■

EPITAPH

Here she lies—the queen ov pies,
Aunt Sally Ann Von Blixen,
Apple, and mince, custard, and quince,
She couldn't be beat in mixen.

Sacred this spot—stir her up not—
Her grace all lay in pie fixen,
Better say i—go without pie,
Than wake up this old vixen.

■   ■   ■

SHORT REPLYS.

DEAR Alice—I know nothing about music. I dont know this tune from the other.

I dont know "Yankee Doodle" from "Now I lay me on the grass," or "Mary had an infant sheep."

I am uncommon sorry tor this, but dont think that i am to blame for this.

I have melody in me somewhere, for any body can make me cry if they are careful.

I love the tender az i do a rare boiled egg.

I have shed many a tear, without any body knowing it, over some mother's catch, or simple lulaby.

But this iz called mere weakness by the artistics.

I have seen wimmin in opera, and also have seen them in fits, and prefer the fits, for then i know what tew do for them.

You must git some professor ov music tew answer your letter, for i don't know any more about classical music then i do about being a mother-in-law.

These are two very hard things tew comprehend.

I understand all about ice cream, and if you ever come down our way, we will have a bowl ov it together.

It dont seem tew require any brains tew love ice kream and i dont know az it does tew love music.

■　　　　　■　　　　　■

I cant see what woman wants any more rights for; she beat the fust man born into the world out ov a dead sure thing, and she can beat the last one with the same cards.

Pensive Rebekker.—I got your letter bi mistake, for the letter you sent me, you wrote for the other fellow.

I am only sorry on the other fellow's account, for your description ov him, which i should have received, may worry him.

It don't hurt my feelings tew be called a "*pokey dunce.*"

I never was much ov a favourite, not even with miself, and often think i am what you call me, a "*strapping monster.*"

Dont let this little mistake on your part worry you, for i love frankness, and think just az much ov you az i did before.

Artless Jane.—In reply tew your long letter, i will state promptly, I cant see any objections tew your lover kissing you, not if you want tew have him.

These things are all regulated by the law ov *supply* and *demand*.

If there iz a demand for it, the supply iz generally on hand.

I dont think it iz best tew be too extravagant in theze matters, for kissing iz like all other highly concentrated goods, a little ov it goes a good ways.

Too much kissing is like molassis candy, it spoils the hanker for plain vittles.

But your own good taste will decide when you hav bin kisst,

enough.

■   ■   ■

There iz only one good substitute for the endearments ov a sister, and that iz the endearments ov sum other pheller's sister.

■   ■   ■

Gay Betsey.—Mi opinion ov oysters, on the half shell, remains unchanged. I consider them better vittles than ever jupiter, or hiz wife juno, swallowed, altho they had the pick ov all the best provishuns in their day.

But i cant say that a woman can take an oyster, off from a shell, without spoiling the effect.

It iz one ov them gymnastic feats, that they should always practice fust, for a long time, in the subdued stilness ov sum private pantry.

I cant tell you whether an oyster has got any feelings, or not, but i know they have excellent taste, especially the saddle rocks.

They have more taste than judgement, and tho they are called muscles, they have no muscular strength.

They are also called "bivalves" bi the unlearned, but this iz a vulgarism.

The true name iz "good-bye valves," a term of affection applied tew them, when they was fust swallowed whole off from the half shell.

If you will ponder into history, az i have, you will find many such thing az this tew provoke your gratitude and wisdom.

Giv mi love tew your sister Amelia, and tell her, that i say, she has got what but phew wimmin have who have got az much beauty, she has got a sweet temper.

A sweet temper always grows brighter with age, while beauty iz extra hazardous, and perishable goods.

■   ■   ■

Happyness consists in being perfectly satisfied with what we hav got, and what we haint got.

■   ■   ■

It iz hard work for us tew luv a man who haz no faults nor failings.

■   ■   ■

Blessed are the single, for they can double at leizure.

■   ■   ■

Caroline.—Yu ask me why i dont write sweet, and sentimental,and lovely things.

I aint built right, Caroline, for that kind ov labor.

I am tew round-shouldered, tew write perfumed sentences.

When i git hold ov an idee, i hav tew let it go out, into the world, like a bird off from mi hand, bareheaded, and barefooted, a sort ov vagrant.

If i should undertake tew dress it up in fine clothes, some folks would say i stole the idee, and other folks would say i tried tew steal the clothes, tew dress it in, and got catched at it.

I make no pretentions tew literature, i pay no homage tew elegant sentences, i had rather be the father ov one genuine, original truth, i don't care if it iz az humpbacked az a dromedary, than tew be the author ov a whole volume ov glittering cadences, gotten up, for wintergreen-eating schoolgirls tew nibble at.

■　　　■　　　■

Bare necessitys will support life no doubt, so will the works support a watch, but they both want greasing once in a while, jist a leetle.

■　　　■　　　■

Prudes hoard their virtews, the same az mizers do their money, more for the sake ov recounting them, than for use.

■　　　■　　　■

It iz eazier tew be virtuous than it iz tew appear so, and it pays better.

■　　　■　　　■

"Matilda."—Kissing is one ov the rudiments, babys ar learnt it instead ov the alphabet, but they dont understand the strong points in it, yet they seem tew love it without knowing why, this iz a tricky argument that kissing iz one ov nature's most natureal notions. I can't tell you whether there is any perticular etiquette to be observed in administrating a kiss or not. Between lovers it iz sumtimes usual to kiss and hang on, but it strikes me that the best way iz tew cum up front face, in single file, then fire and fall back one pace, this gives the patients a chance tew get the flavour. The great beauty ov a kiss lies in its impulsiveness, and in its impressibility, two pretty big words, but worth the money.

I haven't done any thing in the kissing line, (ov an amateur nature) ov late years, and there may be some new dodge, that i aint posted in, but the old-fashioned, 25 year ago kind, i remember fresh, that kind didn't have any mathematicks in it, but was more like spontaneous combustion.

Kissing, az a general thing, iz not very interesting tew bystanders, and iz sometimes even looked upon, by a third party, az uncalled-for.

■   ■   ■

Flattery is like ice-kream—to relish good we want it a little at a time, and often.

■   ■   ■

Caroline.— You ask us, "Which iz worth the most tew a woman, beauty, or modesty."

For a quick return, perhaps beauty iz, but for an investment, for the sake ov the interest, we recommend modesty.

Modesty never grows stale, but beauty iz like buckwheat cakes, aint good cold, nor warmed up next day.

We consider beauty one ov the best *collatterals* that a woman can possess, but if she haint got nothing else but beauty, she ain't no better off than she would be with a life insurance policy, which was forfeited for the non-payment of premiums.

Beauty alone wont *wear* well, and there iz a great deal of it now days that wont *wash* at all and keep its color.

■   ■   ■

The strongest propensity in woman's nature iz to want to know "*whats going on!*" and the next strongest, iz tew boss the job.

■   ■   ■

MARRYING a woman for her money is very mutch like setting a rat-trap, and baiting it with your own finger.

■   ■   ■

Blessed iz he who has got a good wife and knows how to sail her.

■   ■   ■

ELIZABETH MEACHEM.

Lib Meachem (az she iz familiarly called in the township where she resides) iz one ov the rarest gems ov extenuated mortality that has ever been mi blessed luck teu encounter.

She iz not so old az Bascomb by about two years, being only about 194 years old. Next to Lot's wife she iz the best preserved woman the world contains.

I reached her place ov residence early in the morning, and in one minute after i told her mi bizzness her tongue had a full head ov steam on, and for 3 hours it run like a stream ov quicksilver down an inclined plain.

I asked her a thousand questions at least, but not one ov them did she answer, but kept talking all the time faster than Pochahontas can pace down hill to saddle.

Az near az i could find out she had lived 194 years simply becauze she couldn't die without cutting short one ov her storys.

I asked her teu show me her tongue—I wanted to see if that member was badly worn; but she couldn't stop it long enough teu show it.

This woman has reached her enormous age without any particular habit.

She haz outlived everybody she has come accrost, so far, by out-talking them.

The only subject that I could for a moment arrest the flood ov her language with, waz the fashions; but this waz a subject upon which i unfortunately wasn't much.

As a last hope ov drawing her out upon some facts az to her mode ov life, i touched upon that all-absorbing topic teu both old and young—i refer now teu matrimony.

Her fust husband it seemed, waz a carpenter, and, tew use her own words, "waz too lazy tew talk, or tew listen while she talked, and so he died."

Her second husband waz a pretty good talker but a poor listener, and, therefore, he died.

Her third husband waz a deaf and dumb man, and, az she remarked, "either he or she had got tew die, and the man died."

Her fourth husband undertook tew out-talk her, and died early.

In this way she went on describing her husbands, 12 in all.

Az i rose tew depart i said tew her sollemly:

"ELIZABETH MEACHEM, you have been much married, and much an inconsolate widder—at what time ov life do you think the married state ceases tew be preferable?"

She replied:

"You must ask sumbody older than i am."

The world would be more happy, and the mass ov them equally wize, if they would whissell more, and argy less.

WOMAN.

Woman is the glass ware ov creation. She iz luvly, and brittle, and she has run up everything we really enjoy in this life from 25 cents on the dollar to par. Adam, without Eve, would have been az stupid a game az playing checkers alone. There haz been more beautiful things said in her praise than there haz ov any other animate thing, and she is worthy ov them all. She is not an angell tho, and i hope she wont never go into the angell bizzness. Angells on earth dont pay. The only mistake that woman has ever made iz to think she iz a better man than Adam.

Adam iz captain, and i am ready to admit, that he iz often a dreadful poor one too. Woman iz the power behind the throne, she holds all the best playing cards in the pack, and her own good sense ought to teach her not to be in any hurry to play them. I have always said, and i believe it still, that the time to be carefulest iz when you have a hand full ov trumps.

The more babes in a family, the easier and better they are

raised—one chicken always makes an old hen more clucking and scratching than a dozen does.

■   ■   ■

No woman yet waz ever satisfied to be a prude, who could be a successfull coquet.

■   ■   ■

Cheerful old girls, are the bridesmaids ov sosiety.

■   ■   ■

The strongest propensity in woman's nature iz to want to know "*what's going on!*" and the next strongest, iz tew boss the job.

■   ■   ■

THE OLD MAID.

The old maid iz the last gooseberry left on the bush, ded ripe, and reddy to fall off at the fust good shake. She iz sumtimes a leetle hard to suit, but iz quite often the most charming relick in the naborhood. Next to mothers in law, old maids hav been abuzed more than enny thing human, but they all ov them hav a warm spot in their hearts, that enny decent person iz welkum to krawl into, and sun themselfs.

■   ■   ■

You might az well undertake tew drown a knot-hole out, bi pouring water into it, az tew outtalk some wimmin I know ov.

■   ■   ■

No woman yet was ever satisfied to be a prude, who could be a successfull coquette.

■   ■   ■

Woman has no friendships. She either loves, despises, or hates.

■   ■   ■

Tongue-tied wimmin are very scarse and very valuable.

■   ■   ■

THE COUNTRY SCHOOL MOM.

The country school mom is always about 23 years, and six months old, and remains rite there for a term ov years. She wears her hair either cut short, or hanging around in ringlets, and iz az precise in every thing, az a pair ov Fairbanks' improved platform scales. She never laffs out loud, and seldom even smiles, and when she does, she does it according to the rules laid down by Murray, for speaking and pronouncing, the English language properly. She iz the very oil ov propriety, and would rather be four years behind the fashions in bonnetts, than to spell a word wrong, or parse a sentence incorrecktly. The country school mom seldom dies an old maid, she gits married to some man who has less learning than she has, and he thinks (az he ought to) that there aint another such a learnt woman az his wife iz, in all creation. With all her precise foolishness i love and respect, the country school mom, she taut me while i waz stupid, she soothed me when i waz fractious, and she often (good soul) give me a titbit from her luncheon at noon time. May Heaven bless, and comfort her, for she iz poorly paid, and iz stepmother to every body's young ones.

■   ■   ■

Most ov us, when we repent ov our sins, think it iz a change ov heart, when in fact, it iz only a fear ov punishment.

■   ■   ■

Good common sense iz az healthy az onions, we often see those who are good, simply because they haint got sense enough tew be bad, and those who are bad just because they haint got sense enough tew be good.

■   ■   ■

It iz a great deal eazier tew look upon those who are below us with pity, than tew look upon those who are above us, without envy.

■   ■   ■

It iz easy enough, perhaps. for us tew tell what we admire, esteem and respect, in a man, but tew tell what we love ain't so easy.

■   ■   ■

Looking at pictures iz a cheap way tew think.

■   ■   ■

Hope and Debt are partners in trade—Hope hunts up the customers and Debt skins them.

■   ■   ■

The fust thing in this life tew be desired, in the physical line, iz a happy set ov bowells, after that, virtue, and brains, are in order.

■   ■   ■

Advice iz like castor-ile, easy enough to give, but dreadful uneasy tew take.

■ ■ ■

There iz few, if any, more suggestive sights tew a philosopher, than tew lean agin the side ov the wall, and peruse a clean, fat, and well disciplined baby, spread out on the floor, trying tew smash a hammer all tew pieces with a looking glass.

■ ■ ■

Angels handle the dice when doublets are thrown in the cradle.

■ ■ ■

Don't give outward appearances all the credit, the spirit ov a handsome boot iz the little toot what iz in it.

■ ■ ■

Nature never makes any blunders. When she makes a phool she means it.

■ ■ ■

Thare iz no sure kure for Lazyness,—but I hav known a seckond wife, to hurry it sum.

■ ■ ■

MARRIAGE.

MARRIAGE iz a fair transaction on the face ov it.
But there iz quite too often put up jobs in it.
It iz an old institution, older than the pyramids, and az full ov hyrogliphicks that nobody can parse.

History holds its tongue who the pair waz who fust put on the silken harness, and promised tew work kind in it, thru thick and thin, up hill and down, and on the level, rain or shine, survive or perish, sink or swim, drown or float.

But whoever they waz they must have made a good thing out ov it, or so many ov their posterity would not have harnessed up since and drove out.

There iz a grate moral grip in marriage; it iz the mortar that holds the social bricks together.

But there ain't but darn few pholks who put their money in matrimony who could set down and give a good written opinion why on earth they cum to did it.

This iz a grate proof that it iz one ov them natural kind ov accidents that must happen, jist az birds fly out ov the nest, when they hav feathers enough, without being able tew tell why.   Some marry for beauty, and never discover their mistake; this iz lucky.

Some marry for money, and—don't see it.

Some marry for pedigree, and feel big for six months, and then very sensibly come tew the conclusion that pedigree ain't no better than skimmilk.

Some marry tew please their relations, and are surprized tew learn that their relations don't care a cuss for them afterwards.

Some marry becauze they have bin highsted some where else; this iz a cross match, a bay and a sorrel; pride may make it endurable.

Some marry for love without a cent in their pocket, nor a friend in the world, nor a drop ov pedigree. This looks desperate, *but it iz the strength ov the game.*

If marrying for love ain't a success, then matrimony iz a dead beat.

Sum marry becauze they think wimmin will be scarce next year, and live tew wonder how the crop holds out.

Some marry tew git rid ov themselfs, and discover that the game waz one that two could play at, and neither win.

Some marry the second time to git even, and find it a gambling game, the more they put down, the less they take up.

Some marry tew be happy, and not finding it, wonder whare all the happiness on earth goes to when it dies.

Some marry, they can't tell why, and live, they can't tell how.

Almost every body gits married, and it iz a good joke.

Some marry in haste, and then set down and think it careful over.

Some think it over careful fust, and then set down and marry.

Both ways are right, if they hit the mark.

Some marry rakes tew convert them. This iz a little risky, and takes a smart missionary to do it.

Some marry coquetts. This iz like buying a poor farm, heavily mortgaged, and working the ballance ov your days tew clear off the mortgages.

Married life haz its chances, and this iz just what gives it its flavour. Every body luvs tew fool with the chances, becauze every body expects tew win. But i am authorized tew state that every body don't win.

But, after all, married life iz full az certain az the dry goods bizziness.

No man can swear exactly whare he will fetch up when he touches calico.

No man can tell jist what calico has made up its mind tew do next.

Calico don't know even herself.

Dry goods ov all kinds iz the child ov circumstansis.

Some never marry, but this iz just az risky, the disease iz the same, with no other name to it.

The man who stands on the bank shivvering, and dassent, iz more apt tew cetch cold, than him who pitches his head first into the river.

There iz but few who never marry becauze they *won't* they all hanker, and most ov them starve with slices ov bread before them (spread on both sides), jist for the lack ov grit.

Marry young! iz mi motto.

I have tried it, and know what i am talkin about.

If any body asks you why yu got married, (if it needs be), tell him, *yu don't recollect.*

Marriage iz a safe way to gamble—if you win, you win a pile, and if you lose, yu don't lose any thing, only the privilege, ov living dismally alone, and soaking yure own feet.

I repeat it, in italicks, *marry young!*

There iz but one good excuse for a marriage late in life, and that iz—*a second marriage.*

■   ■   ■

I never argy agin a suckess,
When i see a rattlesnaixs hed
Sticking out ov a whole, i bear
off to the left, and say to miself
that hole belongs to that
snaix.

JOSH BILLINGS

■   ■   ■

SAID TO BE A TRU COPY
OF THE FIRST LETTER
EVER WRITTEN.

Edonia, December, Year Two

Dear Eve:

I have been on the rampage now one month, prospecting for our new home, and have seen some ranches that will do pretty well, but none of them just the ticket. The old garden is a hard place to beat, but we have lost that, and are turned out now, to root hog or die. We will fight it out now, on this line, if it takes all summer. Eating that apple was a great blunder, but, my dear girl, let bygones be bygones, there is hope for us yet. Just as soon as I strike a good claim, I will come back to you. Watch over Cain closely, he is a brick. The weather is raw and cold, I feel that I am too thinly clad.

No more now from your loving
ADAM.

P.S.—Has Cain cut another tooth yet?

■   ■   ■

Honest poverty has this advantage, all it owes it owes to Heaven, and dont owe mutch there.

■   ■   ■

KISSING.

I HAV written essays on kissing before this one, and they didn't satisfy me, nor dew I think this one will, for the more a man undertakes tew tell about a kiss, the more he will reduce his ignorance tew a science.

You cant analize a kiss any more than you can the breath ov a flower. You cant tell what makes a kiss taste so good any more than you can a peach.

Any man who can set down, where it is cool, and tell how a kiss tastes, haint got any more real flavor tew his mouth than a knot hole has. Such a phellow wouldn't hesitate tew describe Paradise as a fust rate place for garden sass.

The only way tew describe a kiss is tew take one, and then set down, all alone, out ov the draft, and smack your lips.

If you cant satisfy yourself how a kiss tastes without taking another one, how on earth can you define it tew the next man.

I have heard writers talk about the ecstatic bliss thare was in a kiss, and they really seemed tew think they knew all about it, but these are the same kind ov folks who perspire and cry when they read poetry, and they fall to writing sum ov their own, and think they have found out how.

I want it understood that I am talking about pure emotional kissing, that is born in the heart, and flies tew the lips, like a humming bird tew her roost.

I am not talking about your lazy, milk and molasses kissing, that daubs the face ov any body, nor your savage bite, that goes around, like a roaring lion, in search ov sumthing to eat.

Kissing an unwilling pair ov lips, iz az mean a victory, az robbing a bird's nest, and kissing too willing ones iz about az unfragant a recreation, az making boquets out ov dandelions.

The kind ov kissing that I am talking about iz the kind that must do it, or spoil.

If you search the records ever so lively, you cant find the author ov the first kiss; kissing, like much other good things, iz anonymous.

But there iz such nature in it, such a world ov language without words, such a heap ov pathos without fuss, so much honey, and so little water, so cheap, so sudden, and so neat a mode of striking up an acquaintance, that i consider it a good purchase, that Adam give and got, the fust kiss.

Who can imagine a greater lump ov earthly bliss, reduced tew a finer thing, than kissing the only woman on earth, in the garden of Eden.

Adam wasn't the man, i don't believe, tew pass such a hand.

I may be wrong in my conclusions, but if any body can date kissing further back, i would like tew see them do it.

I don't know whether the old stoic philosophers ever kissed any body or not, if they did, they probably did it, like drawing a theorem on a black board, more for the purpose of proving sumthing else.

I do hate to see this delightful and invigorating beverage adulturated, it iz nectar for the gods, i am often obliged tew stand still, and see kissing did, and not say a word, that haint got any more novelty, nor meaning in it, than throwing stones tew a mark.

I saw two maiden ladys kiss yesterday on the north side ov Union square, 5 times in less than 10 minutes; they kist every time they bid each other farewell, and then immediately thought ov sumthing else they hadn't said. I couldn't tell for the life of me whether the kissing was the effect ov what they said, or what they said waz the effect ov the kissing. It was a which, and tother, scene.

Cross-matched kissing iz undoubtedly the strength ov the game. It iz true there iz no statute regulation aginst two females kissing each other; but i don't think there iz much pardon for it, unless it iz done to keep tools in order; and two men kissing each other iz prima face evidence ov dead-beatery.

Kissing that passes from parent to child, and back again seems to be az necessary az shinplasters,* (to do bizzness with; and kissing that hussbands give and take iz simply gathering ripe fruit from one's own plumb tree, that would otherwise drop off, or be stolen.

Therefore i am driven tew conclude, tew git out ov the corner that my remarks hav chased me into, that the oil ov a kiss iz only tew be had once in a phellow's life, in the original package, and that iz when. . .

Not tew waste the time ov the reader, i have thought best not tew finish the above sentence, hoping that their aint no person ov a good education and decent memory, but what can recollect the time which i refer to, without any ov mi help.

■   ■   ■

Hearts and dimonds are the two strong suits for a woman to hold—klubs and spades for man.

---

*slang for paper money

■　　　■　　　■

An American luvs tew laff, but he don't love tew make a bizzness ov it; he works, eats, and luvs—luvs on a canter.

■　　　■　　　■

Sumthing new, sumthing startling iz necessary for us az a people, and it don't make mutch matter what it iz—a huge defalkashun—a red elephant—or Jersee clams with pearls in them

■　　　■　　　■

There iz two things in this world for which we are never fully prepared, and them iz—twins.

■　　　■　　　■

Remember the poor—it costs not

■　　　■　　　■

Cherries are good, but they are too mutch like sucking a marble with a candle to it.

■　　　■　　　■

It iz alwuss safe to follow the religious Beleaf that our Mothers taught us,—there never waz a Mother yet, who taugh her child to be an Infidel.

■　　　■　　　■